STAIRCASE

OF A

THOUSAND

STEPS

BlueHen Books

a member of
PENGUIN PUTNAM INC.
NEW YORK

STAIRCASE

OF A

THOUSAND

STEPS

a novel

Masha

Hamilton

BlueHen Books
a member of
Penguin Putnam Inc.
375 Hudson Street
New York, NY 10014

Library of Congress Cataloging-in-Publication Data

Hamilton, Masha.
Staircase of a thousand steps : a novel / Masha Hamilton.
p.   cm.
ISBN 0-399-14725-X
1. Girls—Fiction.   2. Grandfathers—Fiction.   3. Midwives—
Fiction.   4. Jordan—Fiction.   I. Title.

PS3558.A44338 S73   2001   00-064161
813'.6—dc21

Printed in the United States of America

1   3   5   7   9   10   8   6   4   2

This book is printed on acid-free paper. ∞

Book design by Judith Stagnitto Abbate and Claire Vaccaro

ACKNOWLEDGMENTS

Thanks to Elaine Koster for her determination and persistence, and Fred Ramey and Greg Michalson for their wise suggestions. Thanks also to the most insightful readers/critiquers any writer could hope for: Nancy Wall, Steve Hanson, and Dan Gilmore for the exhilarating Wednesday nights, the inimitable Rebecca Lowen, Lisa Brener, Jennifer Stewart, and Rupert and Arra Hamilton. Also thanks to David Orr for his support on every level, and to Briana, Cheney, and Daylon for letting me write.

To Hilma Granvquist,

1890—1972

"I needed to live among the people,
hear them talk about themselves. . . ."

Staircase

of a

Thousand

Steps

In this land of the Koran

and the Bible and the Torah,

of women turned to salt and men drowned in

suddenly closing seas, one is wise to accept

whatever is handed down from above.

—HARIF EL JABR—

JAMMANA

Steam rises off a dirt floor made shiny with sheep's blood. A lantern casts contorting shadows. It is a room unknown to me, a time uncertain. Faridah is kneeling. Her eyes are pinpoints of concentration, her cheekbones lofty and distinct. I stretch toward her, then pull back when I see her arms rigid between a woman's thighs.

Faridah, blind to me, yanks her hands free. She flings off her silver bracelets, and they scatter like the Seven Sisters of the sky. "I have to . . ." Her murmur rolls past, blurred at first, but clear by the final word. "Now." She reaches into a reed basket, holds her hand over the lantern, and sprinkles brittle leaves into the fire. Once, twice, and again.

The flame flashes violet, then silver. The room reeks of stinkweed and decay. From between the writhing legs comes a choking sound. I glimpse a crowning head covered with feathers of hair. "Faridah, please," the woman on the ground begs. Faridah stiffens. Her headdress slips, revealing black-berry hair turned glossy from crushed rosemary oil.

The tiny head strains, struggles and stops, trapped. The one on the ground arches her neck and lets loose a howl that speaks of fury more than pain. I press my hands to my ears, but moans seep between the cracks of my fingers. "Do something!" I cry out. Faridah doesn't seem to hear. So I beat back fear, brush past her, enter clinging wetness and grip with both hands. I squeeze my eyes and tumble backward, dragging into this world, onto Faridah's lap, a plump form with a hint of bone. The merest suggestion of determination to come.

Faridah lifts it up. Her gaze is laced with dismay. An infant stares back with tiny novas that hover below eyebrows.

"A girl?" The woman lifts her shoulders from a coarse blanket folded like a pillow. She strains forward, her voice insubstantial as smoke, but victory in her eyes. "I'll name her Rafa."

Neither midwife nor infant listens. They study each other until Faridah bows, tearing the cord with her teeth. Forever severing the link.

In this way my mother was born.

Countless times I've relived this memory of a birth in the Samarian village of Ein Fadr eighteen years before my own, seeking its truth about my mama and the midwife I loved. It distorts all that came later—each life, every death. The last funeral, Grandfather Harif's, was chanted two days ago during the Islamic Month of Great Division. A fitting coincidence of which I've just learned.

Now I'm alone, and I know, I know I should darken my face with soot, tear my hair, throw ululations to where sky joins heaven. But I can't mourn in the elders' way. I'm no longer that child Jammana. *She* was accustomed to the din of donkeys, the jab of sharp stones beneath bare feet, the music of men praising Allah as one. *I* live in Providence in a new century, American now, disdainful of unrestrained grief and skeptical of an omnipresent Allah.

Yet somewhere within me resides Grandfather and the midwife Faridah. And even a shred of that distant girl Jammana. I cannot abandon her entirely, not yet. Her sorrows, fresh and ancient, press against me like secrets demanding to be told.

The three travelers aim their donkeys true like well-thrown stones. They ride fast over hot hills west of Nablus and pause only when they are closer to the sea than the river.

Jammana wipes the back of her neck with the checked bandanna wrapped on her wrist, and shakes her hair, glad she keeps it short in defiance of propriety. Mama and the merchant Abu Sa'id crowd beneath a limp terebinth tree, but Jammana refuses the shade—part of her campaign to demonstrate she is more capable than her eleven years suggest. She drinks from the water skin Abu Sa'id offers. Mama, veiled for the trip, bends over and presses the hem of her dress to her forehead. Abu Sa'id smoothes his robe, then brushes dust from his trimmed mustache with a single fingertip.

Parched hues of tan and ocher collide in the landscape;
no other colors survive. The silence overwhelms—birds are
grounded, lizards barely breathe, even bees won't hunt for
nectar in this dry expanse midway between Jerusalem and
Lebanon. Abu Sa'id looks back. "Drink quickly. We must
move on."

Mama waves a hand vaguely. "He'll not chase us. He's
working now."

"He's my oldest friend. Naturally, I didn't want his wife
and daughter wandering out here alone." Abu Sa'id, palms up,
seems to be practicing the explanation Jammana suspects he
will offer later to Father. "You said you'd cross the desert
without me if I refused to escort you."

Mama nods. "I'd already sent word to my father and
Faridah to meet us halfway. So, you see, my husband will be
grateful to you. If he's angry, he'll aim it at me. And soon
enough, he'll"—she stumbles—"forgive."

Jammana detects doubt in Mama's tone and recognizes
her duty to provide distraction. "*Ya*, what I'd give for some ice
cream," she says unwrapping the bandanna from her wrist.
"Remember your first taste, Mama? Father brought it wrapped
in ice and burlap. You took a spoonful and told him it was
sweet like molasses and"—she giggles—"salty like love."

Mama smiles. "And he promised to provide that flavor
anytime." She studies her daughter, and her voice deepens.
"But that was long before you were born. Seems a century
ago. I'd forgotten all about it."

"Who told you the story, then?" Abu Sa'id has dismounted and is watering the donkeys from his cupped hands.
"Your father?"

"I thought of it myself," Jammana says. She's surprised—she thought he knew.

"Memories come to her," Mama adds quickly. "Memories of events that happened decades ago. No one tells her. She just recalls on her own."

Abu Sa'id glances at Jammana. Only the twitch of his mustache gives away his skepticism.

"Such gifts of insight run in my clan," Mama goes on. "Surely my husband told you. It's a family characteristic, simple as the curve of an eyebrow or the shape of a lip. Only this one skips a generation. My father has special visions, as did his grandfather."

"Is that so?" Abu Sa'id asks politely.

"Small memories, usually," Jammana says. "Once, after a rainfall, I smelled the scent of a flower and knew it was my great-grandmother's favorite. Another time, a sip of water tasted sour and I understood Faridah must have chewed on lemon balm as she delivered her first baby. One morning, I remembered when a strange woman passed Grandfather Harif on a staircase and reached to tug his earlobe."

Abu Sa'id looks away.

"Everyone will believe my memories someday," Jammana says in a tone she knows uncertainty makes too insistent.

She does not speak of the memory she doesn't understand, the one that calls into question all she knows about Mama and Faridah and herself. But Abu Sa'id notices no omission. He is busy checking his donkey's hooves with more concentration than necessary. Jammana is used to this; people invariably shy away if she reveals that the histories of others lodge in her mind like footprints clinging to a beaten trail. Once, she thought all children were like her, gathering the fleece of faded moments in their daydreams. She considered it compensation for being a child, for all the other insights denied. That was before she mentioned her memories to neighborhood children, before they began to look at her and snicker. Now she knows her far-flung recollections are as unlikely as the birth of a savior.

Her memories may be a gift, as Mama says, but they make Jammana feel a misfit. Her most steady playmate is her shadow; no one else invites her into games. Mama says never mind, she'll just have to bear it, and Grandfather Harif has been treated like an outcast, too, from time to time. As if this should be a comfort.

"Are we ready?" Abu Sa'id asks. Jammana knows he'd like to be back in his shop when her father walks by on the way home from work, both to diminish his role in this trip and to salvage the remainder of a business day. One can never tell, Abu Sa'id says, when someone will stop in with something to sell or barter, and only he can ferret out the honey-soaked tobacco, embroidery thread, and bags of pistachios in his shop's clutter. Only he can find, tucked away in corners, the James Bond poster, the well-thumbed surfing magazine, and, before Jammana bought it, the redchecked cowboy bandanna from America. Mama asked him to escort them since he often travels the desert on bartering missions and knows it well. Jammana suspects he agreed, at least in part, because he relishes gossip. She's counted eighty-two coffee cups stacked in the back of his shop—one for each friend who visits in the late afternoons. Missions like this, Jammana thinks, are fodder for the garrulous men of Nablus.

The travelers start out again, still headed west. "I thank the All-Merciful for the chance to help Ahmed's family, of course," Abu Sa'id says after a moment. "Still, why couldn't we tell him we are going?"

"He would have forbidden it. He says,"—Jammana deepens her voice, mimicking—"'Ein Fadr is a primitive village—no telephones, no real beds, no *hygiene*—and Harif is a superstitious old man.'"

"Jammana!" Mama tries to look serious, but Jammana can hear the amusement in her tone.

"And Faridah," Jammana goes on, "she is—how does he put it?—'without moral base.' They'll be of bad influence. I'm a delicate child, you know."

Even Abu Sa'id can't suppress a smile as he says, "Still, he's your father. You must do as he says."

"I take it as my responsibility," Mama says quickly.

Jammana knows Abu Sa'id is wise to be wary of Father. She knows well. Once, when she was four and unable to swim, Father took her to the Lebanese seashore at Tyre. He stood with waves hitting his knees and, without warning, tossed her in. Cold water and topaz darkness entombed her. Drenching salt burned her nostrils. Hair like soggy bread clogged her mouth and eyes. At last he pulled her out, gasping and grateful. Then he began to swing her again. "One . . . two . . ." Jolly voice. She screamed and gripped him. But being held with such urgent need seemed to be the moment he sought. "And three!" He tossed, rescued, pried loose her fingers, and tossed again. Until she stopped begging. Until he wearied. He told Mama later how much fun Jammana had in the waves, and she was afraid to contradict him. Only in his presence does she fear speaking out. But she admits to a grudging admiration for his will, strong enough to allow him to paint the world in his own colors.

Besides, she must acknowledge that his frustration and cruelty are partly her fault. The men who visit him are all Abu Haseem and Abu Sharif and Abu Abdul. He cannot be Abu, the title conferred only on the father of a boy.

It is early afternoon, and the air has begun to smell rank. Jammana peers ahead. Two large falcons are devouring the remains of one of their own. Only the dead bird's head is untouched. One falcon looks up as the travelers approach, but neither bothers to fly away. Black-and-white-striped feathers are strewn at their talons.

Jammana stares. "Do they know what they're eating?" Mama averts her face.

Abu Sa'id hurries them past the feast and then slows so their three donkeys walk apace. "Forget the birds," he says to Mama comfortingly. "Forget, even, whether Ahmed will be displeased. Entertain me with an account of your birthplace. I know Ein Fadr was founded by a grandson of Adam. The Prophet Abraham stopped there, I've heard, to listen to the tales of its silver-tongued villagers."

"Ein Fadr." Mama gazes unseeingly to the slopes beyond. "Yes, it is ancient, and without wish to join the modern world. In fact, the past holds a strange vitality." Mama's voice grows bitter. "Once, a woman shamed the village by stealing cucumbers from a traveling merchant. Her young son craved them, but her husband held tight to their money. The village leader ordered the fingers on her right hand sliced off. Her offspring are still referred to as 'Descendants of the Impure.'" She puts a hand to her throat. "In other places, last night's embers may be today's ashes, but in Ein Fadr, the buried live on. Eventually it becomes hard to breathe."

Abu Sa'id studies Mama carefully. "Such is the way with small villages," he says at last.

Mama shakes her head. "No other place is as thick with grudges."

Jammana knows Mama's moods and has heard Mama talk like this before, though for her, Ein Fadr is filled with extremes that entice. Tortured alleyways give way to manicured olive groves. Harsh caves scar the gentle hills. Faridah is the taste of red pepper on an inexperienced tongue, while Grandfather soothes like olive oil.

"I'm fortunate to have married Ahmed and escaped," Mama says it stiffly, like a verse of the Koran repeated so often it has lost its meaning. She reaches up nervously to finger the edge of her veil.

"Mama's tired," Jammana tells Abu Sa'id. "Umm Mahir walked again last night."

That's all the explanation Abu Sa'id needs. Everyone knows how Umm Mahir's high-pitched cries can pierce her neighbors' slumbers. Ten months ago, Christians stormed the Moslem quarter. Umm Mahir's son, Jamil, lost hold of his father's hand and was trampled to death. Jammana's chest hurts every time she thinks of this. Jamil didn't speak much—he was even more shy with other children than she, and that gave her a kind of confidence. She'd told him of her displaced memories, and he hadn't laughed. He'd stared at his feet as she'd spoken; now and then, he would lift his head and smile. Jammana had wondered if their parents would arrange their marriage one day.

In death, Jamil grew large. A week after he was killed, men from their neighborhood stabbed three Christians and dumped their bodies at the Masri mill among sacks of flour. If they expected Umm Mahir's thanks, they were disappointed.

During the day, Umm Mahir blames her husband for the deaths of both her son and the Christians. At night she blames herself. Wearing red high-heeled shoes from Cairo that she saves only for this, she walks the street, tugging painfully on the silver loops in her ears. Her fish eyes, wise and wild at once, fill with tears that rain down the hills of her brown cheeks. She wails and walks until Mama goes down the street to gather her up, hum in her ear, and take her home.

"Umm Mahir." Mama shakes her head. "First her son, then the other three."

"Her son is dead because those Christians killed him," Abu Sa'id says.

"*Those* Christians?" Mama asks. "Who knows? Maybe those three weren't anywhere near the riot."

This is an old argument, and troubling—not a single neighbor agrees with Mama and Umm Mahir that avenging the boy's death was wrong. Even Jammana isn't sure, though she is loath to admit it. She changes the subject by picking up in the middle of a story she'd been telling Mama earlier. "The ferociously brave heroine was startled when a *jinn* leapt from behind a rock," she says. "But she didn't halt her donkey. She just turned to her companions and said, 'What a lovely trip.'"

This story-telling is a favorite game between mother and daughter. Now, however, Mama shoots her a warning look, a reminder that Father can't abide silliness in front of his friends. Abu Sa'id doesn't seem to notice. He is stroking his mustache, and probably wishing he'd insisted on more information before setting off this morning. "So why," he asks, "must your daughter go to Ein Fadr so urgently?"

Mama's tone is indulgent. "Why not let her spend a few weeks in the village? She's safe there. Nablus is growing tense, now. Besides, she tells me she *needs* to visit her grandfather. And Faridah."

Abu Sa'id directs his gaze at Jammana, and it is her turn to feign preoccupation. She ties the bandanna around her neck and bends to stroke her donkey. After all, she has not told even Mama yet about the memory. It is difficult to think of speaking aloud the question that runs through her mind: Why did Faridah refuse to help when Mama was ready to be born? Jammana has a plan. First she will ask Grandfather. After all, he knows of odd visions. Then she will face Faridah herself. But now it is a raw spot, not to be touched.

Abu Sa'id's stare demands an answer, so after a moment, Jammana gives one that is partly true. "I need to say my good-byes."

"It is certain, then?" Abu Sa'id asks Mama. "You're moving?"

Mama bites her lower lip. "The Troubles" is all she offers. It is enough. Abu Sa'id knows their full weight, as do all the men who gather in his shop by day or in Jammana's own home in the wash of evenings. Men, legs crossed beneath *jallabiya*s, the mouthpieces of water pipes between their lips, bearing secrets of stones and alleys and maleness. Men mulling over their struggles with the Jews and the Christians and the Brits and the Turks, the murmur of their voices punctuated by pronouncements from the town's finest doctor, Father, and its most widely respected merchant, Abu Sa'id.

Two reports of gunfire echo, then. "We are closer than in Nablus," says Abu Sa'id, referring to the border with Israel. He looks at Jammana. "Are you frightened?"

She lifts her chin. "Certainly not." Her disavowal is not just for show. Whenever demonstrations erupt in front of their home, Jammana presses her face tight to the window to watch. Neighbors become strangers with fists raised above heads, mouths twisted as if in pain. Tear gas creeps into the house, and helicopters swoop overhead like steel vultures.

She has heard Father say the Jordanian king has little patience with those he considers his guests, even in their own homes. She knows Abu Sa'id, too, has no use for the demonstrations. He closes his shop hours early on those days, shaking his head as he tugs down the heavy metal shutter that reminds Jammana of an eye refusing to see. But for her, the protests thrill with their passion, their current of danger. Their whiff of a remote adult world.

They are moving slower, now, headed north. A low-lying dust cloud comes into view ahead. Jammana squints until she can make out Bedouin—half a dozen camels and perhaps ten men. They are in a loose group, traveling the same direction as Jammana and Mama and Abu Sa'id. "Of the Bani tribe,"

Abu Sa'id says. "They come in close because it is drier than it's been in many years."

Mama pulls her donkey back, but Jammana speeds up. She's never met a Bedouin. She imagines they speak in poetry and smell musty, like earth after rainfall. She is so busy urging her donkey forward that she almost misses the man sitting alone under a tree. Her attention is drawn by his music—high notes that are, to Jammana's ear, tuneless. His legs are crossed, the heels of his callused feet facing the heavens. His mustache rambles, though his beard is closely trimmed. He holds a *rabab* on his knees, and slides a bow along its single string.

"Greetings and blessings to you and your father and your sons," Abu Sa'id calls from behind her. "May Allah bring wealth and happiness to you."

The man gazes upward with dense eyes.

"Would you care for water?" Abu Sa'id asks. "Surely you are thirsty. One must accept whatever gifts Allah allows to fall upon one's shoulders. We would be honored to share."

The man does not seem to notice them. He sets down his instrument and lies back on the ground. Tethered to a tree some distance away, a camel is camouflaged by its surroundings. "Is that yours?" Jammana asks. "Are you with the Bedouin?" The man's eyes close.

Abu Sa'id shakes his head in frustration. "You need our help?" he asks loudly one last time. Receiving no reply, he turns to Mama. "Let's go. The desert has become a place of deviations."

"It always has been so," Mama murmurs. "Nomads and wild-eyed prophets."

They fall silent. Abu Sa'id pulls from his pocket a tiny black box—his transistor radio. Tuned to a station far south of them in Cairo, it improbably emits into the heat the moan of a male voice singing sorrowful, comforting notes. Abu Sa'id rarely plays the radio because he has few spare batteries. He is, Jammana knows, treating them.

The desert has fallen silent again, and thirst returns to Jammana as a figure appears on a hilltop riding toward them. "A woman?" Abu Sa'id asks, his voice arching.

Jammana can tell from Mama's eyes that she is smiling.

"Out here alone?" Abu Sa'id disapproves.

"Faridah does as she wishes," Mama answers.

Inadvertently, Jammana's chest leaps with eagerness. Faridah doesn't treat Jammana like a child—she is loath to scold, and seldom instructs. She can be counted on to look into Jammana's eyes and listen closely, as though Jammana is worthy.

Jammana kicks her donkey's ribs, riding ahead of Mama and Abu Sa'id. Faridah raises her arm in greeting, and Jammana is captivated by the fingers that reach impossibly far and the shiny metal that dances at Faridah's right wrist. In a moment, Faridah draws up to Jammana and murmurs her donkey to a halt. "Mine of mine," she says, studying Jammana with eyes the color of toasted sesame.

Jammana tumbles to the ground, and Faridah dismounts, enfolding her like a flower. She smoothes Jammana's frizzy hair, and they trade a moment so protected that Jammana knows instinctively she'll miss its passing. Then Jammana makes herself push away and crosses her arms over her chest. Faridah's eyebrows rise in surprise, though she says nothing.

Mama and Abu Sa'id reach them. "I thought she was coming with your father," Abu Sa'id says to Mama.

Faridah's cool stare slides past Abu Sa'id. "Harif is behind me," she says. "He stopped to pray. I kept going because I knew Divine could find you." She places a hand on her donkey's neck.

Faridah and Mama embrace. Then Faridah pulls some mint from her pocket and feeds Divine, stroking his side with fluttering fingers.

Grandfather Harif and his donkey emerge from a *wadi*. Thin and tan, he blends with his surroundings, except for his beard, which is whiter than the desert. Tied to the sides and back of his donkey are a rolled prayer rug, a water skin, a coffee pot, and a ladle for roasting beans.

Grandfather shakes Abu Sa'id's hand and lifts up Jammana. "You smell fresh," he says, laughing. "My sheep will gladly follow you." Then he hugs Mama. "So, he's making plans for America, your Ahmed?"

"Safer for the child, he says," Mama answers. "Better for a physician's career. He has a good friend there."

Jammana makes a face. "A doctor who can't find any work except selling shoes," she says under her breath.

"That won't happen to Ahmed," Mama says. "He's not just a doctor. He's the hospital director." And though Jammana knows Mama doesn't want to move either, now she squeezes her daughter's hand, demanding silence in front of Grandfather and Abu Sa'id.

"And you?" Grandfather asks Mama. "You have agreed?"

Mama studies Jammana a moment before answering. "I'm happy in Nablus," she says carefully. "But Ahmed . . ." She breaks off, turns abruptly toward Abu Sa'id. "You watered the donkeys?" she asks.

Grandfather grunts. He pulls amber prayer beads from his pocket and presses first one, then the next, down the strand. "Farther from Allah," he mutters. "That's what you will be."

"Leave her alone now," Faridah scolds.

Grandfather sighs. "Shall I make Allah's nectar?" he asks of no one in particular.

Abu Sa'id shakes his head. "No coffee. I'd rather return, if you are willing," he says to Mama.

Jammana cleaves suddenly to Mama's skirt. Mama needs her. Mama is her responsibility. Jammana has known this since her vision. Sometimes Jammana fears that if she's not paying sufficient attention, Mama will disappear.

Mama rests a hand on Jammana's shoulder. "Two weeks, *faraashe*," she says. My little butterfly.

"Will you be all right without me for that long?"

"Think of a shooting star," Mama says. "Time will race that quickly."

"No, it won't," Jammana says. "Don't go." Or perhaps she only thinks it, because no one responds.

Grandfather lets his prayer beads erode his fingertips as the donkeys carry them toward Ein Fadr. Faridah, chewing on a mint leaf, has ridden ahead and waits near a boulder.

Now Jammana can ask a question that's been nagging her, that she'd rather not have Faridah hear. "Grandfather?"

"Hmm?"

"Are my visions of the past always true?"

"Have you ever had one that was not?" Grandfather replies.

Jammana shakes her head. "But do you think I could change something that happened before I was born? Make it turn out differently?"

Grandfather pulls his donkey to a halt and studies Jammana. "Now, that's a different matter." He dismounts, stretches on the ground, and she follows. His body seems to sink into the earth, with only his feet protruding like sandaled stones. His hair lies like rain-softened twigs. Sitting next to him, Jammana imagines planting a seed in the furrows of his face. She's sure she will never become as worn as he is, as she suspects he always has been.

Though Grandfather's eyes are closed, Jammana knows he's not sleeping. After a moment, he sits up. "Clasp your hands and twiddle your thumbs," he says, and waits until she's doing so. "See how loosely your fingers are woven? How your thumbs roll and bump against each other? This is how time moves. Not in a straight line, no. It is past rolling over future and coming to the front again. We move within it and call it now." He rises, then, mounts, and clucks his tongue to start his donkey. Faridah has ridden back to meet them. "Come along, Jammana," Grandfather calls.

This is the way Grandfather always replies to Jammana's questions, his answers buried deep under words. As Jammana climbs back on her donkey, she wonders how angry

Father will be when he learns she has gone to Ein Fadr without his consent. It is best if she is home when her parents quarrel. She can calm Father, protect Mama. She can act silly and childish for a good cause, and blow the sour winds over the mountains and out to sea.

"You know what worries me about Allah?" Jammana says as she catches up with Grandfather and Faridah. "He seems to care more about men than women."

Faridah laughs.

"Sometimes it's the kind of caring you can do without," Grandfather says. "He has an unruly sense of humor, you know. Shall I tell you about my first encounter?"

Jammana knows the story well, but she's eager for it again. Grandfather loses himself in his own tales, recounting each with fresh surprise as though he were hearing it for the first time.

Still, Jammana shrugs, trying to affect the casualness of the mature.

Grandfather winks to show he is not fooled. "Oh, to breathe that time again!" he says. "Life seemed varied as a chameleon's colors, and loss was unknown to me."

"So begin, then," Faridah says, easy scoffing in her tone.

He nods. "The year was 1930. I was thirteen years old and spending my days in Jerusalem's Old City, helping my father tend an olive stand.

"The *souk* sizzled with excitement, especially for a village boy." He gestures widely, as though the scene were before them. "Soldiers from the Pasha's camp paraded through streets with chins raised arrogantly high. Donkeys with bells around their necks bore bundles of leather sandals from Jordan. Syrians slipped through the multitude with silks folded over outstretched arms. The calls to prayer from the Dome of the Rock merged with the clatter of coffee beans spilled onto brass scales. It was there I tasted my first cup of Turkish coffee." Grandfather pretends to lift a cup of coffee to his lips. "There I mastered the skill of balancing a cup on my knee so it remains in place as though glued, even when I shift or cross my legs. There I learned, Jammana, that true coffee must be hot like love and bitter like death."

"The story, old man," Faridah teases.

"Tric-trac," Grandfather says. "You know the game?"

Jammana nods. Like backgammon, it's played with dice and counters on a wooden board. Men in Nablus sometimes compete on card tables set up on a sidewalk.

"It was the most popular pastime in the Old City," Grandfather says. "As a boy, I focused all my energy on mastering its strategies. I concentrated so intently that only the good will and honesty of my father's customers prevented our olive stand from being robbed clean in the midst of a match." He lowers his head modestly as he adds, "Eventually, I bested all in the *souk.*

"Came the morning when a merchant from Riyadh arrived with three sons and many carpets loaded on the backs of camels. All the traders, including my father, left their stalls and went to the rear of a rug shop to eat sweet cheese *kenafeh,* smoke water pipes, and observe the shop owner's cagey inspection of the Saudi carpets. While they were inside, the traveling merchant's youngest son wandered until he came to the stall where I sat playing tric-trac with a friend."

Here, Jammana can pick the story up herself, because of both what Grandfather Harif has told her before and her own memories of his past. The boy from Saudi Arabia watched while Grandfather played two games. "You aren't too bad," the boy finally said, adding, "for one so young," though he himself couldn't have been more than two years older. Harif gave a friendly nod, taking in the boy's filed nails and uncommonly clean robe. "But I'll wager I can defeat you," the boy said.

"What's the wager?" Harif asked.

"If you win, you may have . . ." The boy appeared to ponder for a moment. "One of my father's prayer rugs. If I win, I get all the olives my camel can carry."

Harif considered the proposal. "A new prayer rug," he mused, "just for playing tric-trac." He thought of presenting the rug to the village; he thought of what his best friend, Nabeel, the *mukhtar's* son, would say. He grinned at the boy, and nodded.

The boy bowed his head and rubbed the corners of both eyes before making his opening move. Harif, in an improvised gesture for luck, placed one hand on the rough wood of the olive tub next to him. The boy shifted pieces with hesitation, while Harif took his turns with grins of confidence. Two Jewish lads with long side curls joined the Moslem youths who gathered to root for Jammana's grandfather. A nun paused for a moment, hands clasped below her chin. From Jaffa Gate to St. Stephen's, donkeys stopped braying, chickens quit squawking. The terra-cotta dust of the passageway drifted to the ground—even the air seemed to wait. At last a sacred silence settled on the *souk*.

Grandfather's voice grows loud, capturing Jammana's attention again. "I remember clear as this morning's dawn the look on the Saudi boy's face right before he made his last move. Swaggering joy. It was not the move, Jammana, but his expression that made my heart tighten and dive. When the men emerged from the shop, I stood shoulder-to-shoulder with my challenger. As my words spilled out, my father grew hard as stone. We were far from poor, but he was responsible to the village. He cringed at the thought of giving away two large saddlebags of olives on a whim of his only son. After a silence worth more than a day of lectures, he went to fill the bags for the Saudi merchant and his son. We left Jerusalem that evening, and he did not speak on the ride home."

"Were you sorry?" asks Jammana. They are getting to the heart of the story.

"I berated myself," Grandfather says, "for my naiveté, for not noticing how my challenger studied my meager strategies before he offered to play. But the most important lesson I failed to learn immediately."

"And that was . . ." Jammana, on cue, urges him forward.

"Up until that moment, I'd invoked my prayers in the lazy manner of youth, without much faith or even thought. I'd trusted completely in myself. The match, although it took me months to recognize it, marked my first encounter with a Will that would many times overpower my own."

They are quiet now, lost in their separate thoughts. The story has taken them most of the way to Ein Fadr. The sun is lowering in the sky. Jammana sees the Bedouin setting up their black tents at the outskirts of the village.

"What, do you suppose?" Faridah asks, gesturing toward the tents.

"It's too dry, even for Bedouin," Grandfather answers. "They want a turn at our spring."

Then the slope of the village comes into sight. Ein Fadr, where houses cling to one another and tenacious shrubs find life between the stones of walls. Where farmers as complicated as the earth itself flow into the fields each day as they have through generations.

Ein Fadr, where Mama warns that voices of the dead travel on breezes, and Grandfather Harif intuits each neighbor's history of troubles as surely as he senses the changing of seasons. Where once, nearly three decades ago, Faridah caught Mama as she tumbled into the world. Faridah helped by Jammana, though no one but Jammana seems to know this.

Small bodies covered with dusty scraps of cloth leap around them as their weary donkeys trudge toward the arched entry to Grandfather's courtyard. Jammana leans toward the village children, hoping they will talk to her, but at that moment they scatter as if in response to a signal only they can hear.

Great-aunt Khalah, Grandfather's sister who lives with him, is waiting. She carries the scent of bread, and her cheeks are dabbed with floury streaks. "Come, eat," she says to Jammana, and then, to Faridah, "It is Baraka's time." To Grandfather, she adds, "A Bedu seeks you."

Grandfather's eyebrows rise in question.

Khalah nods. "He asked for you by name."

"I must go find a baby," Faridah says.

Jammana steps to Faridah. "I'd like to see that," she says.

Faridah studies Jammana, then shakes her head. "One must enter a birthing room calmly but with energy."

"I have energy—as much as you," Jammana insists, though she has been riding since early morning and feels it.

Faridah's eyes show amusement. "Another time, perhaps. Now, rest."

"Eat something," Grandfather tells Jammana, putting an end to the argument. "I'll join you once I see what he wants, this Bedouin."

HARIF

Harif heads toward the tree that rises like an affirmation to Allah—Moses' Finger, mulberry of twisted trunk, purple fruit, and one bough that soars above the others. By day, women peel its bark to make brews against worms that hide within their children's bodies, or crush its heart-shaped leaves for juice to treat serpent bites. At evening, it is the *fellahin* who gather there, lids half closed in poses of thoughtfulness as they smoke, gossip, and debate with idle passion. Sometimes they summon the women and children to receive their decisions, and then Harif joins the others circled beneath the tree. Even the shepherd is wanted then. Moses' Finger is meeting place and more: a symbol of Ein Fadr's cohesion, of women who sustain their men, and

men who bravely bear the burden of leading. It is where a Bedouin awaits Harif now.

Faridah, two steps head of him, tosses her words behind her. "Nabeel may not approve of a visitor who wishes to be greeted by you instead of him."

Harif himself is puzzled as to why a Bedouin has asked for him by name, but he says only, "Nabeel's father carried on that rivalry, not he."

Faridah halts and faces him, her eyebrows raised skeptically. "You are still blinded by a boyhood friendship."

"Allah knows who I'd rather be blinded by."

Faridah gestures as though to brush him away. He hadn't expected anything else. "Let's talk seriously," she says. "Jammana's troubled."

"Of course she is. Ahmed plans to steal my daughter and granddaughter away." Harif is surprised by the vehemence of his own voice.

Faridah shakes her head. "It's not that. But I don't know what yet. Send her to me tomorrow."

"You'll discover it is simple. Jammana will never belong on the other side of the ocean, and she knows it. Didn't you see how she's ready to soak in my words like a caked patch of earth?"

"And you have words enough to flood," Faridah says lightly. Harif laughs. "I'll come bid good night to Jammana when I'm finished birthing," she calls as she moves with long strides toward Moses' Finger and beyond. Her shoulders shift with each step in a way that makes her seem to dance. Harif relishes the sight of her backside, slender as a girl's—perhaps because she never bore children.

A Bedouin astride a camel is staring after Faridah. Harif

studies the long, noble nose, the pronounced cheekbone. A leader, surely. The Bedouin turns. Only once before has Harif seen eyes like those, liquid as molasses, nightmare-dark. "By the breath of Allah!" Harif says. "Lafi abu Arudi al-Salman!"

Arudi al-Salman dismounts and kisses Harif three times on his cheeks. His voice is thick with emotion. "My friend. I took a chance you still lived."

"My sheep keep me strong. And now your presence blesses me and my family and neighbors."

"Who was that bold-looking woman?" Arudi al-Salman gestures after Faridah.

"Our midwife. Have you someone in need?"

The Bedouin laughs, and shakes his head.

"Then come. I'll make us coffee."

As soon as the Bedouin and his camel reach the courtyard, Jammana hurries over. The cloth she'd been wearing at her neck is now tied around her hair. Next to it, her face looks pale. "I know you," she says to Arudi al-Salman. "We passed you today. You were playing an instrument."

Harif's guest studies Jammana. "I was playing a *rabab* in the desert today, it's true. Only the music held my interest. I had no time for passing strangers."

"This," Harif says, "is my granddaughter, Jammana, visiting from Nablus. And my sister, Khalah. Allah has blessed us with the presence of an old friend, Lafi abu Arudi al-Salman."

Khalah, who has arrived with figs and bread, nods and disappears. Harif knows it would be proper for him to send

Jammana away now, but he doesn't. He is pleased by Jammana's assertiveness. His mother always spoke her mind, too—and from an early age, just like Jammana.

As the Bedouin chews on a fig, Harif drops a handful of coffee beans in his ladle and begins to roast them over the courtyard's small open fire. "And so, my friend, how have you passed these many years?"

"Moving, always. A village raid, from time to time." The Bedouin winks. "Trying to avoid the Hashemite soldiers, of course. And you? You've stuck to your home, I hope?"

"Once was enough," Harif says. Both men laugh.

"Once of what?" Jammana turns to Arudi al-Salman.

"He hasn't told you," the Bedouin asks, "how we met?"

"He pulled me from the desert's sea," Harif says. "May Allah always protect him." He spills the hot beans onto his mortar, and grinds. "I was a young man with no knowledge of the desert's tricks, sent on a mission to Beersheba. On the third day of my trip, sand began to move." He tests the size of his coffee grains by rubbing a pinch between his thumb and forefinger. "An easy breeze became a bitter wind, with muscle enough to uproot tents, bury fires, and transport the entire earth. The sky turned murky red. My camel vanished even as I gripped its neck. I pulled the invisible beast down, and we both lay waiting."

He drops the grains into his pot of steaming water and adds cardamom. "As it fled, the dust devil stole my footprints and sense of direction. When the wind stopped, clouds remained, and I began to travel in circles, not knowing if I was pointed toward the Gulf or the Galilee."

He places the pot back over the coals, closes his eyes briefly. "My camel and I ran out of food in two days, water in five," he says. "My tongue turned to saddle leather. I wore sand inside my body and out. I dreamed of home until thirst scrambled all thoughts." He wipes one eye, then the other, as though removing the grains that once blinded them. "It was too late for me. I knew it. Then I rounded a dune and smelled meat cooking. Desert spirits playing a trick on me, I believed. But my camel, thanks be to the Merciful, knew to aim for the scent."

"You cried like a baby when we dripped water from a rag into your mouth," the Bedouin recounts.

"It burned like fire, after so many days of thirst," Harif says. "But you were wise. You kept wrenching my mouth open to shake in more drops."

"Exposed to the desert's danger, my friend, you survived and toughened," the Bedouin says.

"And it is a joy equal to prayer for me to see you so well now," Harif answers. He places a leaf as a filter over the spout of his pot, then pours a cup of coffee and passes it to Arudi al-Salman with a bow of his head.

Jammana holds a cup out to Harif. "Grandfather?" she says. Before he can object, she adds, "But only, please, if it is hot like love and bitter like death."

Harif laughs in spite of himself, and pours her a small cup.

"I want to live with Bedouin," Jammana declares. "I've heard you are accepted as a grown-up by the time you're ten."

"Don't romanticize it, child," Arudi al-Salman says. "I would guess you are more comfortable here."

"Of course, Arudi al-Salman would never give it up," Harif says.

"No, never," the Bedouin agrees vehemently. "I have no

wish to be civilized. But some turn their back easily on our traditions. I've even heard of a tribe in the eastern reaches where the chief has traded his camel for a devil's tool—a pickup truck."

"But how will he get the fuel?" asks Harif.

"Exactly. And when this truck dies without the warnings that a camel gives, he and his passengers will be caught in the desert and we will find skeletons in the sand." The Bedouin spits. "He deserves the dagger."

"Blessings under Allah." A voice interrupts them. "We heard you had company, Harif. My uncle Nabeel, who leads our village, welcomes your guest. And I, as the future leader, greet him also."

Adil, nephew of the *mukhtar*, Nabeel, bows his head slightly as he steps from the evening dusk into the light given off by the fire in Harif's courtyard. He is a lean man with compressed eyes. Nabeel, behind him, nods in greeting. Harif does not smile.

"So, I have upset village protocol by calling on you directly," Arudi al-Salman murmurs to Harif as he rises.

Harif shakes his head. "It's fine." He turns to Nabeel and introduces his guest.

"May we join you for coffee?" Adil asks rhetorically. Harif pours two cups. "Rafa's daughter?" Adil asks after a moment, gesturing to Jammana with his chin.

"And she can speak, too," Jammana murmurs near Harif's ear. She knows how to amuse him, but her timing is poor. He coughs to cover his laughter.

"Jammana, fetch us more figs, will you?" he manages after a moment.

Jammana shoots him a displeased look, but rises to do as he asks.

"Under Allah, we could use some rain," Adil says.

"It will come," Arudi al-Salman answers.

"If it pleases Allah," Harif says.

The men sip their coffee silently. After a moment, Adil turns to Arudi al-Salman. "The last time Bedouin came to our village, fifty-six years ago, they stole three sheep and one woman. What do you seek now?"

Arudi al-Salman's face tightens. He rests his hand on his dagger and leans forward. "What do you insinuate?" he asks coolly.

"Forgive my young nephew," Nabeel interjects. "His wife is with the midwife even as we speak. A child soon will be born. He is on edge."

Arudi al-Salman turns slowly from Adil. "It is true times are dry," he says to Nabeel. "We would welcome a morning at your spring. But only that. We know how to fend for ourselves in the desert."

"Of course," says Nabeel.

"We are no more than passing clouds," the Bedouin continues. "My cherished cousin, a childhood playmate, was visiting Amman as part of a delegation to the king when he fell ill and died. We are on our way to collect the body."

"You were mourning, then, when we saw you," says Jammana who has returned with the figs.

"You are welcome to stay, my friend," Harif says, "as long as you want."

"That is right," adds Nabeel. "It is our joy to welcome you here."

Adil leans forward. "Forgive my suspicions," he says, though he still wears caution on his face.

Arudi al-Salman keeps his eyes on Adil as he takes a slow sip of coffee. At last he nods. "May Allah bless you for your hospitality," he says.

"How do you happen to know Harif?" Adil asks.

"This is a topic of little interest," begins Harif, hoping to redirect the conversation. He sends Arudi al-Salman a pointed look, but the Bedouin doesn't notice.

"I rescued him in the desert once, uncountable moons ago," Arudi al-Salman says. "He lost his way to the Beersheba district."

Adil visibly struggles with this information. "*You?* How can—? But I thought—" He turns to Harif. "That's not what you told us. You said," —his voice is raised in accusation— "you made a trade with a sand spirit. That's why you were allowed to stay."

"There are many spirits in the desert sands," Arudi al-Salman says. "The Bedouin is king among them."

"You were a boy at the time, weren't you?" Harif says, striving to keep his voice mild.

"I've heard the story. We all know it well." Adil's lips grow thin. "The elders let you stay among us only because your link to the lower world was gone. That's what you said. I wonder what they will think now." He turns to the Bedouin. "You see, we are an ancient village. We've managed to survive because we are righteous. The impure among us are . . ." He pauses. "Dealt with."

"Adil," Nabeel interrupts, rising to his feet. "We can delay no further. We must check on your wife." He nods at

Harif. To the Bedouin, he says, "Your presence is a gift from Allah. You are welcome at our spring."

"For a morning, you said?" Adil adds.

Arudi al-Salman rises also and bows his head until they have left. Then he turns to Harif. "So, my friend?"

"A piece of trouble is coming for me, I suspect," Harif answers.

"Because of a sand spirit?" The Bedouin's eyebrows are raised.

"I didn't like the eyes of the younger one," Jammana says.

Harif drops his prayer beads back in his pocket and lets his fingers tangle his beard. "Here it is," he says. "May the All-Knowing vouch for my honesty. I was born with the gift of seeing the future, just as my granddaughter was given the ability to see the past. By the time I was a young man, I'd foreseen misfortunes here, so they distrusted me. They said I brought evil to the village. They sent me on a mission, believing I would die traveling alone in the desert. When I returned alive, some were angry. They asked how I survived. I admitted I'd gotten lost, but I invented a sand spirit. I said I'd traded my gift of prophecy to the spirit, who, in return, guided me to safety. The elders met at Moses' Finger and allowed me to stay."

"Sand spirit! Wonderful story!" Arudi al-Salman laughs loudly until he notices neither Harif nor his granddaughter join him. "It was decades ago," he says. "It no longer matters. Surely."

Harif shakes his head. "As Adil said, the elders believe our village has flourished so long because it is pure before Allah. Ein Fadr is where my parents lived and died, and their parents, and so on. It is to me what the open desert is to you. But I know it also as a place of suspicion. Old grudges linger here. They lie dormant so you nearly forget. Then they rise suddenly. They move like a slow burn across the fields where men are working. They cling to the laundry women spread on roofs to dry. In this way they enter every home."

"Mama says that, too," Jammana says. "But why did you lie to them, Grandfather? Didn't you think they would find out someday?"

"Nabeel doubted my story from the start," Harif says, "and I didn't hide the truth from my family. But it was enough to satisfy the simpleminded ones—those most likely to try to drive me away. After some time, I hoped they'd just forgotten about my visions, my tale."

"And now?" Arudi al-Salman asks.

Harif has a sudden imprecise premonition. He sees a violet, sun-stained piece of glass flashing in the sun. The air turns fragile as it vibrates with sound—the caw of a bird, perhaps? Then anguish rolls in, unrelenting as the sirocco that blows from the Libyan desert. He senses coming despair, just as he did before the deaths of his mother and his wife. Who it will be this time, he cannot tell. Why in the name of Allah have they become so vague, these images of the future? He tries to erase the uneasiness from his expression as he turns to Arudi al-Salman.

"And now," he says. "You entertained me with poetry when I fell into your path. Let me return the favor. I know many tales. Only it must be a true one, because in stories, truth is as powerful as a well-watered camel." He reaches to smooth Jammana's hair. "When young, who can fathom being old? Who, healthy and strong, can picture death? Imagination is weak, and made-up tales are pale as rock-scrubbed cotton. Memory—that's what satisfies."

Jammana nods, momentarily seeming so much older than she is. Then she reaches to his beard, tugs it insistently. "Tell your first vision."

"That? It isn't what I had in mind." Harif looks to his guest.

Arudi al-Salman has removed the saddle from his camel and dropped it on the ground. He sits and leans against it. "Tell," he agrees. "I'd like to hear more of this gift of yours."

Harif hesitates. That is a story he has never told, not even to Rafa. There was no need . . . It's village history, and others could inform her.

Jammana, insistent child, waits, expectant. He studies her. Why not? This time, why not let the dung mix with petals of jasmine? If through the merging he achieves a sliver of sweet clarity, Jammana might forgive eventually.

Because he knows the time will come for absolutions. It always does.

So he nods once and loses himself in the story, in that Harif of youthful days.

Even before Harif was born, his grandfather Shunnar predicted he would have the power to peer into the future. Shunnar himself had a gift: He was known as far away as Cairo and Beirut for his ability to foretell not only the gender of a pregnant woman's unborn child but its temperament. During Alula's previous pregnancy, Shunnar had placed his hand on her distended belly and said, "This girl shall have the patience of an angel and will be an unparalleled cook."

When his hands rested on Harif within Alula, Shunnar smiled and said she would have a boy this time. Then he moved his fingers, and his face creased. "Harshest of visions," he said. "He must witness troubles twice."

More than that, Shunnar would not say. But Alula vowed before her husband and her father to make sure by the time this unborn son reached manhood, he could handle whatever Allah dispensed. So when she heard of the tric-trac game and the lost wager, she ordered Harif to her side for a year.

Alula's husband, Bahir, opposed her plan when she revealed it in the relative privacy of their single-room dwelling. "You have spoiled Harif by treating him differently all these years," he told his wife while their son and daughter, still and wide-eyed, lay listening on their mats. "If he is to have the gift your father predicted—and I'm not saying I believe that, Alula—he must be tough and disciplined. Summoning him to the protection of your skirts is not the answer now." Bahir stood straight over Alula, who sat cross-legged, weaving a basket.

"Such things you believe!" Alula scoffed at her husband in a way a woman never could in front of an outsider, and few dared even in privacy. "My daughter and I join you at harvest time, don't we? We climb the trees to beat down the olives. We work a full day in the sun and then return home to cook."

"All work as one at harvest time," Bahir said.

She put down the basket, dipped her fingers in a cup of olive oil, and rubbed it on her hands. "You had the first chance to lead Harif to manhood," she said. "Now the turn is mine."

The marriage of Harif's parents had been arranged, of course. But Bahir, eleven years older, had known Alula all her life and loved her as long. He had watched her as a carefree three-year-old toddling through the village. With growing interest, he'd observed her as a ten-year-old whose smile held a dual promise of openness and wickedness. When she was thirteen, curves began to emerge in her body, and she rebelled. One day, Alula left her female work in the courtyard and sneaked to the fields, where she found her brother sleeping as his flock wandered. She gathered and hid every sheep. She even managed to place one poor, bleating animal in a tree, although how, no one ever discovered. When her mischief-making was revealed, most villagers clucked their tongues. But Shunnar only laughed, and Bahir, her future husband, vowed to himself that he would love her forever.

Alula wore her strength like a fine embroidered vest, and that night Bahir knew that arguing further would be like yelling in a sandstorm. Besides, although he prayed five times a day, his devotion to Allah was undeniably second to his adoration of Alula.

He turned toward Harif, who lay quietly, awaiting the outcome. "Do as she wishes," he said. "A year will fly by."

Harif did not complain. He was not dismayed. He'd always been deeply curious about the women's hidden world and felt eager to see where this effort to tame him would lead.

His mother instructed him to join her the next morning at the village well. When the women saw Harif struggling to balance an earthen pot atop his head, they giggled in dismay.

The well was a female sanctuary, and males older than three years were not welcomed. Only there could the women find solace in sharing the salt and stone of their days.

Alula explained her problem to her sisters and cousins and friends. "My son needs guidance only we women can provide," she told them. "I ask this not for his own sake. Don't forget, he is to be a seer, and if we share our wisdom now, he will be able to give more to all later on."

At one time or another, Alula had helped most of the women who were gathered. She worked as hard as five men to bring in crops or build a new home. Beyond that, she had a gift. The songs she sang in her husky voice carried the scents of clover and verbena, the sense of freedom and desire. The melodies within her could still a dust devil, gather the stars, persuade an olive tree to drop its fruit. She was summoned at moments of birth and death to soothe newborns or elderly ill with her music. Ein Fadr was a taciturn village, its people rarely given to praise. But among the women, Alula was loved with extravagance.

So when she asked this favor, the inclusion of her son in their group, the women agreed. Harif knew his own respectful manner helped them in their decision. He almost never spoke at the well, but listened with an interest that the wives and mothers and sisters recognized all the more for its rarity among men or boys. They soon grew comfortable enough to talk in his presence nearly as freely as before. Over time, he learned of monthly discomforts, herbs boiled and consumed in order to bear sons, even complaints against husbands— daring topics to share with a boy.

Each morning after drawing water, the women adjourned to their own courtyards to carry out the day's work. In the *taboon*, the cramped communal oven house shared with the extended family, Harif helped his mother with chores. Alula's specialty was *kibbeh*, small, egg-shaped meat pies stuffed with ground lamb and pine nuts. At her side, Harif grew to appreciate the potency of spices and herbs. He learned to select cardamom pods whose scent reminded him of trees listing in the wind, and cloves smelling of the tangy sweetness of early morning. But most of all, he gained at last a conscious sense of Allah's power. He saw that even though his mother never varied the recipe, every *kibbeh* emerged from the oven tasting slightly different. The fate of each one, he understood, rested in the hands of something infinitely larger than even Alula.

Thus Harif's days settled into a routine, until the autumn morning when he sat crosslegged in the courtyard grinding wheat, his mother near him weaving a reed mat. He was listening to her hum when he felt a flash of heat, followed by a shiver of chill. His right arm tingled and went numb. He dropped the pestle. Perspiration beaded on his forehead as a vision flooded his mind.

"What is it?" Alula asked, kneeling. He flung himself upon her. His black, curly hair stood out like a halo, accentuating the sudden whiteness of his skin. "Where is the pain? Your stomach? Your head? Can't you tell me anything?"

He shook his head, so Alula lifted him and carried him into the house to his sleeping mat spread on the floor. Once inside, he would not loosen his grip on her. Alula touched his forehead and ankles, felt the pulse at his wrist, and studied deep inside his mouth. Seeing nothing unusual, she instructed a neighbor to prepare soothing tea flavored with wild sage. Harif held the cup with one hand, while the other clenched the rope that belted Alula's dress.

By nightfall, neighbors and holy men came. Most spoke with quiet concern, but the voice of one held annoyance. "What, in the name of Allah, is troubling you?" demanded the *mukhtar* curtly. This venerated man of fifty-two felt unable to contain his temper around the el Jabr clan. He had heard Alula predict that her son, Harif, would one day become *mukhtar*, a post he intended to reserve for his own son, Nabeel.

"Why do you lie here, clinging to your mother as though you were a nursing babe?" the *mukhtar* asked.

At this, Alula calmed herself and pronounced that as in most fits and stages with children, the less attention paid to Harif's odd behavior, the more quickly it would run its course. "Go home," she told those gathered. "He shall be at the oven again soon."

The neighbors left. But the *mukhtar* would not allow himself to be dismissed by a woman. He looked directly toward Bahir.

"Our house is honored by your visit," Bahir said. "May Allah the All-Merciful grace your days with length and joy." Here he paused. "But now . . ." He shrugged, and nodded meaningfully toward Alula.

Grunting his disapproval, the *mukhtar* left.

Alula sent her daughter, Khalah, to gather a large bunch of stacte blossoms, as it was March and the shrubs were in full bloom. The snowdrop flowers were Alula's favorite, and she thought they might soothe Harif. She sent Khalah back for a second armful, and then a third. Finally, the sticky scent overwhelmed the room, but Harif remained pressed into his mother, inhaling deeply, trying to memorize the smell of her skin, its subtle mixture of roots pulled from moist dirt and freshest olive oil. Alula told Bahir that if it were possible, Harif would crawl back into the womb.

For three days and nights, Harif clung to his mother. Alula stroked his hair and sang songs that turned into tales and carried the two of them from the Yemeni peninsula to the camel's hump of Turkey. She dozed occasionally, and Harif watched her, his grip always firm. Khalah took over all household duties.

Harif battled sleep with every weapon he had. He bit his lips painfully. He bent his fingers back toward his wrist. But he could not forever forestall the drop of determined eyelids, and on the fourth day, he descended into a fitful slumber. His mother touched his forehead. She rose, and arched her long, slender back. She twisted silver bracelets onto her wrist, smoothed a headdress over her polished copper hair. She promised Khalah to return in a few minutes.

"Allah be praised, he is better? We miss him at the well," said a cousin as Alula emerged into the courtyard. She smiled, nodded, and strolled languidly over the rock-strewn hills toward the village's terraced olive grove, humming softly.

She may have gone through the grove's center or skirted along its edge; what is certain is that as she reached the far side of the fields, the sky changed twice, to white and then black, and a storm thrust itself over a hill. A pitiless wind propelled tiny pellets of rain that ricocheted off the ground. Alula ran under an olive tree that stood apart from all the others, and hugged its trunk with arms and legs.

The women back in Ein Fadr gazed upward. The wind thrashed their hair and dresses. Then came a low, unrelenting buzz. Partly woven baskets and fresh-baked bread slid from their hands as they ran to their homes.

The rain lasted only minutes. The sky unleashed a single jagged stroke of lightning and a bellow of thunder.

Harif awoke shivering. Khalah covered him with an extra rug. "Mama will be back soon," she said, but he flung off the rug and bolted through the door. He plunged through the courtyard to the hills, his sister following, the women watching him go. "Harif, you are still ill. Stop," Khalah called, her voice shrill. "Oh, Mama will be angry that I've let you out." Harif did not respond.

The air felt new as it does after a shower; the birds returned to their harmonics. Harif was not fooled by these pleasantries. He headed up one slope, down another, directly to the far edge of the olive grove. By the time he stopped, his bare feet were bloodied by sharp stones. He did not notice. Filled with two contradictory emotions—a child's inability to understand and an adult's grasp of loneliness to come—he looked.

Her body was slumped against the blackened trunk. Steel-gray fingers branded the insides of her arms. Her hair was singed, shoes blown off by the force. The smell of scorched flesh saturated the air.

Harif is startled by the sound of a jagged breath—his own. He had forgotten his listeners. Now he sees that Jammana's fists are clenched and the eyes of the Bedouin are lowered.

"We buried my mother before sunset," he says, "her face turned toward Mecca. Ein Fadr's scribe recorded the numbers of her life: thirty-four years old, married nineteen years, with only three stomachs, and two of the three—Khalah and me—surviving.

"Ein Fadr trembled with the women's ululations. The *mukhtar* canceled weddings for a year, and seasonal feasts were muted affairs. Of all the children and cousins and elderly who gathered at the funeral, only I did not weep. I wrapped my arms around my chest, trying to shrink, but I did not cry. The *mukhtar*, muttering under his breath, surmised that I had links to the *jinn* of the subtle world and was myself only half human. But in fact, my sorrow was as great as anyone's, perhaps greater since it was coupled with guilt. I couldn't help wondering: If I had not been so constantly at my mother's side, would I still have envisioned her death? Without the vision, would my mother have died?"

No one speaks for several moments. Then Arudi al-Salman rises. "Allah bless the teller and the tale," he says. "May you now leave this sorrow behind in our hands."

Harif does not reply.

"I must return to my own now," the Bedouin adds after a minute. "I will say good-bye tomorrow, and the young villager will see his cattle and women are left in place."

After the Bedouin leaves, Harif turns to his granddaughter. Her cheeks, he sees, are white as an October sun. "And my mama?" she asks. "Can you see what will happen to her when I'm not there?"

Harif dusts off his hands and clears his throat. "No, child, I cannot direct my gift." He gazes upward then, struggling to still the inner pounding that always comes when he recalls Alula's death. At last he heaves a breath. "I thought Faridah would have stopped by now to say good night," he says. "Let's find her, shall we?"

FARIDAH

Faridah, impatient, turns her reed basket upside down and shakes it. Out spill a grinding stone and a dozen palm-sized burlap bags. "Coltsfoot," she mutters to herself. "Eucalyptus. Some ribble grass? Ah, there it is." Her fingers skip, feverish as a gust of premonition before the *khamsin* winds.

No time to spare. She is tolerated in Ein Fadr only because of her clear head and quick hands, which the women say make her the most skilled midwife between Jerusalem and Beirut. But every birth is a fresh test, and this one, she can tell, will challenge as few do. Not due to the life she's dragged from the womb—that seemed healthy enough as she rubbed its body with salt and oil and filled its ear with the necessary prayer. *"La illaha illa Allah . . ."* There is no God but

Allah, and Mohammed is his messenger. No, the problem is not with the infant but the mother, Baraka, who lies in the center of the room. Delirious. Coughing up blood.

Grind, grind. Faster.

Baraka wheezes. A dull yellow phlegm streaked with bright red oozes from the corner of her mouth. Pausing in her work, Faridah gently dabs at Baraka's lips. Baraka opens her eyes wide. "Off with you," she shrieks. "You want to hurt me!"

"Of course not," Faridah says soothingly. "You're fine. You have a boy."

Baraka jerks away. "Don't touch me!" Her voice turns guttural. "They've told me about you, the shadow that hovers near you . . . the death angel."

Ya, Harif! How Faridah wishes he were here—that annoying old man, that endearing old man who tarries always at the edges of her thoughts. But Harif is busy pouring a cascade of words upon his granddaughter. As though the story of another's life could be salve to the child's wounds. As though words could solve anything! Even Moses, sacred stutterer, couldn't persuade without a miracle or two.

"No, Baraka. No death angel here," says Baraka's younger sister, Manara, who is settling the baby. Then she mutters to Faridah: "I told Adil this cough was worsening. They refused to fetch you until the last moment."

This doesn't surprise Faridah. Baraka is, by marriage, one of the *mukhtar's* clan. Faridah herself was of them for six long years, also by marriage. Then she was cast from her husband's home for failing to bear children. But she refused to go quietly, and now the clan's men view her with the unreasonable loathing the sun feels for the moon that overwhelms it each night.

Baraka shivers, her face scarlet and hot as euphorbia coals. Faridah dips the hem of her skirt in a cup of water, dabs below Baraka's eyes. The mother's chest heaves, then rattles harshly. It sounds worse even than the noise of skin ripping, as it sometimes does when a baby emerges. Manara presses her fingers hard against her cheeks.

Faridah moves to the fire by the door, tosses her ground herbs in a pot. A few dashes of boiling olive oil to moisten and heat them, and then she will paint Baraka's chest. Silently, she begs the flames: *Warm! With speed!*

She spies the copper bowl of water Baraka's husband, Adil, left her. He washed his feet in it and told Faridah that his wife must drink it directly before birth. "A mere sip will bind the dust of the new child," he said. A custom of their clan, she knows.

Faridah didn't answer him, but now she lifts the bowl and flings its contents into the corner.

"Faridah, my sister must drink of that—Adil will ask," Manara begins urgently, but Faridah waves her to silence. Faridah may not always know what will cure, but she knows instinctively what will not.

Adil once sought to marry Rafa. What joy Faridah felt when Rafa refused! Of course, Adil is not the only superstitious villager. Faridah has struggled long and hard against the ridiculous customs that flourish in her adopted village, and had some success, especially with the younger ones. No longer do the villagers protect an infant from illness by cutting off a piece of its ear, baking it in a loaf and leaving it out for the hyenas. No longer do they ensure a safe pregnancy by storing crushed newborn dog, dried and salted, in the corner of the room. Let other villages cast such spells. The midwife won't allow that nonsense here!

Faridah returns to the fire, tests a drop of the oil and herb mixture on her wrist. Eiya! A little too warm! She blows on it—hard.

She dabs at Baraka's face with the edge of her damp skirt. Baraka doesn't object this time—her eyes are closed and she seems to rest. The baby, too, is quiet. Manara brushes by Faridah, pacing, and rubbing her hands.

"Child," Faridah says. "Sit. Grind me some comfrey root."

Manara rushes to Faridah's basket in the corner and sets urgently to work. Faridah had hoped to calm her, but it may not be possible.

The tension in this room stems from more than Baraka's sickness. From more, even, than the helicopters that sometimes growl overhead or the explosions they hear to the west, where the cease-fire line lies. A dank warning scent floats in Ein Fadr, dirtying Faridah's hair and skin. She can't place it but knows it is responsible for a nightmare she's had for three nights now. In it, she sees Harif surrounded by an angry circle of men. She hears the female ululations that signal the death of a villager. Then she wakes, sweating.

Faridah rarely remembers the dreams that dash through her mind at night, and she refuses to ponder the meaning of this one. She forces it from her thoughts as she removes

Baraka's *thobe* and pushes aside her thin vest. Better to con-
centrate on coating Baraka's chest with the herbal mixture.
Thick as Koranic verse it must be. Heavy as rock on the Temple Mount, and warm as dung from Mohammed's heaven-
bound steed. Because only with help from above will Faridah
cure this woman.

She covers Baraka's chest again. Now she will mix the
torchweed blossoms with the comfrey root, and the woman
will drink. Drink until it's gone, and then Faridah will make
more. Whether through infusions or rubs or sheer determination, Faridah will force Baraka back to health. In all these
years only one mother in her care has died, and she can't bear
to let another slip away.

Besides, if she loses Baraka, she'll be gone, too. She
knows what nonsense the elders whisper: that *ghouleh* taught
her how to deliver babies, that she consults with them at
night behind boulders. She doubts they really believe their
own stories, it is simply that they can make no sense of Faridah. Faridah's mother was a woman in the way men ordain:
her voice a whisper never raised, her step quiet as a moth's,
her very sneeze suffocated into silence. At work to the end,
she died while mending her husband's shirt. Faridah hasn't
been that meek in decades, and it confuses the men. How
satisfied they would be to cover her skin with soil.

She doesn't believe in prayer, but she cannot still the inner whisper: *Please, Allah—or whatever deciphers the lives of
women—please, don't allow this illness to lie beyond my herbs and oil.*

Faridah lifts Baraka's head, puts a sip of tea in her mouth. She turns to Manara. "Give her this, one swallow at a time until it is gone. She must sip, then rest. Then sip more. She will recover, don't fear."

Manara nods. Her eyes fill with tears. "Thank you. I wish I could do something in return."

This Manara already looks like a mother, though at sixteen she is still unwed. She dresses in gray pants under a plain brown dress—no embroidery, none of the bright colors the young are so fond of. Perhaps because her sister is tied to the *mukhtar's* conservative family, she denies herself freedom.

But as Manara leans forward and speaks in a low voice, Faridah sees a hint of independence in the girl's eyes. "You know, a Jordanian captain came to the village a day ago. He told Nabeel the Hebrews believe someone here is organizing attacks. He warned it must stop or there would be trouble for all."

Silent, Faridah begins to gather her herbs and collect the bracelets shed during delivery.

"They walked off together," Manara says. "Nabeel and the captain."

Faridah suspects her expression betrays impatience. She can never still the twitching in her eyebrows when she is bored. "We are a tiny village, a mere grain of sand," Faridah says. "Those who would rule us will soon forget us."

"They want a name this time," Manara insists. "Someone to blame." She scans the room. "Once, I felt safe here. So far from the troubles of others. Now I sometimes imagine a snake rings Ein Fadr with his long body and waits to eat us." She steps closer. "Nabeel may be looking for someone to sacrifice. In the name of Allah, take care."

"Me?" Faridah stares hard at Manara, who finally cannot bear such a direct glance and bows her head.

"Just take care," Manara mutters.

Faridah tucks her basket decisively under her arm. She will not be intimidated! She never would have survived this long if she allowed threats to rattle her.

"You're as nervous as a shroud sewer," she tells Manara. "Eat a dozen onions over the next four days. I promise you'll sleep like a rock badger."

She declines to hold the baby—she's not given to coddling—but she kisses Manara's cheeks. On her way out, she sprinkles a bit of lemon balm in the corner. It should bring a measure of harmony.

When Faridah emerges into the night through the arched stone door, Manara at her heels, two men are waiting—Baraka's husband, Adil, and the *mukhtar*, Nabeel.

Adil does not push past Faridah into the room, as many new fathers do. He fidgets uneasily. "May Allah the Protector watch over you. Our home is honored by your presence," he says formally.

Faridah waves her hand, brushing his words away.

"What news?" he asks.

"What was created arrived."

"Don't make me wait further. Which is it?"

"Boy," answers Faridah. Adil grins proudly, but Faridah goes on grimly. "We've been tending the mother. Why wasn't I told about the cough?"

Adil glances at the *mukhtar* before meeting Faridah's

gaze. "She wasn't coughing before," he answers firmly. "She was fine."

A fighter plane flies just above the hilltops, then banks sharply toward the Dead Sea, drowning out Faridah before she can reply, so she shoots a pointedly skeptical glance over her shoulder to Manara. Manara, however, has arranged her face in a noncommittal expression. This girl cannot be expected to have the courage to contradict her brother-in-law. But Adil! Either he lies or he pays no attention to the women around him. In either case, he isn't worth Faridah's bother.

"Go see them," she says to Adil with a flip of her wrist, glancing up at the heat trail left by the plane. "I'll be to you later this evening." Adil hesitates, biting his lip as he glances uneasily at the door to his room. Faridah laughs. "Don't fear your baby," she says. "It doesn't carry a rifle."

Adil reddens, and anger crosses his face. Then he passes. Manara grips Faridah's arm. "Why must you make your tongue so sharp?" she whispers. "It's dangerous."

The girl may be right, but Faridah refuses to bridle her thoughts any longer. For many years she sought acceptance from the elders. Except for an occasional loss of temper, she performed all the necessary mincing, bowing, exchanging pleasantries. She even endured being called Barren Woman of Many Children—a false label, since she did carry a child once, though only Harif knows it. All her efforts brought no reward, so Faridah has decided to stop even trying. She speaks her mind. Let them do their worst.

"Onions," she says to Manara. "With every meal. Then you won't worry so."

"Come, Manara," Adil demands.

Manara shoves a lit lantern into Faridah's hand. "To

guide you home," she says. With a shake of her head, she disappears inside.

How Faridah's words concern them! It makes her smile, because she finds language to be frail, elusive. She's a woman of action, not phrases. She cannot suppress a satisfied nod at *that* thought.

Nabeel remains facing Faridah, blocking her way, hands crossed over his chest. "Something went wrong with the birth?" he asks.

Faridah raises her eyebrows.

"Something that caused the cough?" Nabeel goes on.

"You didn't hear me? She had the cough earlier."

Nabeel shrugs. "Her husband says no."

Faridah snorts. "Her husband is a simple boy. He wouldn't notice if a dozen holy Sufis rode into Ein Fadr on asses."

The hint of a grin plays on Nabeel's lips.

"They say you've chosen him to be the next *mukhtar*," Faridah goes on. "Hoping to look wise by comparison?"

Nabeel's mouth turns into a puckered line. "I, too, visited Baraka two days ago. I noticed no cough."

Faridah groans. "Do you really think a child removed from here"—Faridah gestures broadly toward her own thighs—"causes a cough from here?" She indicates her upper chest.

"Why not? They both meet in the middle." Nabeel points to Faridah's stomach.

Faridah tosses back her head and laughs. "Nabeel," she says, "you should have schooled more when you had the chance."

Nabeel glares, his face becoming his father's, full of

grudges, without memory of joy or mischief. "Insults are your calling. That's been true from the day you"—his voice deepens—"spat at my father."

Ah, yes! Faridah can't restrain the smile that comes unbidden to her lips. It's been decades, but still it pleases her to remember gathering the saliva into her mouth, spraying spit toward the bottom of the *mukhtar*'s robe. The widening of his eyes, the gaping of his shocked mouth. A foolhardy act, undeniably, but it filled her with such joy!

"You were only a boy," she says, and starts to move past him, but he grips her by the arm. That startles her. Nabeel has never touched her. Only two men ever have.

His hand feels callused and cool. "Watch yourself, Faridah," Nabeel says. "I feel the villagers readying to visit the past again. Old suspicions will be recalled." His voice, sneering, reveals its own echo. "It is not wise for you to arouse new anger."

The words she barely hears. His eyes disturb her, though. They hold many drops of water: one of determination, another of guilt. A third of nostalgia. A fourth, sorrow.

The guilt troubles her most.

She pulls away from his hold, steps back.

"Faridah!" Someone calls her name. It is Jammana. Harif trails behind. "We came looking for you," the girl says, moving past Nabeel to take Faridah's hand. Then she seems to see something in Faridah's face, or perhaps Nabeel's. "Did the newborn die?"

"No, child." Faridah, eyes steady on Nabeel, squeezes Jammana's hand. "The baby is fine."

"What, then?" Harif asks gruffly. Faridah can feel his

stare. No one replies. Nabeel remains facing Faridah, his back to Harif. At last, he lifts his chin.

"May Allah the Great Interceder see to your safety, Faridah," he intones.

"And to yours," Faridah says, allowing her skepticism to be heard. "Also to yours."

JAMMANA

Jammana hears the shuffle of approaching hooves and the restrained whinny of a patient beast pulled too sharply to a halt. Faridah raises her eyebrows. "Who's come in a rush?" She flings the door wide to the Samarian hills, and strides into her courtyard.

The Bedouin Arudi al-Salman towers on his camel. A *keffiyeh* wrapped around his head trails down beyond the shoulders of his robe. He nods regally at the woman and the girl, then begins to speak.

> "For three days I've not touched food,
> My liver's been long dry.
> My heart's been restless since she left,
> My soul leaks away."

Jammana glances at Faridah, who seems as perplexed as she. The Bedouin saturates his words with gestures, recounting a tale of a woman at a well and the warrior who wins her love. He describes the warrior's devotion with enormous feeling. Jammana cannot look away. When he finishes, he joins his hands on his lap. For several minutes, the only sound is that of his camel sniffing the ground.

Faridah speaks at last. "I know you. You're the one who brought great trouble to Harif. All the village is muttering against him because you made him seem a liar." Her hands sit on her hips, and each time she says "you," she says it hard.

"That was not my intention. Further, it's not why I'm here now." Arudi al-Salman smoothes his robe. "We go today to Amman. We will return in a week's time. I would like you to join me then."

At last, Jammana understands. So this is how men propose! She wonders if Faridah will mount the camel immediately and depart with the Bedouin. She wonders if she could go, too. There is a musical pause of possibilities—the crisp beating of a wing above, the slight rustle of a passing lizard.

When Faridah speaks, however, she wrinkles her nose. "You want to marry?"

The Bedouin king gives the barest of nods.

"Perhaps you have not noticed," Faridah says. "My days for weddings are gone."

Jammana studies Faridah, remembering with some surprise that she is as old as Grandfather. But her body bends easily as a sapling, her fingers can fly faster than sight, and her light-colored eyes reveal a quality, fierce and untouched, that makes her seem a girl.

"Nonsense." The Bedouin sweeps his hand as though to

dismiss the issue. "What is time but the changing of the sands? Your spirit moves me, its strength and intensity."

"What do you know of my spirit?"

"I've seen you walk," the Bedouin says. "Heard you speak—evidence enough."

Faridah waves her fingers through the air and chuckles. It is a dismissive sound. "You say you know me. Yet you believe that I would choose to spit sand from my supper all my remaining days? To rise before dawn and draw your morning milk from the udders of cranky beasts? All this to become Wife Number—what? Four? Five?"

Faridah's merriment is so infectious, Jammana almost laughs herself. Instead, she glances at the Bedouin. Suddenly, he looks nothing like the man who played his instrument, nor the one who gave audience to Grandfather's story. Certainly not the one who just captivated Jammana with his proposal. His eyes are hooded. His mouth, stretched in anger, almost disappears. He draws himself up, handling the saber at his waist. Jammana backs away. "This is a cruel response to the compliment of my proposal," the Bedouin says. "You have insulted an honorable man."

The camel lifts his head warily, and then, as if realizing the Bedouin's anger is not aimed at him, lets it fall again.

"If you think to frighten me," Faridah replies, "you know nothing of my spirit."

The Bedouin raises his chin so high, his eyes are only slits. "Springs should run dry in your sight," he says. "You should end your days bent, like lavender without water." Jammana reaches for Faridah's skirt. *"Yallah!"* the Bedouin calls to his camel, and the animal haltingly turns away.

"Come." Faridah turns to Jammana, a smile still at her lips.

Jammana shudders as she watches the Bedouin ride away. "Will he try to hurt you?"

"He'll be gone by lunch, and we'll never see him again." Faridah links her arm through Jammana's. "A Bedouin stays nowhere for long, and certainly not where his pride has been wounded. Still, let's not mention it to anyone, Jammana."

Another secret. Jammana can't keep many more.

In the two days since she arrived in Ein Fadr, nothing has been revealed, nothing has become clearer. In fact, she's more confused. The memory of Mama's birth remains unresolved, and, worse, she's had a second vision, its images sharp as pottery shards piercing her palm. She pictures a tree stump where women have gathered to plead. On the ground nearby lies a piece of glass stained violet by the sun. Then she has a nagging sense of a shadow vanishing at midday, replaced with hues of emotion: amber of guilt, steel-white pain, crimson regret. Jammana knows her nights will be quieter once the meaning of her memories becomes clear. But it has been difficult to ask Faridah the questions that trouble her now.

"Listen to them quarrel," Faridah says as she joins Jammana at the arched doorway. The snarl of jackals can be heard more clearly in Faridah's home than in any other. That is due to the village hierarchy, Jammana knows. Traditionally the *mukhtar*'s family takes the rooms highest on the hill and closest to Moses' Finger. Below the tree in intricate descending social order come the quarters of the others. Dwellings are passed from one generation to the next, so it is easy to tell which family has been valued the most and which the least. Grandfather lives with Khalah in the rooms their parents once occupied, just below Moses' Finger. Faridah's home is at the village's very fringe, the lowest spot on the slope.

"Sit, now," Faridah says. She leaves the door open, and glossy shafts of light invite themselves through high ventilation holes, warming the room to an almond color. She begins to sort herbs, touching one to her tongue, sniffing another, testing for freshness. "Your grandfather thinks you are troubled about America."

"I don't want to move," Jammana agrees. "In Nablus, I have my lemon tree to climb in the courtyard, and the field of wild lavender to lie in behind our house." Often at early morning, in the final drowsy stage before waking, she finds herself reciting verb conjugations. *Ana antemee ila,* I belong to. *Enta tantamee ila,* You belong to. *Howa yantamee ila,* He belongs to.

Still, the move has been overshadowed by other worries. "It doesn't seem real yet," she says.

Faridah nods. "If you go, who will you miss?" she asks.

"Grandfather." Jammana pauses. "And you."

"No, I mean in Nablus."

"Umm Mahir," Jammana says. "The one who lost her son. She's our best friend, Mama's and mine. Mama says it is because Umm Mahir is Egyptian, not from Nablus, and Mama isn't either. But I think what Mama most admires is that Umm Mahir refuses to keep her sorrow hidden."

Faridah pitches herbs on her grinding stone. "Are there no children you will miss?"

Jammana looks away. "I liked Umm Mahir's son," she says, and her voice comes out cross.

"And your father?" Faridah asks after a moment. "He's determined to go?"

"Father's always determined." Jammana warms to this subject. "I remember a story he told me. When he was my age, a Scottish missionary came looking for a boy to be lowered into Jacob's Well, the one the Christians like to visit. The missionary said he'd lost something and offered a reward. But no one would help because they thought spirits lived in the well. Finally, Father agreed. The missionary got eight men and four lines of camel rope. He tied the ropes around Father's waist, and the men lowered him down the well. Father said the air became thin and rancid, and he felt sick spinning to the bottom. But he rested only a moment. Then he began tugging rocks aside, groping in the dark. It took nearly an hour to find what the missionary wanted: a dirty book three inches thick. When they pulled Father up, he saw it was a family Bible, generations old. You know what he did?"

Faridah shakes her head.

"He threw it down the well again." Jammana says each word slowly. "He said if he'd known what the Scotsman sought, he'd never have agreed to help. The missionary was so angry that he sprang at Father, and the men had to pull him off."

This is not an event Jammana has dreamed—she has never been able to dream Father's past unless it is connected with Mama's. But she can imagine how Father looked, back stiff, eyes aflame. So unrelenting. No one is more determined than Father.

Jammana, feeling Faridah watching her, tries to redirect the conversation. "Tell me about bringing babies. Tell me about"—she takes a deep breath—"when Mama was born."

"How about when you came into this world?" Faridah doesn't wait for a reply. "That night I will never forget. January. Clear, full of stars. Stars and fighting!" She chuckles, a sound of stones skipping across the surface of water. "Your

neighbors—a carpenter and his wife—were yelling and wailing. The usual noises of men and women together. I asked
your mama if she wanted me to silence them, but she said,
'No. This is a night for life.'" Faridah shakes her head, smiling. "With you, your mama had her way. Her miscarriages
were in the hospital. That's where Ahmed wanted you to be
born. But Rafa was afraid of the hospital. This one at home,
she told your father. First time she ever stood up to him, I
think."

This isn't what Jammana wanted to discuss, but despite
herself, she is drawn in, wondering if the story may hold a
candle to the enigma of how others' memories come to her.

Faridah's eyes soften. "You two were linked," she says,
"even after I cut the cord. Some newborns shut their eyes
tight against the world; others gaze around without recognition. Some fasten on me as though I were responsible. You—
you were born with old eyes, like your mother. You began
playing with her hair. She whispered in your ear some secret,
I guess, and you made a laughing sound. 'Look, Faridah,' she
said. 'Allah the Beneficent has given me one at last to increase
both my joy and my pain.'" She smiles, then begins grinding
her herbs.

"But what is it like?" Jammana insists.

"Bringing the babies?" Faridah holds up a palm and wig-
gles her fingers slightly. "First the olive oil," she says, "to
massage into a woman's body. Then depths of darkness and
blinding light, with only your hands to guide you."

"Frightening." The word slips out inadvertently as Jammana thinks of the shadows and groaning when Mama was
born.

But Faridah shakes her head. "Not at all. A baby, they

say, is made of dust from three places—where he was conceived, where he is born, and where he shall die. He is also made of the substance that sets his nature—either sky or wind, fire or stone. So the whole course of his life is present at birth." Faridah lifts one hand, palm up. "That's what they say. I know only when I reach into the womb in that last moment before one becomes two, I feel the opposite of fear. I am reaching to the other side, caressing the essential. All answers seem accessible." She laughs. "A moment of sacred illusion."

"To have answers," murmurs Jammana.

Faridah looks at her sharply. "You had them, once," she says. "Newborns do. By the time they can talk, they've forgotten. By then their minds are too full of mundane lessons. I've seen it again and again." Then onto Faridah's face floods a look of regret. "All those babies, and only once . . ."

Jammana holds her breath and leans forward. Faridah, eyes cloudy, doesn't meet her gaze. "What?" Jammana asks. She hears the urgency in her own voice. Perhaps Faridah will explain now. The leaves in the fire, the choking sound, how Faridah didn't help Jammana's grandmother.

Faridah shakes her head as though releasing a memory. "Maybe you will be a midwife someday." She smiles, and her voice takes on the tone adults use when trying to soothe. She strokes Jammana's frizzy hair. "You'll be skilled at many things."

"Faridah! I'm old enough. You can tell me. What happened only once?"

Faridah, though, has finished. Mint sprigs clutched in hand, she walks to Divine's stall in the corner, separated from the rest of the room by a half wall. "Want to feed him?" she calls.

Jammana shrugs, unwilling to resume easy friendship. But finally she is unable to resist the pleasure of feeding the donkey. She follows Faridah and takes the mint. As Divine nibbles carefully from Jammana's hand, Faridah presses her cheek to his. She strokes the egg-white spot on his brown nose.

"My beauty," she says. "No *automobile* could ever replace you." She smiles at Jammana. "That mint gives Divine the sweetest breath of any ass on either side of the Jordan River." She reaches deep into her pocket. "I nearly forgot. For you. I've been working on it evenings."

She pulls forth a doll made of cotton with an embroidered face. Jammana cups her hands, and Faridah places the doll in them. Jammana is too old for dolls—surely Faridah knows that. But this is a curiously grown-up doll, more like a companion than a plaything. It has delicate wrists and ankles, and its expression is neither happy nor sad, but serene. How, with an embroidery needle, did Faridah do that?

Jammana presses it against her cheek, inhaling the sharp, reassuring scent of orange rind and earth. Faridah watches with satisfaction. "What shall we call her?" Faridah asks. "If she is to be polite—more than I, for example—she could be Melek, for angel. If you think you will whisper her secrets at night, perhaps Samar, for quiet one."

Jammana knows the name she wants. "Asima," she says. Defender.

Faridah studies her, then nods.

Jammana examines the doll, noticing odd stitching at the neck. "What is this?" she asks, holding Asima out.

Faridah leans forward to look. "My fingers slipped with the scissors when I was nearly done. I had to mend it."

Jammana touches the doll's neck and feels, unaccountably, a sharp pain in her own. Then it is gone. She doesn't mention it. She knows Faridah doesn't believe in omens. Faridah is a woman devoid of nonsense, with a will sharp as an embroidery needle. Jammana's memories make her certain of that. Especially one of Faridah as a young woman.

Ein Fadr, 1929. Faridah, eighteen years old, huddles on the floor of this very room. She cries like a girl still dangling from childhood, still needing a mother's cool finger to wipe away fiery tears. But soon enough, she stops. She gathers herself up. She stiffens her shoulder muscles and begins, clear-eyed, unpacking belongings her husband flung out their door. Possessions that once lay naked for the village to see but that from now on—she nods firmly—will be revealed only here.

Humming softly now, Faridah unrolls one sleeping mat stitched by her mother, a wedding present given six years earlier. Folded inside: two extra dresses and three head shawls. No cookware; she will make or trade for that in the days to come.

Then Faridah reaches into her right pocket, removes her hand, and shakes it. "Good-bye, shame," she says. She reaches into her left pocket. "You, too, confusion." She presses her hands together between her breasts, each no larger than a man's fist. "Fury, you stay here," she says. "Stay until I need you."

Jammana feels a rush of love, then pulls herself back. She releases her words without calculation, in a jumble. "What if you think someone tried to do something wrong, like throw a rock down on someone's head? But you aren't sure, maybe the rock just rolled on its own. You keep having bad dreams about it. What should you do?"

Faridah tilts her head, puzzled. Then her face clears. She reaches forward, takes Jammana's hands in her own. She positions Jammana's arms as though Jammana were hugging herself, and draws back. "There's only one person you can be sure of," she says. "You are touching her now."

Jammana drops her arms, steps away. "I don't believe that. I don't think you believe it."

"It's been my hardest lesson." Faridah looks out the doorway to the hills. "It is easier to strip thorns off a tragacanth bush at night than to learn that."

"What about Mama? Grandfather? You can't count on them? What about me?"

Faridah studies her. "Mine of mine," she says, "if there's anyone I can count on, it is you. Still, even you are going to change. Who knows? Once you move away, maybe you will consider us ignorant and foolish."

"I won't!"

Though Jammana speaks loudly, Faridah doesn't seem to hear. "We exist alone, Jammana," she says. "Even in this village, I'm the stranger-woman, a sore in the side of the elders, nothing more."

"You're the midwife."

"I'll always be the one from somewhere else. Odd, undisciplined. A *ghouleb*, even." A look of anger crosses Faridah's face. She moves her hand across her mouth as though to wipe it away, then her eyes clear. "I don't mind. Isolation brings its own gifts. Don't waste time trying to change your enemies, or even understand them. Just outlast them." Faridah crumbles a dry leaf beneath her fingers, lets it fall to the floor. She nudges the fragments with her toe. "Outlast them," she repeats.

Jammana shakes her head at the surprises grown-ups carry inside. Of course, she remembers, she too has a secret no one knows. Something lives within her that she never has spoken of, though she's felt it many times. She thinks of it as a serpent—powerful, potentially cruel, coiled between collarbone and belly button. It is content, so far, to be mostly quiet. It waits. She wonders if something lives within Faridah, and if it struck out the day Mama was born.

A shuffling summons their attention, and the room fills with the scent of freshly baked bread. Jammana's great-aunt Khalah. She is panting, and Jammana is startled to see she's been running. Khalah's legs, thick as tree trunks, are made for standing, not haste. In fact, though Khalah is constantly busy, she rarely seems to move. Jammana realizes she's never noticed how Khalah gets from one place to another.

"Have you come for this one so soon?" Faridah asks.

Khalah shakes her head. "We must talk." Her voice is flat as always. She turns to Jammana. "I'm sorry, child." She steps just outside the door, and after a moment, Faridah follows. Jammana, left inside the room, cannot make out the words, but she recognizes the thread pulling them taut. She's familiar with that tone of secrecy. She's heard it in Father's voice and the muted conversations of the men who visit him at night. She draws closer.

Her movement is noticed.

Faridah pokes back inside the room. "Jammana, check on Divine. Give him more mint."

Jammana nods. But when Faridah moves outside again, Jammana inches toward the doorway. Away from Divine.

The rise and fall of indistinct murmuring is punctuated by a stray syllable or two. Jammana is certain—almost certain—she hears the names of her parents rolling through their words.

She slides still closer. The women suddenly stop and step inside the room. Jammana looks from Faridah to Khalah. Faridah rests a finger on her lips thoughtfully. Khalah smoothes her eyebrows, the tear-shaped blemish on her right cheek softening.

"What's happened?" Jammana asks a little too loudly.

Khalah leans forward to touch Jammana's cheek briefly with her own. Jammana feels the melancholy that always comes from Khalah—fragments of her past. Khalah is a golden expanse of sand, supporting wanderers willingly but growing no trees of its own. She is mostly silent, but Jammana knows her love through the meals Khalah sets before her. "Come, child. I'll take you home," Khalah says now. "Bread, humus, and cucumber salad to fill your belly." She turns and walks out the door.

Faridah leans forward, takes Jammana's hands. "You must rely on yourself. Whatever is worrying you, remember you are the child of strong women. You'll survive."

"It would be easier if people would stop whispering in

my presence. Stop acting like I'm too young to understand."
Jammana raises her voice. "If someone has a secret about my
mother, they should just tell me."

Faridah's eyes widen in apparent surprise. After a moment, she says, "If the secret were mine, I'd tell."

"But it *is* yours," Jammana insists.

Before Faridah can reply, they hear Khalah call Jammana's name. "Come. No time to spare," Khalah says.

"Why are we in such a hurry?" Jammana asks.

Faridah just shakes her head and gestures toward the
door, the bracelets on her wrist colliding violently. "We'll talk
later. Now to your grandfather," she says. "Go!"

HARIF

*Y*a-aaaah-ah-hoooo yaliiii!"

When his sister appears in the scalded late afternoon, Harif is cajoling his sheep into the courtyard with his voice alone. His body rigid as an entombed patriarch, he concentrates all his energy into a herding song—a wordless chant of his own invention that the sheep now accept as the intonation of Allah.

"Ya-aaah-ah-hoooo yayaaah!" Come, ye ones, to meet nightfall.

Harif is sure Khalah will not interrupt. She knows if he stops singing, the sheep will break and scatter. He glances at her and notices she is fingering her cheek: the cocoa-colored blemish that appeared overnight after he failed to prevent

the death of their mother, Alula, and grew darker the year he married Hannan.

"Ya-aaah-liiii yaaaah-hooooo!"

It fills him with satisfaction to watch his sheep pass before him at day's end, a mass of bowed heads. Though the elders made him shepherd as punishment, that chore has become a blessing. These sheep are more than his charges. They are his link to the earth. To see them bland-eyed, grinding fingernail-sized leaves begged from a stingy shrub, one wouldn't guess at their depths. But they are able to sense his every mood, especially the three smartest. When he is somber, those three ewes poke him with noses damp and inquisitive. When he is full of life's joy, they prance. When he prays, they hold to a respectful distance, their own heads lowered. If he becomes inattentive for too long, they scale sharp rocks to gaze upon him in longing and despair. For them, this works—he dashes to save them from dangerous heights. For humans, Harif has found, such precarious appeals to the All-Mighty are likely to fail.

"Yali yali yali."

All are in the courtyard, now. Harif smoothes his thick white eyebrows, clasps his hands behind his head, and stretches. As he turns to Khalah, he thinks—not for the first time but always with guilt—that in the four decades since their mother's passing, he has never heard his sister hum. Or giggle. Neither does she seem especially pained. She is simply shed of girlishness. Neutral, adorned in perpetual calm.

Now, too, her face betrays nothing as twilight revolves around her. He is alerted only by the way she reaches out and grips his arm, wordlessly but painfully tight, as if to prevent him from falling into a pit only she can see.

His body becomes a held breath as he recalls his premonition: violet glass, shimmering air, and pain. Someone is hurt. "Jammana," he says, his voice dark.

Khalah loosens her grip, shakes her head. "Trailing behind. She'll be here soon."

He exhales. "What, then?"

Khalah speaks in a monotone. "Rafa . . ."

Again his shoulders tighten.

". . . is here," Khalah finishes.

"She left him?" Harif's voice rises in surprise, though he understands his sister's meaning immediately. He feels a flush of pleasure: Soon he may no longer be connected to that arrogant man who married his daughter. At the same moment, he's struck with a shock of fear. A divorced woman plows the fields without aid. Isolated, even despised, as is her child. Harif had planned for Rafa and Jammana to escape the curse of the outcast. He'd considered it his duty as father, as grandfather, to make sure they always found a haven in the village of their ancestors. He'd thought of it as Ahmed might consider money in the bank, insurance that his family would be provided for after he himself was gone. But Harif's efforts suddenly seem as pointless as rainfall after a month of storms.

Because there is little chance that Rafa will be accepted here if she is divorced. She might be better off, then, in America, or certainly in Nablus, where people die and events fade. In Ein Fadr, the past is constantly sharpened, ready at all times to be hurled like a weapon. In Ein Fadr, a mere moment can live forever.

Khalah is silent. Harif would like her to volunteer the information he needs, but he cannot out-wait her. "Where is she?"

"Not now, Harif."

"She's my daughter."

Khalah shrugs. "She seeks her own counsel."

"Can't I at least make sure she is safe?"

"Safe? She's with Faridah." Khalah's voice holds finality.

Harif feels his shoulders grow leaden. "I can help. It's time for discussions, planning." He cannot keep the pleading from his voice.

Khalah gazes at him blandly. "It's time when Rafa decides," she says. "So not a word to Jammana."

"Khalah, in the name of Allah! I can't see her. I can't mention her. Why tell me, then?"

Though Khalah's mouth remains a line, amused acknowledgment softens her eyes. But she says only, "I thought you should know."

At that moment, Jammana tumbles in, silencing them. If his granddaughter is worried about moving, as Harif suspects, she's forgotten it now. She hugs him, smiling. Nothing can make a child unhappy for longer than a morning—at least, as long as its mother lives.

Khalah heads to the door, then turns to Harif. "I'm going to sit with Baraka tonight," she says. "Don't forget, you must leave the other matter alone."

Harif tells Jammana to wash off the dust. Then he climbs to the rooftop. He can see the lump of Faridah's house at the eastern edge of the village—she's the only person in Ein Fadr who never sleeps outside. He wonders if his daughter is there, and is seized by a sudden desire to sprint as fast as his old legs will take him through the courtyards and spindly paths of Ein Fadr. Pound on Faridah's door, begging entry. As he did once before—one exalted night, the night of his wedding. No, he will not throw himself at Faridah's door again. And he will not violate Rafa's wish to be left alone.

Ahmed was the first topic he and Rafa ever really argued about, and even then they didn't fight in the way Harif and Faridah sometimes do, with firecrackers and flailing wrists, and afterward, moods like vegetables spoiled to mush. Harif only rued aloud the day a donkey stepped on his foot in the crowded Nablus market and he bent to look at the injury and a man approached to announce he was a doctor. Harif regretted that he had brought Rafa with him to Nablus that day. That was when his daughter met this stiff creature in white coat and headdress, a Koran in one hand and a black bag in the other, who prided himself on greater comprehension than he actually held.

"He is tedious, without humor," Harif had complained to Rafa. "Besides, how can you even think of marrying a man who sounds like metal when he walks?"

"It's the soles of his shoes, Father. They aren't of leather."

"No honest man," Harif replied, "wears shoes like that."

He knew his words were petty, but when it came to Ahmed, Harif couldn't think how to dissuade his daughter. So Rafa married, lured by Ahmed's modern world—not only the exotic promise of cars and radios but the distance from one's neighbors, something one never feels in Ein Fadr.

No other father would have permitted a daughter the freedom to defy his wishes in the choice of a mate. Is that where Harif erred? He remembers Nabeel saying Harif made a fool of himself by not disciplining Rafa properly. "Pampering a girl disgraces you," Nabeel had said. "You should have forced her to marry Adil and stay in Ein Fadr."

Jammana, damp at the temples and finished with the dinner Khalah left for her, flies up the ladder and lands on the roof. She stretches on a mat, and Harif hands her juicy sections of an orange for dessert.

Perhaps because she spent the day indoors with Faridah and didn't walk the fields with him, Jammana is not tired enough. Her eyes remain open. She rolls, stretches bird arms to the sky. Cups her body, straightens it, then cups it again.

"Look what Allah's done," Harif says, pointing at the moon. "Cut off a fragment of His fingernail and left it dangling in the sky."

"And there's one of the beautiful dancing sisters," Jammana says, "wearing a see-through veil and a dress of pure silver. See?"

"You know what a shooting star really is?" Harif asks. "A spear thrown by an angel to drive away devils who try to sneak up to heaven and steal Allah's secrets."

For a moment, they both consider that idea. At last, Jammana says, "Tell me everything, Grandfather."

He laughs. "Now?"

"Tell me," Jammana insists, "about Faridah. When you first met her."

Harif hesitates, then decides. Why not let more of the past bleed into present? Jammana's eagerness moves him. Tonight he will explain not only to Jammana but to all the villagers. Perhaps, if only in their dreams, they will hear his words and understand. They will forgive him for envisioning sorrows and for lying about the sand spirit, a deception the men have been pondering. Most important, they will not punish him by venting their anger on those he loves—like his now-vulnerable daughter, Rafa.

He begins the story.

His mother, Alula, became a *wali* within four days of her death. First, black ants erected three large hills around the scorched olive tree. Then a rock badger burrowed a home at the base of the stump. The charred portion fell away, and the underlying wood turned glasslike. These were taken as sacred signs that Alula was, indeed, a saint. Women began appearing with prayers, requests, offerings of bread or fruit. They rolled large rocks around the shrine to support their backs while they spilled forth woes. As the months fled, they constructed an earthen hut and covered it with crooked branches of turpentine trees.

The stump where Alula died became an altar unlike any other. There, at the site of violence, it became possible for women to discard accepted notions of compromise. To plan extreme solutions—even ferocious ones—in total serenity and without shame. One timid wife decided to challenge her brothers for a share of their parents' inheritance. Another sat three days in stony silence, refusing to cook her husband's dinner until he apologized for heartless words. A third, too old and weary, squatted for long hours reviewing her options, and then, against the wishes of her sons, gathered poisonous leaves from the Jericho Rose and vanished into the desert one last time.

The men, discussing matters beneath Moses' Finger, agreed they were pleased by neither the hours women wasted at the stump nor the nature of decisions made there. The *mukhtar* suggested the tree's remainder be yanked from the ground and buried far away. Under his orders, three farmers rose before dawn, harnessed cart to donkey in darkness, and made for the edge of the grove. As they approached Alula's shrine, a wheel of their cart sank into a sudden pothole. The men gathered behind to push it free, then felt cold air punch from the opening in the ground. They knelt over the cavity, peering in, and a moist breeze blew back their *keffiyeh*s. Three leapt back as one. "In the name of Allah," each muttered, hands clutching neck, chest, robe. "The All-Merciful, the All-Powerful."

"The Earth breathes here," one said at last. "She will punish us if we go further. Our crops will surely fail." The others agreed. They led the donkey back home. After this omen, the *fellahin* settled for avoidance. Grumbling, they stopped tending to the nearby olive trees and abandoned the area to the village females. Passing women often held their hands over the opening to feel the earth exhale.

The women were grateful to Alula for providing them with a sanctuary removed from the village and its duties, and to the earth for saving their shrine. For them, Alula continued to live, a satisfying part of their daily lives. But Bahir needed a wife, not a saint. Alula had been the elegant curve of calligraphy at his center; without her, all turned indecipherable. After the day of the funeral, he did not weep. He rose each morning, dressed in his *jallabiya* with neckline embroidered by Alula, ate breakfast prepared by Khalah. He visited the groves, journeyed to Jerusalem, sold olives. He knew Harif had foreseen Alula's death, but he never asked about it. He rarely mentioned his wife's name.

In fact, his voice grew rusty from disuse. His arms forgot how to embrace. He regarded his children with the same interest he showed a cooking pot. To urgings from relatives that he take a new wife, Bahir simply turned on his heel, leaving his companions to offer persuasions to the wind.

Harif did not blame his father. Even then, he recognized that those who had loved Alula would continue somehow, even if in a lesser manner. For Bahir, there was to be no recovery.

Harif was fortunate that two villagers stepped into the space left by his buried mother and absent father. They were his cousin Musa and the stranger-woman Faridah.

Musa, at thirty-six years old Ein Fadr's finest farmer, had a round face decorated by a mustache so astoundingly long it resembled droopy leaves on a thirsty tree. Musa's formal name was Abu Samir, the father of Samir, because after four daughters, his wife had finally given birth to a son. But he had been simply Musa for so long that people of the village often forgot to call him by his new title. Musa was a good-natured farmer; although he had waited long and anxiously for a son, he did not insist on being addressed formally. Musa was a name the villagers uttered with great affection.

Two weeks after the funeral, he called on Harif. "Shutting yourself up like a bat in a cave is not the answer," he said. "True solace lies in the land." He led Harif to the courtyard beneath the almond tree. "I'll teach you the magic touch. Here is the first lesson. Treat the trees as if they have feelings." He stroked the tree's long leaves. "Never shake branches to free the fruit. Pluck with gentle gestures instead. In this way, you can eventually persuade a tree to grow from rock." He patted Harif's shoulder. "Now, tomorrow to the fields."

Under Musa's guidance, Harif began to toil not as a boy of thirteen but as a full-grown farmer. He worked hard and gained height, weight, and strength. Despite Musa's kind-hearted attention, however, Harif never felt comfortable among the other men. Often when he approached a group, a hush fell. Behind his back, the *mukhtar* muttered that Harif had brought evil to Ein Fadr, and would again. Musa scoffed at him, but others did not. The farmers debated and chose sides.

So it came to pass that at day's end, when the men conferred under Moses' Finger, Harif slipped away, preferring instead the courtyard and the *taboon*, the enclosed clay oven where women gathered to cook the evening meal. They welcomed him there not only in memory of his mother but as a willing helper. And among that soothing company, he felt his loss less severely.

Faridah, nineteen years old then, lived alone but often joined the women to cook. Harif barely knew her, but she sensed before anyone else the best way to comfort him. She put him to work baking bread, slicing eggplant, grinding rosemary. He responded gratefully to her suggested chores, although he paid no notice to Faridah herself. With all, in fact, he favored a careful distance. He had the idea, vague in his own mind though it was, that if he could curb contact with others and avoid mention of Alula, she would live. Eventually, she would stop being occupied elsewhere and return to him.

One evening, a younger girl unwittingly asked Harif to help her make *kibbeh*. Such a small word. Upon hearing it, Harif froze. The sky darkened until finally he could see only his hands. He backed away and left. Faridah followed, carrying a basket she was making from softened wheat stalks.

Outside the courtyard, he stared at her, trying to remember exactly who she was, wishing she would leave. For the first time, he noticed her high cheekbones, her lips full of vibrant defiance, her wrists. Her skin was burnished, and her hair refused to be bound, escaping from her scarf in bold tendrils.

She motioned for him to sit in the shade of the courtyard wall.

"Please," Harif said. "I don't want to talk about . . . anything."

She looked at him sharply for a moment, and then lowered her eyes to the basket held between her feet. She began to speak, her voice rising and falling hypnotically.

"I came to Ein Fadr," she said, "at age twelve, a bride in an exchange marriage arranged by my father. My mother had been worn by bearing many children, so my father decided to take a second wife. Multiple marriages were rare in our village, just as they are here, but he was determined. However, he was not a rich man. To wed the woman he selected, he gave me to the woman's brother. I saw my groom first on our wedding day. My husband was . . ." She paused, searching for words. "A man of immense demands. Each morning when I swept our home, he insisted I start in the east corner. Always the east. He ordered me to tend to his brothers' clothing as well as his. His mother kept me working, too. I was free from duties only when I walked to and from the spring to gather water. I looked with terrible longing at the children running through the fields. I missed my mother, my home." She paused to tuck an end of a stalk into the spiral she was making to serve as the basket's bottom. "I knew a mistake had been made. I cried myself to sleep every night."

She lowered her head, and her voice grew distant. "But after a few weeks, I became different from the children, too. I belonged nowhere. I tried to fulfill my responsibilities. I did everything as he instructed." A bitter expression crossed her face. "Everything," she said. She rubbed her left arm with her right hand, as though warding off a chill. "The women soon sensed my problem. They suggested eating mandrake and pomegranate on the morning after a new moon, and gave me oils to rub into my skin. I swallowed the herb and fruit and massaged the oils. Still, Allah granted me no children."

Harif had been party to women's talk, of course, by the well when his mother still lived. But he'd never heard words like this before. It was prohibited for a young woman to speak so boldly to a boy. He had the sense that much about Faridah would be considered taboo, but he did not want her to stop.

"Who is your husband?" he asked her.

"The *mukhtar*'s nephew, Abd al Qadir, was my husband. He allowed six years to pass before he decided my childlessness would not be overcome. He divorced me last year, with the *mukhtar*'s blessings."

Harif knew divorce for reason of barrenness was acceptable under Allah's law. Still, he felt drawn to this woman, who, clearly, was as unprepared for the passing of childhood as he himself had been, as perhaps everyone is. "I heard nothing of this," he said.

"Why would you? You were a child. If you'd already been included among the men, you'd have known, because they debated it. Many, including the *mukhtar*, wanted to expel me." Faridah put her work down and shifted to face Harif. "Your mother stopped them," she said. "Alula persuaded them that it would be honorable to allow me a small room at the village edge." She paused, and her voice grew harsh. "The day I moved, I searched until I found the *mukhtar*, and I rained spit at his feet. For Abd al Qadir, who robbed me twice of my home, I wish only the curses of Cain."

"Why don't you just go back?" Harif asked. "Return to the soil you came from?"

She shook her head. "I feel no affection for my father, and my mother died two years ago. Besides, she told me often enough it's better to live with the shadow of a husband than with the shadow of a wall. I will not return home bearing the stigma of divorce. If my husband's family will not be responsible for me, I will be responsible." She rubbed her hands together slowly. "Almost everyone ignores me now. Only your mother was different. We weren't friends. Nor would Alula have wanted to trade places with me. Still, I saw that in some way she did covet my life. My banishment holds one unexpected benefit—freedom. I do as I wish." Faridah dusted off the tops of her bare feet. "Alula gave me a certain strength. A woman pitied as much as I have been—that woman needs to be envied by at least one other." She picked up her basket and rose. Harif stood also. She drew a line in the dirt with her toes, diffident for the first time. "I tell you all this," she said at last, "because of Alula, but also because of you. And because it is the only story I know so far."

And not long after that, she delivered Mama?" Jammana asks. Her voice holds an urgency Harif does not understand. Her cheeks shine in the moonlight.

"No," he says. "It was many years before she became a

midwife. But after that day, I felt in her presence the unlikely confidence of a plump lark resting on a narrow branch. It is natural that we were drawn to each other. We both lost our mothers, were targets of village gossip."

"Except for Faridah, you had no friends." Jammana nods.

"I had a few, but I was to lose them soon." Harif looks out at the night sky. "All it took was another vision."

That came," Harif continues, "in my seventeenth year," the year his voice deepened and the hint of a mustache blurred his upper lip. It was Ramadan, the ninth month on the lunar calendar, when believers reject food and water during daylight hours. By mid-afternoon, weakened farmers give up labor, drag back to Ein Fadr, and lounge under trees.

One such afternoon, Harif met Faridah in his family's courtyard, where she knelt before a clay vessel, carefully fashioning it into a jug. She had not yet found the true work for her hands in those days and was seeking, constantly seeking. He squatted beside her, helping her shape the sides of the emerging container, pinch its top. They worked silently. At last, Harif spoke. "All I want is to be like everyone else. Just a farmer. No more premonitions." He sank back on his haunches and waited until she looked at him. "I've dreamed of a failure in our grape crop. The dream has recurred for seven nights."

Harif did not see his second sight in those days as a mirror of reality; he superstitiously feared that it begot reality. The *mukhtar,* he knew, thought the same. Only the women did not hold him accountable for events he foresaw.

Faridah sat still, thinking. "Let me talk to Musa," she said finally. "As well as being your cousin, he is our finest farmer."

Harif hesitated, well aware that it would be safer for him to secret the dream away. But, burdened by a sense of responsibility, he nodded at last.

Faridah called on Musa that evening, though she rarely visited anyone in those days and to do so without invitation took courage. Musa's wife welcomed her graciously, and Musa too, after hearing her news, thanked her for coming. He rose early the next morning to inspect the vineyard. He could see nothing wrong with the soil or the site; still, he suggested he and Harif take the warning to the elders. Harif opposed that, as did Faridah, but they bowed to Musa's wishes.

The *mukhtar* listened to Musa skeptically and responded with impatience. "All looks well, yes? And even if it is true, what are we to do?" Then, glancing upward, he added, "It is in the hands of Allah, not Harif. Wouldn't you agree?"

Helplessly, Musa nodded. Harif, at his side, bowed his head.

Spring grew surly, and summer pressed down. The villagers took to visiting the vineyard daily and watched in mute horror as, by mid June, all the grape vines had withered, tiny unborn fruit wrinkling on their stems. Songs of anticipated harvest died on lips. The farmers could identify no cause for the damage, no sign of mildew or leafhopper. But never in collective memory had Ein Fadr suffered such a total loss. The great grape failure of 1934 meant no raisin-making that year, no molasses.

The villagers considered the devastation an evil omen. Disgruntled farmers fumed that they had wasted many hours laboring over the vines that were now spoiled. The el Riyad clan, which depended wholly on the grape output, called for a meeting to insist other families share the burden.

Musa and Harif inspected the vines together one evening after the worst was over. "There's next year," said Musa, stroking his long mustache.

Harif snapped off one withered vine, crushed the brown leaves in frustration, and threw them to the ground. "Do you really suppose I'll be allowed to work on the grapes next year?"

His words were prophetic; now even the mildest of the villagers stared at him with suspicion, murmuring about the evil eye and Iblis, the devil born of fire, thrown by Allah from Paradise. All supported the *mukhtar's* order that he be given the job of tending the sheep instead of sowing the fields. Worse, the memory of his mother's death surfaced as vividly as if it had occurred the day before, and the elders pondered Harif's role with an intensity usually reserved for study of the Prophet's life.

But now," Jammana says, "I want to know how Faridah became a midwife."

Harif shakes his head and covers her. "Tomorrow." He strokes her hair.

She fidgets. "I won't sleep," she vows.

"That is as you wish. Only be quiet." He sits next to her and waits with patience until an owl begins to hoot and he finally feels her resistance weaken, until he feels her grow heavy with slumber. Then he rises to survey his village with its tiny homes huddled together, some so ancient that they lean against their neighbors like old men with canes. Ein Fadr is said to be older than Jerusalem, nearly as old as Allah's start with the earth. Villagers claim that Abraham himself drank from the well, ate of the bread, when he stopped for three nights to hear its storytellers spin their tales. Throughout the neighboring hills, Ein Fadr has the reputation of being a place of righteous and eloquent farmers. It is unfortunate that with time, some have come to see themselves as guardians of village purity.

In the moonlight, Harif sees a narrow thread of smoke rising from a neighbor's *taboon*. The night air smells dangerously sharp, but all is still; he may be the only person awake in Ein Fadr.

Except for Rafa. Surely she, too, is having trouble sleeping tonight. Somewhere here, his only child cowers, hoping for protection. Reaching in his pocket for his amber beads, he prays: If it pleases the All Merciful, the Compassionate, the Generous, don't let his neighbors turn their backs on Rafa, or worse. Let them see her as one of their own, come home.

But he knows this village.

FARIDAH

Make haste, girl! Faridah urges Rafa silently, with a quick, broad gesture of her arm. *No one must see you. No stray fellahin dragging from a day's work or child skipping over stones. We have not a moment to sift and soothe.*

A sanctuary is what they want. A refuge, where Rafa can burn a few days without anyone seeing the smoke. The two women have no need for words. As one, they are flying toward a single place. Alula's shrine. It is not to worship or beseech—far be it from Faridah to favor such stagnant action. It is because the scent of possibilities lingers there. Because the men never visit—none save Harif, and he seldom enough these days. And because the hills overlooking the shrine are pierced by the largest caves.

As they dart and skim over the surface of the earth,

Faridah can't resist glancing at Rafa. How pale she is! How she has chewed the tips of her fingers raw! Her cheeks have grown thin, her eyes swollen. She peers east and west, then east, then west again, so that if her gaze reflected the sun's movement, a year would pass in a minute.

But Faridah has no time to worry, now. She tries to stretch her strides long, then longer. Like the lope of Adam, who stood so tall in life that in death his shoulders were buried below Jerusalem but his feet had to be submerged somewhere beneath the Judean hills. Adam—Allah's first of-fering, hang-headed and slow-witted, snared by the whims of others and tossed from the source of cool water. Neverthe-less, what legs! A leap of those legs, Faridah thinks, is what they must have now.

They scramble up a hillside with the speed of nervous geckos, scattering sand and pebbles. Faridah leads the way. They duck their heads and scurry into the finest cave, tiny entrance but large within, and blocked from sight by a boul-der in front. Faridah looks around with satisfaction. The cav-ern smells damp but is large enough, and clean, except for a blackened wall and a few wood ashes near the entrance. With a reed mat on the floor, it will do.

Rafa does not inspect the cave. She immediately leans against the boulder at the entrance and peers out toward the village. This is not a haven for her, but a lookout. Faridah fi-nally has a moment to study her. She's all stiff energy. Her breathing is that of a woman in labor, her wrists so casually fragile. Faridah squints at the new hollowness of Rafa's cheeks, and sees what she mistook for simple shadow: ten-derness below the right eye. Punished skin turned purple.

Faridah's hands ball with fury at the thought of someone striking this woman she considers half her own. She will contain it, she resolves. Best to deal with the practical, hold flames in reserve. Wait for a moment of met minds. Still, she's unable to strain the anger from her voice as she asks: "What have you eaten today?"

Rafa doesn't respond at first, then shakes her head without glancing at Faridah. "I'm all right."

Faridah touches her arm lightly. "I'll get food, be back before nightfall."

Rafa looks up. "No!"

"Rafa! You must keep your strength."

"If someone sees you?" Rafa's voice trembles.

Faridah moves closer, speaks less harshly. "I always travel on Divine, looking for herbs, delivering babies. It's not an unusual sight. But best if I act now, while the sun is still high. Besides, I have to handle the donkey."

"My donkey?"

Faridah hesitates, wondering how precise to be. "He must not be discovered among ours, Rafa, nor wandering the desert in this area. Not while you are trying to hide."

Rafa shudders. "It belongs to my neighbor, Umm Mahir," she says. She looks away, then nods. "She'll understand."

The village swells with the sounds of *fellahin* returning from the fields and Jordanian soldiers on heightened alert who have paused their desert partrols long enough to drink from Ein Fadr's spring. Children flutter around their fathers. Black-eyed dogs, just this side of wild, bark to chase away the somnolence of the day. Roosters strut through courtyards, assuming as always that the commotion is made to honor them.

Faridah walks Divine up the narrow path to the courtyard Harif and Khalah share. Khalah, moist strands of gray hair lying at her temples, squats in the *taboon*, peeling fresh bread off hot stones. A delicate scent of yeast and pepper embraces Faridah. Ah, the blessed odors of Khalah's cooking! It goes beyond mere taste. Her bread, dips, and pastries soothe the soul. Faridah cannot remember exactly when Khalah gained this gift, when some secret knowledge taught her fingers how to knead and spice and give and take. All Faridah knows is that she often craves Khalah's bread when she is agitated. And that bread is what Rafa needs now.

After a moment, Faridah speaks. "She's in a cave near Alula's."

Khalah lifts her head, unasked questions hanging in her eyes. Questions both women know they haven't time to ponder.

Khalah has already placed figs and almonds atop a cotton headdress. Now she adds pine nuts, warm bread, and pastry filled with lamb meat, then rolls up the bundle. It is an offering, Faridah sees, disguised as an inconsequential rectangle of woman's cloth.

"We are watching for Ahmed's approach," Khalah says.

"You've told others already?"

"We take a risk." Khalah spreads her hands. "But I cannot keep watch alone."

Faridah considers, then agrees. After a moment, she asks, "And her donkey?"

"You brought something?"

Faridah holds out a burlap bag. "Wild celery fetched

from the banks of the River Jordan three months ago, joined with Star of Bethlehem buds. Together they should be palatable enough for the beast to eat, and potent enough to accomplish our needs."

Khalah nods. Matter-of-factly. Who, after all, can spare a moment to mourn a donkey? "I'll lead it out of the village just before nightfall, and then feed it. The jackals will strip it by morning."

Faridah squeezes Khalah's hand. She takes the bundle of food, dives from the smoky womb of the oven room, and quickly ties the bundle on Divine's back.

At home, she lashes a water vessel to each side of Divine, and a rolled blanket on his back. She springs back inside, stuffs mint into her right pocket, and heads toward the lantern in the corner. So focused is she that a knock startles like an elbow of pain. She holds her breath as the door, pushed from outside, swings open. A figure stands there. Pale. Oval-shaped. Cold gray eyes.

"Nabeel," says Faridah in a voice of approaching night.

"In such a way you greet me?"

Faridah must summon social skills from somewhere. She recalls her mother's face—she can't remember it exactly; she hasn't been able to for years—but for some long seconds she thinks of soaring cheekbones, winglike fingers, and curling voice. "I'm honored. You bring me blessings, and may the peace of Allah fall upon you. Of course, you've never visited my home before, but now . . . please enter. In the name of the High One. I'll prepare you some tea."

Nabeel smiles thinly. "I come on official business. I prefer to talk outside."

He is a trained falcon, ready to dive for a master Faridah cannot yet see. She keeps her gaze fixed on him as she steps outside. Sky the color of a robin's egg tinged orange around the edges warns her she has little daylight left. She must dispense with Nabeel quickly.

"It is my nephew's wife, Baraka," he says. "She's failing."

This again? Faridah struggles to conceal impatience. "I would disagree," she answers solidly. "I saw her this morning. She's not improving as quickly as I'd like, perhaps, but—"

"She's worse. Adil says you threw away the water he left to ease the birth."

Faridah groans, lifts a hand to her forehead. "Yes, I tossed out the dirty water. It would have made her sicker."

"It's our custom."

"A ridiculous one."

His neck muscles swell. "Such defiance in a village that is not, at root, your own. You managed, too, to offend our Bedouin visitor, Harif's old friend. You are surprised I know of this? My nephew Adil overheard a conversation between you two. You'll pay for it all in time, Faridah." He raises his clenched fists to waist level. "Under the eyes of Blessed Allah, you brought problems the moment you arrived. You brought them to Harif, too, though he can't see it. I don't know where you were born, or how. But I wish you'd stayed away from Ein Fadr."

Faridah studies him a moment. Then she lifts her chin. "Make sure Manara is giving Baraka the coltsfoot," she says.

"You"—Nabeel spits the word—"are so sure of yourself. Always. Quite amazing, for a woman of your standing."

She clenches her teeth involuntarily, but decides to ignore the insult. "Yes, I'm sure of the coltsfoot. I've been a midwife now for . . ." She pauses, letting her mind tumble back. "More than thirty years."

Nabeel takes a deep breath, regaining self-control. He steps closer. "And everything you do is intentional," he says. "When deliveries go well, you are credited. When not, I presume you are to blame."

She squints, trying to vent her frustration in that single, tiny squeeze of muscles. This is no time for argument. She speaks with exaggerated patience. "Many things, Nabeel, are beyond my control."

"Some are not."

She gestures with one hand above her head. "Your words fly on the wings of birds."

"Let me be clearer, then. I refer to a singular tragedy from which you benefited. The death that left Harif a widower."

Faridah holds her breath. In nearly two decades, no one has dared mention it so openly, so callously. She once feared it could be her undoing. Then she'd become complacent, deciding that her one serious mistake, along with her single moment of real wonder and joy, had escaped general notice.

She'd been foolish in her confidence, she sees that. The men of Ein Fadr may worship Allah as their god, but memory is their king. They clutch the image of the guilty to their chests, and wait.

Will Nabeel pronounce punishment? Or perhaps he's not completely sure and hopes Faridah will give herself away. Whichever, she must show no sign of weakness. She speaks three words, loading each with weight. "I. Gained. Nothing."

Nabeel, outwardly calm again, goes on as if he hadn't heard. "The lamb must be sacrificed if the wolf is to survive. Even with Allah's help, both cannot be spared." He curves his lips upward stiffly. "And just when we think everything is hidden, our sins long buried, the mischievous *jinn* reveal our secret slyly, in the color of a set of eyes."

He means, of course, that Jammana's eyes are the same color as Faridah's own. She herself can't be sure how or why that happened, just as she doesn't thoroughly understand the reason for the intensity of her link to Rafa and to Rafa's daughter. She knows only that a man speaking in dark circles signals attack like a jackal raising its tail. Faridah must dive for cover.

She glances helplessly toward Divine, who is swinging his head back and forth impatiently. Divine, loaded for travel, wonders why they aren't moving. Faridah silently chants a name in her head, the name of the one who needs her. *Rafa. Rafa.* With that litany, she recovers. "Your words are irrelevant," she says. "Baraka will soon be well."

"Perhaps not soon enough." He pauses. "You've heard that a Jordanian captain has visited us? He warned that the Hashemite kingdom would punish any political activity from this village."

Faridah wills flames from her eyes. "What has this to do with me? I care nothing for these political struggles, these borders and battles between men. If the village is to be punished, I will survive that—as I have the rest. It is the one called upon to inform and betray who should be worried by such a warning. It is he who will, in time, feel Allah's full fury."

Nabeel laughs, a bitter sound. "Harif has been misguided in as many choices as the olive tree bears fruit," Nabeel says. "Lying to us for all these years. Forsaking my friendship for yours." He breaks off, a distant look in his eyes. Then he focuses again on Faridah. "But in memory of what I once shared with him, I urge you: Take care!"

Faridah drops her hands to her sides, fingers flared outward. In the cloudless late-afternoon sky, a column of shadow sweeps across the two of them. Far overhead, Faridah sees a large cinnamon hoopoe, clearly distinguishable with its fan headdress. A bird from the Nile Valley, hundreds of miles to the southwest, has found its way to Faridah's home. Her words are clipped, booming. "Your many warnings begin to sound like a threat."

"Call them a vision." He smiles. "Yes, like one of Harif's." He glances over his shoulder, motioning toward Divine. "You are taking a pleasure ride?"

"To gather herbs."

"Isn't it late for that?"

"I have just enough moments before nightfall. And so, Nabeel . . ."

Nabeel runs his eyes over Divine again. "Two jugs of water?"

"I had hoped to start earlier."

"Even so. Two jugs?"

Faridah shoots him a glance as cold as his own. "I get very thirsty. Praise Allah the All-Seeing for such needs," she replies firmly.

"And you carry a blanket on such trips?" Nabeel steps closer to Faridah, blocking her way to the donkey.

Faridah knows she has to act or everything will flow away from her. She's always known that. She strides purposefully past Nabeel, mounts Divine. "I assume your predictions of Baraka's future are meant to frighten me," she says. "So I can guess you wouldn't share them with her. Nonetheless, I'll ask: Please don't. Alarming her would damage her health. The very thing you are so worried about." Divine takes a few jerking steps toward the hills, but Faridah pats his neck, willing him to slow. "If you really want Baraka well," she says, "leave me alone!"

She turns from him fully, bends, and whispers in the ear of her donkey. "Now fly."

They coast over hills, Faridah and Divine, sometimes led and sometimes trailed by the shadow of the hoopoe. Faridah pulls Divine up short twice to make sure they are not followed. She knows she must never turn her back for long on a hungry beast. She will not be frightened away, not by anyone, but she will be cautious. She listens with enough intensity to hear springs running far below the earth's surface. No following footsteps, though.

Behind a boulder at Alula's shrine, Faridah dismounts. The ground expels the heavy heat of the day into her sandals. A breeze sighs; on a distant hill, she sees an array of antennas, a listening outpost erected by the Jordanian soldiers. A war is coming, no doubt, but Ein Fadr will tuck in its head, keep out of the way. And anyway, for the moment, all is silent. Satisfied, she hoists a water jug atop her head, slips head shawl under one arm and blanket under the other. She climbs to the cave. Just enough time to deliver these supplies, then she must return.

Rafa starts. She's been drowsing. She has taken off her headdress and laid it on the floor as a sleeping mat. Her eyes look underlined. Her cheeks are the gray of a hawk's underbelly.

"Khalah made you fresh bread," Faridah says.

"Shhh." Rafa rises unsteadily, lurches to the cave's entrance. "I thought I heard . . ." she whispers. "Were you followed?"

Faridah shakes her head. "I checked," she says as she unrolls the bundle and hands Rafa a fig. "He *will* come, you know. Soon."

"But if he finds me now, he'll spill the worst of his anger on me. With the passing of even a day, he'll be calmer." Rafa stares again out the cave entrance. "I would guess he'll start here at first light, though he might not wait."

Faridah sorts the food, sets one jug of water in a corner. "I meant to carry a lantern."

"Better without." Rafa hesitates. "I thought about bringing Jammana here."

Faridah shakes her head. "If she disappears, it will attract attention."

"How is she?"

Faridah knows she disappointed Jammana today. She believes what she told Jammana about trust, but still wishes she'd been more gentle. "Jammana works so hard at hiding her girlishness that even I sometimes forget she's a child," Faridah answers.

Rafa nods. "Sometimes I think *she* feels responsible for *me*, as if she were the mother." After a moment, she takes a deep breath and goes on. "He can't help it, you know. Ahmed wants to be a modern man, but he grew up with old-fashioned beliefs. His father was an *imam* who, in the name of Allah, simply erased his mother. Her wishes meant nothing."

"Most men of this land are of stone," says Faridah.

"Yes. So I must accept and stop struggling."

Faridah shrugs. "There are other choices."

"If I were to leave him, I would be a shamed woman," Rafa says bitterly. "All would avoid me as a thorn. And from childhood, you and my father always said, 'Follow the rules. Do what you must to retain your place in the village.'"

"We thought it best if it were gentler for you than it's been for us," Faridah answers.

Rafa squats before the entrance. "So I'll have to repent for this boldness. Otherwise, I'll never be part of anything solid again."

Faridah studies Rafa's profile. "Perhaps we made a mistake," she says. "Being cast out is not the worst fate, Rafa."

Rafa shakes her head. "What about Jammana? Without a father, it'll be harder to protect her. To wed her. To provide for her."

"Love of a child complicates the decision," Faridah agrees softly. "I know something of that."

A look of pain flashes across Rafa's face. Then it is gone. "I need time," she says. "Time to decide." She gestures toward the horizon, where the sky is turning inky. Her tone turns slightly formal. "You must leave," she says.

"I don't like to desert you."

Rafa shakes her head. "Be in your home tonight. All must be now as it was before."

Faridah nods. Rafa is right. Under the soothing moon-breast of night and the sharp sun-elbow of day, in time's shuddering, all must be as it was before. "I'll bring you more water and food tomorrow," she says.

Night stretches beyond, infinite in its sorrows. How can Faridah not suffer Rafa's anguish? This mother-child robbed too early of her own mother. What would that dead woman advise Rafa now? Harif's wife, with liquid eyes, had a cunning about her. She would not support the flagrant rebellion of fleeing one's husband and hermitting in a cave. She would call for solutions more sly.

These thoughts bring Faridah to the event Nabeel alluded to—the day Rafa's mother died in childbirth. History is supposed to stay in place, but it never does in Ein Fadr. Here it is again, pushing and shoving as though to get to the table first at mealtime, to touch all the food so that when everyone eats, the lamb is already spiced with the past, the sheep's-milk cheese soured by elapsed events, even the freshest tomato bruised by what has gone before. With every bite, the villagers will sink their teeth into ancient moments for which Faridah already has repented. Moments that deserve to be buried.

Something alien once grew in her—that's how she thinks of it. An herb both flowering and poisonous. It lived for many years but gained the upper hand only a single time, when Rafa was born. No one knows of that time, not for sure, and she has no wish to recall.

Far better to remember that when Rafa's mother died, several years later, Faridah and Harif were doing all they could to save her. Khalah, too. Every proper herb, freshest olive oil, and purest words. Faridah even tried cures she didn't believe in, those favored by the old midwife. They'd burned a blue cloth and held the smoking remnant under the laboring woman's skirt. They'd shaken her in a carpet of camel hair to right the baby's position. Faridah prepared *shaade*, the drink of forty ingredients to strengthen the weak. Then she herself had beseeched the heavens, whose gates stand open briefly to all who witness a birth. With tears, Faridah begged for the child to come and the mother to be led away from the grave, so that Rafa would not have to bear the sorrow.

Remember that, if there must be remembering! She flings that thought to an unseen accuser.

And yet.

And yet, even when she returns to the end of that life and can see herself a blur of movement in the shadowy room, sweat beading in the small of her back, Harif by her side, both moving in synchronized concern—even then, the memory is troubled. Because who can deny buried intentions? Who can dismiss the power of an unspoken wish?

"O morning, where are you?" Faridah chants these words until finally a dawn breeze rushes in, disturbing feathers and opening buds. She rises, rolls a reed mat, and ties it to Divine's rump, packs watermelon seeds, herbs, water. Faridah and Divine speed to Alula's shrine. Faridah scrambles up the hill to find Rafa awake, her blanket wrapped around her like a cloak. She seems stronger. Faridah offers silent thanks. "The night passed well?"

"Praise Allah. Food helped. I slept a little."

"Here's more water. And a mat to keep dust down."

Rafa is at greater ease this morning. She hushes Faridah for an instant, and turns toward the cave entrance but doesn't scramble to look out. Instead, she stretches forward to touch Faridah's cheek to her own. "You've always been my staff, ever since Mama died."

Faridah is aware of the fullness in her chest. "It's all I've wanted," she says. Although even in her joy, she knows her words are not quite accurate. She'd wanted to be Harif's staff, too.

The women work together quietly, spreading the mat, folding the blanket. "This village!" Rafa says at last. "I struggled so hard to escape, and here I am again." She shakes her head. "I remember when I thought Father would order me to marry Adil, how worried I was."

"Dung beetle of a man, that Adil." Faridah pulls some bags of herbs from her pocket. "Baraka had her first baby. She's very ill. And still every night, Adil goes to Moses' Finger, puffing himself up with idle talk of politics." She doesn't say that actually, the talk of the men lately has all been about Harif, about the lie that the Bedouin revealed.

"Politics. The Troubles." Rafa spits out the words. "It's like a rabid dog lurking at our doorstep, snapping at our heels. The Troubles make men crazy. He was not always like this, you know." She gestures to her cheek.

Faridah busies herself, covering the water jug with a piece of cotton. The mention of Ahmed turns her mood foul as untreated meat hung too long from the branch. But she thinks perhaps Rafa is right: For the sake of the child, the worn path must be followed.

"We've fought before," Rafa goes on. "We fought much

over whether to move to America. But for this latest, I blame the Troubles."

Faridah is silent.

"Ahmed was furious that I brought Jammana here without his permission," Rafa says. "He said Umm Mahir was a bad influence, encouraging me to act against his wishes. I told him that was nonsense, but he ordered me never to associate with her again."

"Did you agree?"

"The next day, I told Umm Mahir. She wasn't surprised. She said Ahmed felt shame in her presence. Shame for what? I asked. She thought I knew. Ahmed was with Umm Mahir's husband on the night of retaliation. Ahmed himself killed a man. A Christian."

"Men have always been foolish on such matters," Faridah says. "Wouldn't it be better for you to ignore?"

Rafa's voice is razor sharp. "*You* wouldn't have ignored it."

"If I loved him I might," Faridah murmurs, but Rafa shakes her head.

"He claimed it would have been dishonorable to refuse to help his own," Rafa says. "He said it was one more reason we had to get to America, in case his name became known by the Christians and we—Jammana and I—were targeted. Killer. That's what I called him. And then he . . ." Again she gestures to her cheek. Her voice grows even harder. "You don't agree with me?"

"Of course I agree, but in practical terms . . ." Faridah stops. The thought of the argument Rafa and Ahmed must have had makes her stomach cramp as though she's consumed goat's milk turned heavy in the sun. Once, Rafa would have sidestepped such discord, knowing that her husband would never change. But Rafa herself is changing, now, and clearly unable to hold her views to her own chest. "So, what are you going to do?" Faridah asks.

"I know where one of the families lives. I went with Umm Mahir after the killings. A widow with six children. I'm going to help them." She gestures within her *thobe*. "Dinars," she says. "Money for the hospital fund. He keeps it in the house. I took it all."

"You what?" A deep voice startles them both. "Madness!" The word echoes as a shadow steps just inside the cave's entrance.

"Father!"

Faridah leaps to her feet, waving both arms in large gestures. "By the melodies of Allah, what are *you* doing here?"

"I borrowed Khalah's donkey and followed. It was easy. You looked more than half asleep." Fleetingly, Harif grins like a boy.

"Where is Jammana?" Rafa asks.

"With Khalah."

Faridah scowls. How could she be so careless as to allow a man, any man, to trail her? She takes Rafa's hands. "I'm sorry."

"Why do you apologize? I'm her father."

"It's all right," Rafa tells Faridah. But her eyes are smoky. "Just check the entrance."

"No one came after me," Harif says. "Now, Rafa, what have you done? You know I am no admirer of Ahmed. But you are forsaking your own daughter for a family you don't even know."

"I have forsaken no one," Rafa says stiffly.

Harif steps toward her, shaking his head, then halts, studies her profile, and reaches out toward the bruise. "What happened?"

Rafa drops her head. A distant voice seeps into the cave.

"Shhh." Faridah hushes them sharply.

A man calls from below. "Khalah? Harif?" They hurry to the cave entrance and peer beyond the boulder, silent as bats in the daytime.

Nabeel and Adil are circling the shrine and the two tethered donkeys that belong to Faridah and Khalah. The beasts' ears are raised in wariness, and they paw at the ground. The men are talking. Their words are too far away to hear, but Faridah can guess. Words of suspicion. Words that will bring her trouble.

Faridah struggles to still her ragged breath. Nabeel, a hand shading his eyes, stares up toward their cavern, then turns and gazes toward the hills to the south. He inspects Divine, who responds by turning his back. Nabeel and Adil, heads swinging loosely from their necks, pace around the gray boulders that circle Alula's tree stump. They peer into the mud hut covered with turpentine branches. Finally, they set off in the direction of the village.

Those pressed against the boulder slowly pull away.

"I have to go back," Faridah whispers. "Pick some herbs and visit Baraka. Otherwise, they'll return."

"You too," Rafa tells Harif.

With reluctance, he nods. He embraces Rafa. "Allah decides all, but with His wisdom, Ahmed shall be punished for this," he mutters, looking at her cheek.

"It is nothing," Rafa says. "Please, Father, promise me. Do not mention it again."

Faridah brakes with her heels as she skids down the hill. Harif follows closely. When they reach the donkeys, Divine noses Faridah nervously, questioning. Faridah faces Harif. They adopted a light manner with each other years ago by unspoken agreement, and by now they've perfected it. It allows them to avoid talking seriously. But this time, she can't force teasing into her tone. "You broke faith with Rafa, coming here before she was ready. And with me, by following me."

Harif spreads his hands. "She's my daughter. A different kind of man would do worse."

"If you were different, Rafa wouldn't have left Ahmed."

"Meaning I caused this sorrow?" He shakes his head and smiles wryly. "The devil is no match for an old woman!" He turns toward Divine, stroking the donkey's side. "Besides, remember what you told me once? Every union contains the seeds of separation—it's just a matter of time." He moves closer to her. "You still believe that?"

Faridah dismisses his question, waving her hand in front of her face as though flitting away a fly. "She had the courage to oppose her husband and speak her own mind. Be proud! And allow her privacy."

Harif looks back toward the cave. "I can't," he says starkly. "Especially if he comes. And he will."

"So you will leap forward and do . . . what?" Faridah's voice rises incautiously. Divine lifts his head. "This is not a struggle between two men. It belongs to your daughter. She demands your distance."

"You would have me allow him to—?"

"*She* will stop him."

"I must—"

Faridah grunts in frustration, raises an arm to the heavens. "She doesn't want your help."

"Rafa"—Harif's voice echoes—"has few allies in this world. Yes, I know, I know. You survived alone."

"I wasn't comparing—"

"You stood up to all under the seven heavens. But she's not made of that."

"*I* had no choice."

Harif steps closer. His eyes take on an almost angry glow. "You did. Remember? You could have had me."

Faridah opens her mouth in surprise. He's broken the rules, speaking about that time. "I didn't decide alone, Harif. You're the one who had much to lose. If you had really wanted . . ." Faridah breaks off. She senses they are being watched. Overhead, she searches the sky. Perhaps it is the hoopoe, hovering somewhere unseen, which gives her this premonition of danger.

She's not afraid. She's not.

Still, they mustn't delay. "Lingering here, we are pointer stars. Go," she tells Harif, her words a rough caress. "Go tend to your sheep, old man."

He chuckles, then gently lifts her chin so she will meet his gaze. An irresistible moment. She needs to hear Harif laugh from time to time. To feel his eyes lingering on her. It soothes.

He reaches for her hand resting on Divine's mane. Holds it for a second made of seconds. "My hot flame," he says. "Lit with birth juice and war. No murmur about you. Only a shout. But you're always sending me away. Why?" He leans close, and she stares at his lips, so perfectly shaped. "You have no wish," he asks, "for salt and mud and light?"

Of course she wishes. The taste of his shoulder, moonlight exposing the breadth of his chest. The intensity, the safety. Where are you going, O heart, in such a hurry? She cannot ignore its leaping. Never has been able to ignore it. A sudden thirst dries her throat.

"I can't be the only one who remembers," Harif whispers, winds of wanting blowing through his voice. "It is too sacred to keep it by myself."

Remember! That word sobers Faridah. Shadows of the past seem more important to Harif than the ones on earth here and now. "All you want from me is memory, then?" she asks. "Action would still frighten you?"

"No." He takes her shoulders. "I want more. And why not?"

Why not indeed? Because Faridah, fearless warrior woman, is frightened by only one thing: the strength of feelings she once allowed herself to act upon and now must hold in check.

She pulls away. "You named our direction long ago." She throws her skirt over Divine's back as she mounts. "I haven't time for nonsense."

"Faridah. Wait."

She doesn't reply. She doesn't even pause. She doesn't dare pause.

JAMMANA

Jammana is awakened by music charming but insistent, notes that shatter the press of night. Is it the tinkling of coins sewn onto the headdress of a child bride? Or a chiming of bells that hang around the neck of Grandfather's lead sheep? She can't quite place it. But she's accustomed to moments when sound or smell or face seems familiar though elusive. Past crowding out present, trying even to outrun the future.

They are bedded inside because Grandfather gazed at the knotting clouds before darkness and, chuckling at his own humor, announced a premonition of coming downpour. Jammana sees Grandfather's form now, its comforting lift and heave. A blanket of nightfall is enough to keep him warm. When she rises and her own cover drops to the ground, however, the air quickly chills. Holding her companion Asima, she hugs herself. The sheep, gathered in the stable beneath Grandfather's room, stir. She inhales their mustiness as she glides to the open door. A beckoning moon paints the courtyard the color of a fading acacia flower.

A woman stands beneath the almond tree, reaching into its leaves, her back to Jammana. She wears a long belted *thobe* that, in the moonlight, glows velvet with gold embroidery on its flowing sleeves. She is trilling softly, the notes high yet husky. Jammana, holding her breath, moves forward. At times the woman strikes the same clear, expectant notes Grandfather's coffee-roasting pan makes when tapped against granite. At other moments, her voice betrays something sooty.

The woman stops, glances over her shoulder, and smiles. "Blessings of Allah," she says. Her head is bare, which is never seen outside the home in Ein Fadr. Of course, it's night and this woman—unable to sleep or perhaps roused by a fleeting scent, a transient sound—surely has just come from her home. She must be a neighbor, though Jammana doesn't recognize her and her clothes are not those worn to sleep. She looks older than Mama—several gray streams flow through hair of polished copper. Perhaps about Umm Mahir's age, though more slender and, oddly, with a face unlined as a girl's. Her eyes, too, belong to a child; they don't hold back. Her neck is long and narrow.

The woman steps closer. "Look," she says in a tone of light surprise. "I've hurt myself." She holds out her right hand as a child might, and Jammana sees the side of her thumb is freshly red and blistering. Jammana tucks her doll under one arm and takes the offered hand to inspect the injury. The woman's skin shines between shadows of leaves that collide on her arm. She smells like a blossom the day before it begins to dim, its perfume sharp with coming loss.

"What happened?" Jammana asks. "Shall I get some herbs to put on your hand?"

The woman shakes her head. "I scorched myself making *kibbeh* just now." She laughs lightly, turns, and weaves around the courtyard in a swaying dance, a reed in the wind. "I know I shouldn't cook anymore," she half sings cheerfully, "but I used to be so fine at it."

Though the burn looks new, it couldn't be. The villagers allow the oven coals to die out at night, Jammana knows. Suddenly she wonders if this could be a memory that belongs to someone else, though she's never had one quite like this before. Usually she feels herself in another place or time. Now she's still at Grandfather's house. He sleeps inside.

"Did you know a mulberry has always been rooted in this village, as far back as its history reaches?" the woman asks. "Our farmers are a bit superstitious about it. Eventually they will decide it is time to tend one of Moses' Finger's babies so that when the old tree dies, a replacement will be ready. In this way, they believe, Ein Fadr's heart will ceaselessly beat."

Jammana enjoys the woman's lyrical voice, but makes no reply. She cannot imagine the meaning of this talk about Moses' Finger. After a moment, the woman says softly, "All unsettled."

Involuntarily, Jammana's shoulders sag in relief. That's just it! Lately her legs have constantly wobbled, and even fresh goat's milk can't dissuade her stomach from churning. She tries to demonstrate her maturity: She never mentions missing Mama, she never runs to play with the other children. The grown-ups, perhaps in response, don't treat her like a child; but they also do not accept her as one of theirs. They talk in hushed staccato that breaks off at her approach. She feels as though she is in a deserted land, separate from all.

The woman strokes her hair. "You worry."

Jammana nods, grateful for this stranger's unexpected accuracy. Her words come in a rush. "It's my memory. I've tried to ask Grandfather about it. Faridah, too. Everyone treats me like I'm only half here. And I keep dreaming about glass and losing something. I think it's about Mama, but how can I protect her if they won't tell me anything?"

The woman reaches up, twists a leaf off the almond tree. "Such responsibility you give yourself, child. But you must know that temporary disorder is sometimes necessary. And betrayal is often an accident, like burning yourself at an oven. No need to punish yourself—or others. It is not your fault."

Betrayal. Fault. Punish. Who, Jammana wonders, does this memory belong to?

"It is yours," the woman answers.

Jammana steps forward. "But—"

The woman places a finger, long and warm, on Jammana's lips. "This is enough to remember. More would simply confuse. I don't know where your grandfather inherited his love of talking, but it wasn't from me." She stretches an arm around Jammana and leads her to Grandfather's door, where she peeks in, smiling in that crooked way adults sometimes do to disguise sorrow.

"It's he I worry about," she says. Her eyes grow distant. "My bundle."

Jammana steps away from her. "Who are you?" she asks, suddenly knowing.

The woman shakes her head. "Back to sleep now, little one." Jammana starts to argue, but the woman's voice holds a calm authority she can only obey.

At the door, the woman watches as Jammana lies down and places Asima next to her, as she pulls the scratchy wool blanket to her chin and inches closer to Grandfather. The woman with the girlish face and streaks of gray is the last sight Jammana sees before she tumbles into the mysterious valley between childhood and maturity. The ravine of sleep.

Sunlight pries open her lids. She feels leaden, as she often does after one of her odd dreams. Though her body is slender and light—"not filled up yet," Mama says, as if she were some empty jar—her forehead is ponderous as stone. She drops Asima into her pocket and rubs her head vigorously with both hands.

She can tell the sheep in the courtyard have been fed because they are not shifting from foot to foot or bleating with hunger. Grandfather stands with his profile to her, prayer beads sliding between his fingers. He seems to be searching somewhere beyond the fields and hills, the olive trees that soon will be dense with fruit. The air is thick with the sound of a helicopter overhead. Jammana knows the Jordanian planes must be careful because of the border in the sky, as real as the one on the ground but even harder to see. If they cross it, they can expect fire from a concealed foe.

When at last the helicopter vanishes and Grandfather turns, he seems momentarily startled by the sight of her. Then he smiles. "Allah bless you, child." He reaches to a platter on the ground and hands her bread smeared with molasses. "Khalah prepared this for you."

She takes it, sits cross-legged. "Why were you out so early?"

"The sheep woke me before even the sand grouse rose." He strokes his beard. "When I arrived home, you weren't stirring. You must have been tired."

Jammana tilts her head up, hoping to look wise. "A woman came last night," she says.

Grandfather steps closer. "Who? Where?"

Jammana savors his attention before going on. "She had a burn on her hand."

Grandfather kneels, facing Jammana. His forehead is creased. "Did she see you?"

Jammana nods. "She said not to wake you."

"So it wasn't anyone you know?"

Jammana feels her way with her words. "I thought she came from one of the houses, but then I knew she didn't."

Grandfather rises, allows his fingers to wander into his beard.

"She said I would betray someone."

"Betray?" His tone arches. His face falls into shadow.

Jammana drops the bread, untangles her legs, and jumps to her feet in a sudden rush of worry brought on, in part, by Grandfather's single-word response and his disguised expression. "What did she mean? I would tell a secret? Lie? Steal something?"

"You would never do so intentionally. But sometimes betrayal comes as easily as a storm while one is sleeping, child. It is in the care of the All-Knowing. You mustn't blame yourself."

"She said that too."

Grandfather steps to his lead sheep, slips his fingers deep into her coat. "Did she name who you would betray?"

"She said it was up to me. Then she looked in on you." Jammana watches for Grandfather's reaction. "She said she worries about someone—I think she meant you."

Grandfather jerks his head up. She can tell that though she hasn't said Alula's name, he understands now. His eyes hold longing that he quickly hides.

"One of my memories, wasn't it?" Jammana blows air through her mouth in frustration. "Mama calls it a gift, but I don't think so. Why, Grandfather?"

"Why does one seed become a bush while another lies fallow?" Grandfather shrugs.

"Has anyone ever come to you like this? Someone you could talk to and touch?" Jammana asks.

Grandfather shakes his head. "For me it's like observing from a great distance. At least it was in the beginning. Now I catch only a scent, a sound, a feeling sometimes. Nothing more."

"Why do they have to be so incomplete? So hard to understand?"

"It was, even for *my* grandfather," Grandfather says. "We cannot make demands. We must be satisfied with that." But he himself sounds dissatisfied. He rubs his neck and drops his hand to her shoulder. "I have to go now, child."

"Again?" Jammana hears her voice rise in protest. She tries to sound adult-annoyed. "I've been here four days, and your time is always occupied. Where are you going now?"

"You haven't eaten a bite," he says, pointing to the bread. "Finish your food. Then you're to stay with Khalah. She's fetching water, but she'll be back soon."

Jammana clenches her teeth. He won't acknowledge her question. She makes her words formal. "I'll accompany you."

He looks at her steadily a moment. "Not until the afternoon," he says in a tone that leaves no room for discussion. "Then we'll graze the sheep."

Why can't he share his secret? Why can't he—why can't any of them—see how she's growing up? He starts out of the courtyard, then pauses. "Remember, Jammana. Stay here."

Though she likes to sound defiant, Jammana in fact has never before disobeyed a direct command from an adult. Still, her hesitation this time is briefer than a thought.

She hurries into the room to grab her bandanna, which she ties around her neck as she dashes after Grandfather. A rumble of distant fear sends a thrill through her body, the way it does when she watches a protest from the window of her home in Nablus. He may catch her. Then he'll be angry, send her home. Yet she will try. She'll not be held back by an unseen border. She'll pace her steps, keep Grandfather in sight, she vows. Not follow in her usual way, dashing ahead at first and then slowing to examine a moth or the veins of a leaf so that she's always the last to arrive. This time she'll be concentrated, stealthy.

Because it is undeniable, now. There are no tall, broad trees to shade her on this road. No one to take her hand and lead her to the bridge. She has to be the one.

Grandfather scuttles, but Jammana, with her tender goat legs, easily keeps up. Sometimes she halfheartedly attempts to duck behind rocks, though instinct tells her she won't be seen. Grandfather checks over his shoulder once in a distracted way and doesn't notice her.

They soar and dip over hills along the border of the olive grove in a direction she has never taken in her wide wanderings with Grandfather and his sheep. Fleshy clouds dart overhead as though struggling to stay above their own shadows. Then they—Grandfather, Jammana, and the clouds—arrive at an untended section of the grove. Above them rise ragged hills.

Here, Jammana's attention shifts and she forgets Grandfather. She is swept up by the sight in the clearing before her. An earthen plate with figs, not fresh but edible, sits in front of a tree stump slightly taller than her knees. Three stones as tall as she but wider loom like bulky supplicants. A makeshift ramada stands to one side, and next to it four rocks are stacked, resembling a kneeling human form.

She approaches the stump, tentative, and reaches to touch its hard surface cut by veins of deep red, charcoal, brown. It is removed from this life, turning from hot wood to cool stone with the silent intensity that transformation requires. Yet as she touches it, she hears muffled sounds. Hopeless weeping. Heaves of breath. Finally, faint laughter.

Nearby, the earth offers a peephole the size of a young child's spread hand. She kneels there, and wafts of cool air caress her face. Suddenly she knows. Though she's never been here, she recognizes the stump as the remains of the sacred olive tree Alula grasped. The tree chosen by lightning. Where Grandfather heard an inner scream of loss. Where a tear left forever a stain on Khalah's cheek. Where even today, Jammana has been told, women bring secret ambitions, fears, and angers.

It is also, she realizes, that place in her dream.

That place of broken glass, where loss and violence live still, calling for someone.

She can hear it.

She lifts her head to see Grandfather scrambling up a hillside. He turns, searching. Jammana closes her eyes, cringing, certain she will be spotted at last. When she opens them, Grandfather has vanished.

She won't lose him now. She sprints up the hill, her feet setting pebbles into noisy motion. She doesn't stop until she reaches the squared boulder where he vanished as if into a hole. She touches the rough, marbled rock. Begins to circle it. Behind, she sees a shadow, the narrow entrance to a cave. She hesitates, then discards the notion of caution.

The cave feels damp but surprisingly warm. Jammana blinks, identifies Grandfather's back, which screens her. Jammana sees Faridah kneeling in a corner, grinding something on a stone. And against the far wall, someone else—Mama!

Ya, Mama. How Jammana has missed her. She rushes forward.

Mama starts like a mouse in the knowing moment before the viper strikes. She appears older, grayer. "Jammana!"

she says. "How . . . ?" Jammana stops short at the sound of her voice, so far from welcoming. The string of a frozen moment unwinds. How odd, Jammana thinks, that Mama didn't come to her. That Jammana had to find her by accident, as though Mama herself were one of the secrets the grown-ups are keeping.

At last Mama opens her arms and Jammana runs in, trying to dismiss her worries. Mama loves her and has missed her. Jammana shoos away a grain of doubt.

"You brought her?" Faridah asks Grandfather. Each word taut.

"Of course not! Child, I told you to stay with Khalah."

"Check the entrance," Mama says in a breathless voice. "Make sure."

Jammana turns, holding Mama's arms in an X across her shoulders. Grandfather hurries to the cave entrance. "No one below," he says. "Not even donkeys this time." He faces Jammana. "Now," he says, "explain yourself."

Jamman steps away, straightening her shoulders. She won't apologize for disobeying. They've left her with no choice. She speaks with as much defiance as she can summon. "You don't need to keep secrets from me. If no one will tell me, I'll find out myself. If you want to punish me, go ahead."

She wonders what they will do to her. Perhaps Mama will forgive her, but Father will be livid. His body will swell, his lips will grow thin, and he will not speak to her for days, maybe weeks. Perhaps he even will forbid Mama to speak to Jammana. Then it occurs to her. "Where is he?" she asks.

Mama's eyes hold something unreadable. Jammana glances right, then left, looking for signs of Father. She notices a mat on the floor, water and bread in a corner. "What are you doing here?" she asks.

Mama gives a short, curt laugh. "Looking for a donkey with hands."

"What?"

"It means trying to find something that doesn't exist," she says.

Why won't grown-ups offer simple, straightforward explanations? Jammana turns and faces Mama squarely. "I came here to think," Mama says at last. "Like you when you climb up the lemon tree. It seemed this cave might work for me." She spreads her arms. "I wanted to think alone. I didn't tell anyone except Khalah, who saw me first, and Faridah, who brought me here. I didn't tell your grandfather, even. He found me the way you did. He followed Faridah."

"And Father?"

"I don't want him to know, *faraashe.*"

Jammana feels a prickle of alarm on the back of her neck. "He is still angry that you brought me here?"

"He'll manage to forget it," Mama says tightly.

"So everything will be all right between you? Once you are done thinking?"

Mama kneels. "I don't know yet, Jammana," she says, unleashing with her cautionary tone a flood of fear that rushes against Jammana's ears. "Will it be very hard for you if it's not?"

Jammana turns in a circle, staring at the silent faces around her. She senses that Mama, Faridah, and Grandfather are about to be propelled into separate, battering worlds— and that she'll be stranded, cut off from them all.

But Alula was wrong. She will not be the one to betray.

She'll be the one to rescue. It is not too late. "It can't be," she says loudly, causing Mama's eyes to dart toward the cave's entrance.

"Shhh," warns Faridah.

"I remember," Grandfather interjects in a strong but quiet voice that calms Jammana, "when they forced me to leave. I remember going into that moment alone. I'll tell you of it now. A familiar scent brought me comfort then."

"Old man, is this the time for tales?" Faridah asks, her eyebrows raised. "We must take Jammana back."

Mama hesitates. "Perhaps we could allow her . . . ?"

Jammana wants to hear Grandfather's story, but even more, she doesn't want to leave Mama yet. Mama needs her. "Tell us your story, Grandfather," she says, lifting her chin.

Mama nods. "But quickly. Because soon you all must leave, and tell no one I'm here. You understand, Jammana?"

"At least, let me . . ." Faridah moves to the cave's entrance and peers beyond the boulder, her head moving along the horizon. Finally, she turns and shrugs. "No one. Still, I'll keep watch." She sits, drawing her knees up under the tent of her belted dress. Mama drops to the ground also. Jammana pushes her way onto Mama's lap for a moment, then shifts, sitting next to her instead.

"We can survive much, Jammana." Grandfather rests his head against the wall and strokes his beard. "I remember the year I turned eighteen. That was when they flung me from Ein Fadr like a scrap of waste they hoped would soon be buried under desert sands."

H A R I F

Even now, as an old man, Harif can easily recall the weeks after the grape failure of 1934, when the muttering of Ein Fadr's villagers flowed thick as sap from a wounded tree. His visions were widely misunderstood: Some claimed he talked to water; others said he conferred with *jinn* in distant fields. They blamed him not only for the crop loss but for other misfortunes as well—broken tools, sickened donkeys, disobedient children. Farmers decided their ill luck was not a matter of chance but of free will: Harif's will. It was rumored that Harif had insight into Ein Fadr's secret sins and desires. Each man surmised that he was being punished for some transgression previously believed concealed but now somehow divined by this strange son of Alula's.

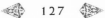 127

Oh, the aversion felt toward one who seems to know his neighbors too well! Harif saw the fear and anger that rode on the *fellahin*'s skins like work-sweat mixed with dust. Ein Fadr wound upon itself tightly as a ball of wool. Some took to tucking beneath their *keffiyeh*s tiny bags of verbena leaves thought to ward off the evil eye. The less superstitious—and their numbers were few—simply recoiled from Harif. Among the men, only Harif's cousin Musa and the *mukhtar*'s son, Nabeel, defended him, although they did so with such vigor—at first—that they were able to forestall the inevitable.

Harif knew that Nabeel, though much doted upon by his father, felt his own shortcomings keenly. A meager, awkward boy, Nabeel had shown little talent for farming—the most respected job in Ein Fadr. Neither could he write or read. He was, by nature, a follower. In their younger days, Harif had without second thought been his leader, the bearer of myriad plans and pranks, and Nabeel hoped for that breath of excitement in his life again.

One evening, Nabeel found Harif as he herded in the sheep. "We're going to the cave," Nabeel said. "Join us?" He referred to a small cavern used by generations of boys. All were welcome and shared there a camaraderie they recognized would dissolve once they tied on the sashes of men, became responsible for the future of the village and burdened by its past. Harif knew that while in the cave, even he would be accepted. But he couldn't imagine finding comfort there. He shook his head and went in search of Faridah and the other women.

Another day, Nabeel strolled along with Harif on the way to the fields. "Remember the tricks we used to play?" he asked. "The time we stole wool from my aunt to make slings? Or when we picked a tree clean overnight, and in the morning no one knew where the olives had gone?" Nabeel laughed. "We had wild streaks, didn't we?"

Harif looked his friend full in the face, then turned away. "I must go." he said, and sent his sheep sharply in another direction. As he left, he saw Nabeel's jaw harden. He'd heard the plea in Nabeel's voice. And he knew his refusals offended, but he couldn't help himself. He simply could not return to the easy, unconscious alliance of their childhood. Nabeel's very presence recalled Harif's vanished years of innocence. Besides, Harif feared angering the *mukhtar*, who had made it clear he opposed the friendship between Nabeel and Harif. Harif already worried about what the village chief would do if he had another vision.

One morning, after the worst of winter had passed and the air was already warming, Harif awoke shivering. Leaving his sheep behind, he fled to the edge of the olive groves not far from the shrine dedicated to his mother. He lay there alone until afternoon, when Musa, who had heard the sheep were not attended, found him. "Come, come," said Musa. "This is not a day of rest or prayer. Your animals must be attended." Harif sat up and, with difficulty, swung his head toward his cousin, his protector. "What's the matter? Are you sick?" Musa asked, with indulgence more than concern.

Having spent hours debating whether to be silent or speak, Harif suddenly decided. He'd failed to voice the vision of his mother, and he'd lost her. "Your son," he said.

Musa rose slightly on his toes, and his voice climbed. "Samir? What about him?"

"Ill."

Musa stared. Then he turned and flew back to the village. His four-year-old son, Samir, was playing in a corner, and his wife laughed at his concern, but Musa slept uneasily that night. Before morning, Samir awoke holding his stomach and screaming as though locusts had eaten through him. Blessed with a nature as cheerful as his father's and an unusual bravery, Samir had weathered earlier childhood ailments—from falls to fevers and rashes—with little complaint, which made his weeping all the harder for his parents to bear.

In the days that followed, Musa and his wife met with a healer from Nablus and two from Jerusalem. Each had cures for the child: He should eat only eggs laid on Fridays; he should drink blessed water three times a day; they should burn the clothes he wore when he first fell ill and rub the ashes on his body. Each proffered remedy Musa tried and then tried again. A cousin carried a tuft of the boy's hair to Abraham's tomb in Hebron; another offered a sacrifice at the Dome of the Rock in Jerusalem.

These were the treatments practiced in Ein Fadr in those days, these and prayer. If once Musa had been so busy in the fields that he forgot to bow down to Allah five times a day, now he did so without fail. He also began fasting Mondays and Thursdays, as had the Prophet Mohammed.

Nothing helped. The pain in his son's stomach eased sometimes, but not for a moment did it completely disappear. The boy often could not eat. He grew weaker. Musa paid scant attention to his duties in the gardens. His own cheeks turned hollow.

Harif, for his part, feared the villagers were right—that

somehow the power of his visions had brought misfortune upon Musa's family, the grape crop, his mother. His shoulders became weighted, his step slurred. He looked an old, frail man. "My life for the life of Musa's son," he told Faridah one evening when he met her on his way home.

"You speak the drivel of bird droppings, Harif," she answered.

"Perhaps I wouldn't if my mother had completed my training." Harif's head drooped. "As it is, I'm unprepared."

Faridah whistled in disapproval. "Such self-pity before the will of Allah!" She crooked a finger and motioned for Harif to follow to her small home. At the threshold, she reached up to smooth her headdress, gazing at him deeply as though estimating the weight of a stone. In the movements of her wrists, the reach of her cheeks, the wash of her eyes, Harif suddenly saw what his preoccupation with his mother's death and his own visions had prevented him from seeing before. He saw Faridah, at twenty-four, six years older than he, a woman of slender curves and dramatic eyes and burnished skin. Then she disappeared through the door.

Harif had never been to Faridah's house before. No one had in the six years she'd lived there—her contact with other villagers came only at the well or in a *taboon*. Now, as Harif stood outside and Faridah waited within, he found his breathing suddenly constricted. He blamed it on a rational fear of stepping through this door without a chaperone. If he were discovered, the outcry would rise to all seven heavens. An unmarried couple alone together in the woman's home would be an offense against Allah, reason to expel both from the village, or worse. Death by stoning. These worries shot through his mind as he stood outside her door. But, compelled, he followed her inside.

She motioned for him to sit on a small carpet on the floor. Stripped of his own will, he obeyed. She stepped back outside, and he looked around. Faridah's room. A chamber nearly empty, filled to its essence. Her sleeping mat lay in a heap, not folded neatly as they were in his home. Pounded dates sprawled in a basket on the floor. Shadows curved teasingly from the corners. A lizard stepped toward the room's center, bold and taunting.

Faridah returned then with a plate of warm *falafel* and a small earthen cup of olive oil. "Eat. Drink," she ordered, only the slight hoarseness of her voice revealing what must have been her own nervousness. Then she lowered herself to the ground.

Sitting across from her, he stared first at her cheeks, then her lips, and began to imagine. Briefly. He clamped his mind shut before even one picture came into sharp focus. Still, he couldn't unfasten his gaze from her, couldn't prevent his eyes from begging answers to questions his mouth would not ask. She stared back, unrevealing. The air in the room seemed to vibrate.

At first, each bite was difficult. The *falafel* did not crumble as usual. It held together as a solid mass, and he had to force it down with breathless gulps of oil, which coated his tongue and throat.

After a dozen bites, he began to feel strength returning to his body and spirit. When finished, he rose and faced her. He stood taller than she again. "What did you mix in this food?"

"Nothing," she replied, though her eyes shone oddly.

"The oil you drank was stored in a clay jar you and I made together, and the *falafel* was cooked in the same. That's all."

"It restored me."

"We made it together," she said. "That's its power, if it has any. Now, let's go."

"Where?"

"Musa."

Harif stepped backward, shaking his head. "Musa can't bear to see me now, not after what I've done."

"So far you've done nothing," said Faridah, her voice sharper than usual. "It's well time for you to act."

Again, Harif allowed himself to be led as they walked the short distance to Musa's home. Musa opened the door, hesitated, then admitted them without the usual effusive greetings. Samir lay sleeping fitfully, cheeks flushed. His stomach gurgled loudly, and even in his sleep, he moved a hand to it. In the corner, one of the male villagers stood quietly reciting the Koran.

Struck by a sudden urge, Harif lurched toward the corner where the boy lay, and reached for the child. Musa stepped between Harif and Samir.

"May I rock him?" Harif begged, turning toward Musa's wife. "Just for a moment?"

She spread open her hands, but only Musa spoke. "Let him lie."

"Please. Perhaps—"

"Don't."

Harif and his cousin stared at each other. Finally, Harif bowed his head in submission.

Musa's wife awkwardly offered tea, which both Harif and Faridah refused. "But may we come again to check on the child?" Faridah asked. Musa turned away. Musa's wife stared at her husband's back for a moment, then silently opened the door.

After they left, Faridah turned to Harif. "Could you offer no advice?"

"Would he have listened to any?"

She shrugged agreement. "What were you hoping for when you asked to hold the boy?"

Harif barely knew himself. "I thought perhaps I could ease the pain," he answered vaguely, searching the hills beyond the village as he spoke.

Early the next morning as Harif prepared to leave for the fields, someone rapped on the door impatiently. He opened it, and Faridah took him by the arm, her fingers feverish and soothing at once. "Come," she said. "Quickly." The command in her touch cut off his ability to reply, let alone question.

She led him through the village, along the edge of the olive groves, and to the shrine to Alula. There, in the shadow of the hills above, stood Musa's wife holding Samir, who twisted and fussed. "Take him," she said, pushing the child desperately toward Harif. "Nothing else has helped."

"Where's Musa?" asked Harif uneasily.

"At the harvest." The wife wiped her cheeks. "The responsibility is mine."

The child quickly quieted in Harif's arms. Faridah took Musa's wife by the elbow. "Let's go to the well so we're not missed," she said. She called over her shoulder to Harif. "I've left you our jar."

Harif looked at the earthen container smoothed by two sets of hands: pinched narrow at the top, spreading out to sides generous and tender as a woman's hips. Hesitating at first, he finally lifted it and gave a drink of oil to the boy. The child's chest was swathed in cotton; Harif lay him on the ground, uncovered him, and began massaging deeply with oil-dipped hands. He kneaded and smoothed the boy's throat and chest and back until his fingers gave out. Then he wrapped the boy again. Samir, cupped in Harif's arms, slept deeply, breathing through open mouth, limbs dangling.

Whether it was pure coincidence, the oil, or simply a case of Allah changing His mind, Harif would never know. Two days later, word emerged from Musa's home that his heir had unaccountably but undeniably recovered. Women filling their earthen jars at the well trilled in celebration, and the sounds of joy and relief rebounded off the hills. Harif, on his way to the fields with his sheep, couldn't stop himself from humming.

Not even Samir's recovery, however, could save Harif now. The *mukhtar* circulated the news of his latest insight: The devil had reached up from the depths to touch Harif at birth, he said, and only a stray breath of Allah's had prevented disaster again.

Two weeks later, one evening while Bahir was in Jerusalem selling olives, the *mukhtar* came to see Harif. He wore a black ceremonial coat, sleeves trimmed in gold that emphasized the majesty of his broad gestures. Nabeel accompanied him.

The two young men bowed slightly to each other, and then Harif turned to the *mukhtar*. "You have brought blessings," he greeted his guest in the customary fashion.

"Allah the Knower blesses you," responded the *mukhtar* woodenly.

"You have brought light to our house," Harif said further.

"The light is yours," answered the *mukhtar*. He held his face stonelike, but Harif noticed the line of sweat above his eyebrows.

"Beneath the Blessed One's eyes, my father and his children kiss you," Harif went on, unable to control a slight twitching of his lips. Such ceremony he was requiring from the obviously uncomfortable village chief!

The *mukhtar*, clearly wearied by the graciousness of the culpable, groaned slightly. "We return the kisses," he said. "May I sit?"

Khalah brought the guests cups of sugary tea and a plate of watermelon seeds, then squatted in the corner of the room while Harif and the other two sat in a circle in the center. The *mukhtar* took a noisy sip and began to speak, his voice smooth but his words sharp as briar. "I have often wondered," he began, "how it is that you are able to foresee only pain and disaster. Your grandfather in his time envisioned more joys than trials. But you—you have foreseen plagues upon our heads."

Nabeel studied his own thumbs as they twirled in his lap. Harif coughed. "Musa's son is well," he said.

"Yes, but that you did not predict."

"I cannot choose."

"And your mother," the *mukhtar* went on without pause. "At her funeral, you did not even cry."

Harif stared at the chief for a moment before speaking. "I am like the olive tree after the Prophet's death." He didn't need to elaborate; the *mukhtar* knew the story. When Mohammed died, all trees save the olive lost their leaves. People became angry because the tree looked as lush as ever. Finally, an old man asked why it felt no grief. "It is not the deepest feeling which displays itself," the tree answered. "My heart is broken. Cut into my bark and you will see." And so it was, for the olive tree blackens and dies from the inside out.

Harif noticed that Nabeel couldn't suppress a satisfied grin; Nabeel admired Harif for the speed of his tongue, even when used against his own father. But the *mukhtar* remained unmoved. He rose and paced the room. "I must speak with the openness this moment requires," he said at last, a cagey expression in his eyes. "The villagers are afraid. You seem to tote misfortune on your shoulders."

The *mukhtar* hesitated here. Harif knew punishment would be hard to pronounce. After all, he enjoyed the status of an oldest son, and in addition the oldest son of the *wali* Alula. Besides, Nabeel was watching, which may have made the *mukhtar* reluctant to demonstrate cruelty. Harif did not act to ease the *mukhtar's* discomfort; neither did he try to make the moment more difficult. He remained observant.

"Perhaps you do not bring misfortune," the *mukhtar* said, as though arguing with an adversary. "But you can't disagree that it seems to follow you at least." He reached into his tunic and handed Harif a piece of paper. "As you know, the teacher in our *kuttab* is too old for the job. I've a message here to be delivered to my second cousin in Beersheba. I'm asking that they send us a new teacher. You will deliver the message and return with whomever they select. You may rest on the way with my uncle's family in Bethlehem."

The fire in the brazier collapsed loudly on itself, leaving only embers. Khalah half stood, but Harif motioned for her to sit. Nabeel stiffened. "Father!" he said. "The desert is home to too many windstorms and too few wells. Only Bedouin, bandits, and fools travel in it alone. Let me accompany him."

"No!" answered the *mukhtar*. "Only Harif. We can spare only Harif. When he returns"—he drew out the last word—"perhaps passions in the village will have cooled."

Nabeel started to protest further, but Harif stood up. "I will go," he said with more confidence than he felt.

The women of Ein Fadr wailed in sorrow that night. They believed the *mukhtar* had blundered, and they sought to alter his decision. But their men, in an overpowering alliance, hushed them.

Harif's father returned from Jerusalem the next day to find his son preparing to leave. Weakened by the loss of his wife, he felt unable to defy the *mukhtar*. So he procured a camel, a beast far more suited than a village donkey to extended journeys across desert expanse.

Khalah gathered the food, and Faridah offered Harif a lump of unformed clay. "Add a little water to it every day," she said. "When you are ready to fashion it into something that will serve you, mix it with straw and sand. Also ground pottery shards, if you can find any. You know how. Take care of it, and your home will always be with you." Before Harif left, she leaned forward and whispered so only he could hear: "Please, Harif, hurry!"

Nabeel, too, came to see the departing Harif. Awkwardly, he held out a hand. "You will not die out there," he told Harif in a voice that broke in and out of manhood. "Our words will take turns again."

Harif, full of doubts, could not answer. His saliva turned salty; his lips felt parched. As he climbed on the camel, a sudden gust lifted his hair, carrying on it the odor of wild herbs and olive oil, fresh *kibbeh* and the essence of white flowers rubbed into women's flesh. Both Bahir and Harif knew the smells of Alula. Bahir bent over in the anguish of loss, unable to look at his son again. But Harif took the scent as a sign of his mother's blessing, and it calmed the fears that had risen to his throat and threatened to erupt in the most unmanly of cries. Only in this way did he manage to leave his ancestral home without a single glance behind.

Harif rises. "So you see, Jammana, support comes from unlikely places."

"Didn't it make you angry," Jammana asks, "the way the villagers treated you?"

Harif sighs. "Bitterness is a poisonous weed."

"Now it's time to go," Faridah says, standing. Harif knows the rest of this story brings her little pleasure.

"Not yet!" Jammana says. "I know you got lost, but what else happened?" Harif sees she's emboldened by having escaped punishment for her disobedience, but he doesn't mind. She may need a sense of her own power, soon. When adults falter on the path, it is the child who must find strength to tote the water skin.

Rafa, watching Jammana, nods. "You can tell a little more."

"All right," Faridah says, her voice tight. "Finish it. Tell Jammana about meeting her grandmother. Tell her about the woman you were saved for." She begins to pace the tiny cave.

Harif follows Faridah with his eyes. Time has refined

her to her very essence. She is both flower and stone. He leans back, eyes closed, recalling in vivid detail how on that trip in the desert, the sands of the Judean wilderness took on the shape of her cheekbone, the hollow of her neck, the imagined curve of her knee. He'd beheld her eyes, as well, in the fires he lit at night. Heard her laugh on the wind. He'd struggled—then and for decades—to shut those images out. He'd made himself believe they were only symptoms of loneliness and fear. Because he always understood that one outcast joined to another would not survive in the overheated air of Ein Fadr, and he would have nothing to pass down to his children, not even a place.

"But hurry, Father. You all must go soon," Rafa says.

Harif shakes his head to clear it.

"Go?" Jammana protests.

"You promised," Rafa says. "Remember?"

The cave grows silent. "You know that Faridah delivered Rafa, of course," Harif begins, and this captures Jammana's attention again. She leans toward him. "But did she ever tell you how difficult a birth it was? So that the next time your grandmother became pregnant—"

"We aren't there yet," Faridah interrupts in a voice that ricochets off the walls and causes them all to stiffen. "You've skipped some details. Shall I tell them for you?" She faces them and gazes, loose-eyed, somewhere above their heads. But when she speaks next, her tone is controlled. "Harif spent many days in Beersheba and found a new teacher for Ein Fadr. On their return, they broke their journey in Bethlehem, as the *mukhtar* had suggested. There, on Daraj al-Alf Darji, the Staircase of a Thousand Steps, he discovered his heart had matured." Faridah gestures, and they all follow the upward movement of her hand. "The staircase starts from the spot where Jesus was born, and ends at the marketplace where merchants cheat and old women plead. In Bethlehem, they say the ascent represents the arc of life, beginning with birth, when one is so cherished, and ending with old age and its inadequacies. Where better to meet your future? Isn't that so, Harif?" Faridah's wrist drops to her side. "He was going up; she coming down, a basket of eggs balanced on her head. Pale cheeks like ashes from a finished fire, yes, Harif? Lashes thick as a fir." Faridah's voice, deadened for a moment, now rises above their heads. Her face is a commotion of fury and love. "Hannan! Your dear Hannan!"

Harif lifts a hand to his mouth. In all these years, Faridah has never spoken his wife's name. He doubts she has allowed herself to think it. "Faridah," he begins in a warning tone.

"Harif and Hannan!" Faridah goes on, her eyes now hard and unseeing. "She must have felt him staring, because she giggled as she passed, reached out and tugged his ear. Such bravery in an Arab girl. The most spontaneous act of her life, I would guess. Her touch left him"—here Faridah gulps—"breathless."

Harif sees Rafa's eyes widening.

"The teacher," Faridah continues, "acted as go-between, along with the *mukhtar*'s uncle, head of a powerful clan. He assumed Harif had been chosen for the Beersheba mission not as punishment but for his bravery and skill. A betrothal was quickly arranged—with such speed, in fact, that Harif had no time . . ." She finishes in a voice that falls to the floor of the cave: "To consider those left behind."

I didn't understand, Harif wants to shout, *that you'd readied my heart and then let me go.*

But before he can think of what to say that will be clear to Faridah and vague to the others, Jammana rises. "Then they came back to Ein Fadr," Jammana begins, as though she's picking up the story, "and had a baby. And that is what I don't understand, Faridah. That is what I've been trying to ask." Her words spill on top of one another. "Why did you refuse my grandmother when she needed you?"

"What?" asks Harif. "Faridah didn't—"

Jammana ignores him. "Why didn't you want Mama to be born?"

What could she possibly mean? With any other child, Harif would pay no heed. Jammana has a gift. Still, she must be mistaken this time.

"What are you talking about, faraashe?" Rafa asks.

"That's why I wanted to come to Ein Fadr," Jammana says. "To know about this memory. I'm old enough. Tell me."

"Faridah loves Rafa like a daughter, Jammana," Harif says. "She would never—"

"Jammana," Rafa interrupts, an edge in her voice. "Did you have a bad dream?"

"It was as real as any of my memories, and they've all been right, Mama. You know that. It was in Grandfather's home, and Faridah put something in the lantern just before you were born, and the air got thick, and then you got stuck, and Faridah didn't pull you out even though my grandmother was begging, and so I—" Jammana sucks in air, as if surprised by her own words.

"No, Jammana. You must be . . ." Rafa breaks off. Harif is watching Faridah. She is holding her breath, a red spot on each cheek. Her eyes are focused on Rafa, and they do not deny Jammana's words. Harif sees Rafa, too, is staring at Faridah. "I've been blind," Rafa says. "Under Allah's sky, I've been a child." She backs deeper into the cave. "I dismissed the rumors, my own suspicions. I admired your strength. I wanted to be like you."

"It wasn't that way. It was only . . ." Faridah, pleading, trails off.

"Only what?" Rafa's voice arches.

Faridah looks to Harif, then, and he reads in her eyes an appeal, but he's too shocked to respond. Faridah reaches toward Rafa. "I'd give my life for you."

"And for him? Whose life would you give?" asks Rafa. "Mine?" The question takes aim between them. Rafa straightens, her tone turning cruel. "It would have been easier without me. You must have thought that countless times."

"No!" says Faridah.

Jammana is staring from her mother to Faridah, her sesame-seed eyes widening. Someone should pull the child away, Harif knows. She should hear none of this. Yet he himself feels rooted. His head begins to spin, and in the midst of his dizziness, the vision of recent days reappears. A violet shard of glass. Pain. A broken quality to the air. He still can't fathom it, yet it is more vivid than ever. Can Jammana see it?

He stares at his granddaughter. But before he can penetrate her expression, his concentration is shattered. A wisp of sour sound magnified by fear: the crunching of pebbles underfoot at the entrance to the cave. Someone gasps, and his own throat clenches as he whirls.

FARIDAH

Khalah." Rafa trills her name like a song of buds opening. "Only Khalah!"

Faridah hears Harif murmur through deep breaths: "*Al hamd li Allah.*" Praise be to Allah.

Khalah ignores everyone but Rafa. "He's on his way."

Rafa stiffens. "Where?"

"Somewhere beyond the terebinth tree. I told some of the women. We've been keeping a lookout."

"We have little time," Rafa says. "To the fields with your sheep, Father, quickly. To a far field, and stay until dark." Rafa, Faridah sees, is a grain of determination. "Khalah, he'll come to you first, I'd guess. Prepare yourself. I won't make you throw dust in his eyes too long." Khalah nods. "Jammana,

you go"—Rafa hesitates just a second—"with Faridah. Stay in her home until Harif or Khalah or I come to fetch you."

"Mama, I think I should—" Jammana begins, but Rafa interrupts:

"Go, Jammana! Now." Rafa doesn't bend to kiss her daughter. She turns away from them. Faridah takes the girl's hand.

"I'll stay," Harif implores.

"No. I'll handle him," Rafa says over her shoulder. "But on my own terms, when I'm ready. Time is the best protection you can give me now."

As Faridah steps from the cave, she hears Harif's voice, hesitant at first and then stronger, quicker. She shifts her head slightly to catch his words. "I honored her, you know that, Rafa. Ever since the moment I saw her on that staircase. I took her away from her village, so I knew I had to be responsible for her. Maybe sometimes we didn't—"

"Father," Faridah hears Rafa interrupt. "Not now."

The weather has stiffened while they've been in the cave. A hungry wind skirts the land. It cuts through Faridah's dress and searches between her legs, reaches for her neck. It stirs a braid of dust—desert spirits in hand-to-hand combat, the villagers say—that whips and tumbles past the edge of the shrine, then dies.

Against her will, apprehension crowds Faridah's chest—*ya Allah*, the resurrections and revelations that will be demanded of her! She grips Jammana's hand and pulls the child down the incline, past Alula's shrine, along the fringe of olive fields, running from a danger sensed though unseen. Hurrying to her home at the very border of the village's protection. How ridiculous to think that this village protects. Yet onward she rushes.

What has she done? In a sanctuary for Rafa, amid the magic of shadows and words, she forgot herself. She recalls, suddenly, the woman in the well.

Some twenty years ago, a traveler fell down a shaft near Ein Fadr. A passing village woman heard his cries and reached to pull him out, but slipped and tumbled in too. When her brothers returned from the gardens, they heard their sister yelling. They rescued her and the stranger from the depths. The traveler was given food, drink, and a night's lodging. As for the unmarried woman who had spent the day alone with a stranger-man, the *mukhtar*, Nabeel's father, ordered her tied to a tree and stoned to death.

Now Faridah herself has fallen down the well of Harif's past; he will be sent on his way while she is sacrificed. But first, just like the woman in the well, she will have to endure the explaining. She will have to take her turn wrestling with words. Harif, Rafa, and Jammana will call upon her to lay out the past in intricate detail while they listen and judge. She could refuse. But if she does, she will read in their gazes unadorned suspicion, and she doesn't know if she can bear that. Let the whole village condemn her, but please, not those three.

At last, Faridah reaches her room. Only there does she breathe again, the constriction of her chest loosening slightly. She glances down in surprise—she's all but forgotten the child beside her. This child of insights whom she always felt belonged partly to her. Jammana is staring up with eyes so like her own, widened now with the first of the tentative accusations.

The door closes behind them, and Jammana speaks. "We ran like wolves with our tails on fire. Are we so afraid of Father?"

Faridah shakes her head. "I don't fear your father."

"Then what?" Jammana spreads her hands. "Faridah, why did you throw something in the flames while Mama was being born?"

Faridah feels the familiar stinging in her throat and tightening sensation behind her nose. It has been decades since she has wept, but not so long since she laughed hysterically, and she recognizes the pinched feeling. She has always managed to free her immoderate convulsions in privacy—not too difficult, as she is so often alone. She tries to put some distance between herself and Jammana. She moves toward Divine's stall as if to check on him. When she reaches her donkey's side, a burst erupts.

Jammana follows. "What?" she asks, forehead creased in puzzlement.

Faridah cannot answer. She is gasping now, her chest a knot of anguish. She kneels, rounds her body, tucks her head, and through enormous will, forces all sound to bury itself inside her. Her shoulders shake silently. She pinches her eyes, but tears betray her and fall onto the dirt floor of her room, where they are absorbed and expand.

In the past, such drops nourished the dill she planted in a corner of her room, each a single taproot, one long hollow stalk and dozens of taunting sunburst flowers. She was in her twenties then, the period of tears. By the time she learned what purpose the dill served—how to boil the seeds in water so nursing mothers could drink the infusion and increase their flow of milk—she'd almost stopped crying for good.

Now something is clawing at her cheeks, prying open her eyes. Faridah realizes with astonishment it is her own fingers. The world seems a silver blur. Jammana comes into focus, Jammana standing over her, confused and frightened. Faridah rocks herself. "A moment. Just a moment," she manages, but she isn't even sure her words can be understood.

Jammana, Jammana. What shredded scraps of childhood lie at her feet today. That thought pulls Faridah back into this world, allows her to calm herself. She rises.

"Faridah? Should I fetch Khalah?"

Faridah doesn't respond. She is setting resolve into place: It is decided. She will speak of the past—at least a part of it. She's left without choice. She's cornered herself. She secures her headdress, smooths her *thobe*.

"Faridah?"

Faridah strokes the hollow at the base of her neck with the fingers of one hand to slow her breathing. She wills the muscles of her face to soften. "First, some tea," she says.

She moves back across the room, reaches for bags of herbs stored beneath the table built by Harif, lights the brazier, and sets water in a pot above. As she works, she wonders how to express it. Because words have always been, at worst, her enemies; at best, a disguise worn over her passions.

How, for instance, would she explain why Harif still stirs her after all this time? She could call him a man of angular body, hollow cheeks, with eyes of music, but that would reveal so little. No, she would say instead: *Think of a silent woman, veil covering her eyes. Imagine she has lived with the veil all her years—let's give her fifty-five, as I myself hold. This woman is allowed outside only in evenings and only as far as the courtyard of her home, a place of stone and dirt and a single almond tree. No matter—she's accustomed. She does not dream of more. Now, imagine a particular evening and a warming breeze that, for a single moment, blows aside the veil. She beholds shadows of tree leaves pirouetting under a full moon—a simple sight to others but the clearest vision she's ever seen. Then the veil falls back. Wouldn't she wait until the last bend of time for the breeze's return?*

These are the words that tell her truth, but who would understand them? Best to try to explain their history, hers and Harif's, in a more straightforward way. Best to say that when Harif began his trip to Beersheba—riding from a mother's grave, a father bent by loss—he had to locate within himself an immense bravery. Leaving always takes courage, whether on the back of a camel or on the shoulders of death. But the one left behind needs to summon strength, too. For the abandoned, there remains a dangerous sinkhole. Faridah had to take great care to save herself from vanishing in that pit while Harif was gone.

Yet she has no wish to represent herself as a hero. Anything but that.

Faridah returns to the fire. She pours hot water over the herbs.

Jammana follows closely. "You'll tell me?" she asks, challenge hanging on her words.

"It will take a long while for this story," Faridah warns.

"We have time," Jammana insists. "Mama said to stay here."

"It's *not* that I didn't want her to be born."

"I dreamed, Faridah." Jammana's words worm their way into Faridah's heart. "You did nothing to help when—"

"It's not that simple, whatever you dreamed." Faridah thought she was untouchable, but she's not. It hurts to hear the condemnation in Jammana's voice. Jammana should know the truth of the past. If Faridah must be sucked into the waves of yesterday, even drowned there, so be it. Let time bend. Let the dung merge with the sweet jasmine. Faridah will—she raises her chin in resolve—uncover all.

"We'll start at the beginning," she says. "I never planned to be a midwife. That was someone else's will."

When Harif left Ein Fadr under the *mukhtar's* orders, villagers doubted he ever would return. Only Faridah scanned the horizon with each spare moment, searching the line of land for a tiny distortion that would become Harif.

One afternoon as she squatted at the edge of the village, she heard a voice call her name. She turned to find a girl who smelled of dandelion, with thick hair hung in a long, oiled braid. Faridah recognized her as Suha, the bride of Faridah's own former husband, Abd al Qadir. Suha grabbed her sleeve. "I need help."

Faridah rose and tried to pull away, but Suha would not release her. "Come," she implored. She led Faridah to a large courtyard and then to the door of the very room she'd once shared with Abd al Qadir, the room where Suha now lived. Suha pushed open the door, but Faridah, not wishing to enter, stiffened her legs. Suha held up her hands and said, "We need you."

"Me? For what?" Faridah asked.

"My sister is to give birth."

It occurred to Faridah that Suha taunted her, alluding in such a sly way to her own inability to bear fruit. "And what of the midwife?" she asked.

"She's ill. Old, too, and her mind wanders, sometimes even as she readies to bring a child into the world. She won't be much longer at her work, they say."

"Then let the baby come on its own."

Suha nodded. "Sometimes that's possible. Sometimes only light from Allah is needed to guide." She stepped closer. "Other times, help is necessary on this side. We can't know which one this will be. Did you know my grandmother was a midwife here many years ago? When she reached to deliver a baby, Allah was beside her. She brought me into the world, and all my brothers and sisters. After she passed to the other side, my mother had only one more stomach, and died while giving birth."

Just then Faridah heard a low moan. "She's afraid," said Suha, gesturing with her shoulders to the room behind. "And she's ready."

"Why me?" Faridah struggled to keep her voice steady. "I've not spent time around babies."

"You have the hands," Suha insisted, "quick, with long fingers. And the temperament. Besides, you are clean."

Faridah knew what she meant. Only barren women or those past the age of possible conception were permitted to be midwives in Ein Fadr. Still, she shook her head. "I'm not skilled. Do it yourself. You must know how from your grandmother."

"I have some idea," Suha acknowledged. "That's why I want us to do it together." She paused, leaned closer. "Then," she continued softly, "when you deliver my baby, it won't be the first."

"Yours?" Faridah took a step back and inspected Suha's belly, but it looked flat to her. "You carry one?" she asked.

Suha lowered her head slightly and nodded shyly with just a hint of a smile. "It is past the time, and I'm craving lemons and radishes."

Now Faridah felt convinced the girl was flaunting her pregnancy to make a joke of Faridah's barrenness. She gave Suha her back.

"Wait, please," Suha cried, and something plaintive in her voice made Faridah hesitate. "I haven't explained it well," she said. "From the moment I found I was pregnant, I knew you must be the one to deliver the child."

"I can think of nothing less appropriate," Faridah replied stiffly.

"We have shared much, perhaps the very essentials."

"And come away with quite different impressions, I suspect," Faridah said.

Suha disagreed. "If there's any difficulty—with me or the baby—you'll know how to handle him," she said.

Faridah wanted to ask what kind of trouble, but the moaning inside the room grew louder. Suha tugged her in.

She saw a girl sprawled against a pillow on the floor, trembling with a violent seizure like a spider carelessly dropped by Allah. Even Suha seemed shocked to discover her sister thus. "With your help," she murmured, "yours and Allah's . . ."

Faridah knelt at the side of the writhing body, settled the head onto her lap, and, pulling up her skirt, dabbed sweat from the face. Her own mother must have touched her in that way during some forgotten childhood illness, because the motions seemed natural though she did not recall having made them before. After several moments, she could see from the girl's face that the pain had rolled back slightly and stood waiting. The girl's eyes held dazed appreciation. "Praise be to Allah," she said, perhaps believing in her insensible state that Faridah was the midwife arrived at last.

Faridah turned to Suha, who remained standing behind. "Yes, I will help you. And in this way: I'll fetch one of the women to deliver the baby."

"No," said the girl on the floor. She reached forward and gripped Faridah's hand with surprising strength. "You can't leave." She was breathing rapidly again, now.

"Then I'll stay with this poor one and you go." But Suha did not move. By now, Faridah was becoming desperate. "I've told you," she said, "you mustn't put your confidence in someone as ignorant as myself."

"You're strong," said Suha. "The strongest woman in this village. No matter what they say or do, you stand up to them."

The girl, still holding on to Faridah's hand, began to pant ever more loudly. The time for talk, Faridah knew, had fled.

"Rinse your hands in the pot by the door," Suha ordered Faridah. "And chew this." She handed Faridah some lemon balm leaves.

Then Faridah and Suha pulled the girl to a squatting position. "O Prophet Noah, divide one spirit from another," Suha called. Faridah felt the world narrow to the tiny corner of a room in which she herself had lived, barren and unhappy, for six years. The sister's knees reached for opposite walls. Faridah massaged and coaxed in time with the beating of her heart. The girl tossed back her head in confusion, not knowing who or how to fight. Urgency exploded, and tears erupted from unlikely places. Faridah held a baby girl on her knees.

Jammana sits silently a moment, then speaks. "So, this was the first."

"Yes. Suha told the villagers I had a natural talent for helping a baby find its way into this world. It wasn't true; she simply wanted me to practice before her own came." Faridah laughs. "Her extravagant praise reached the ears of the old midwife, who appeared at my door. For forty minutes she questioned me; for four more hours she shared her secrets—what to do with the afterbirth, the phrases a midwife must recite, when the pregnant woman must eat fresh eggs prepared by her mother-in-law." She shakes her head. "Delusions, most of it. Later I would chase those ridiculous customs out of this village. But on that day, I listened carefully, and when she emerged from my home, she announced she was retired. So it happened that as Suha's belly grew visible, other women whose time had come began calling on me. The men thought I'd bewitched the old midwife into giving me the job—they think that still. But it was Suha. Wittingly or not, she provided me with my place in the village. She also gave me confidence. Oh, I knew everything then!" Faridah rises. "A heady herb, confidence is. Beware of it, Jammana, for it deceives."

There's more she'd like to say—that Jammana herself is at the age when one can become dangerously sure of oneself. That the intentions of others may seem clear when they are not.

Then she reminds herself that she believes experience is the only teacher, not words. She lets the moment pass.

"Unfortunately, babies were not born every day in Ein Fadr," she says. "I still squandered many hours missing Harif. Then one morning, as the other women and I were gathered at the well, a boy ran up shouting at Khalah, 'He's back. He's come back.'"

Faridah falls into silence, remembering how the news of Harif's return made her feel as elated as a breeze permitted to carry the rich scent of earth after rain. She abandoned her water jar and ran to Moses' Finger. Her enthusiasm escaped notice only because all were running, eager to see both Harif and the teacher he should have brought for the mosque school.

When they reached the mulberry, Harif had not yet dismounted. Khalah knelt in front of him. "I cannot kiss Heaven, so I kiss earth," she said, stretching a hand up, dropping it to the ground, and putting it to her lips. Other women did the same. Faridah remained standing.

The villagers parted to give space to the *mukhtar,* who ambled forward. Another man rode beside Harif, and they were followed by a flock of sheep. "Praise the Compassionate One for your safe return, Harif," the *mukhtar* said, fingering his amber prayer beads. "It seems you've accomplished your mission."

"Praise Allah for His bountiful mercy," Harif answered. "This is Kamil Ben Sa'id al Abahrami. He has brought with him three Korans."

The new teacher, not much older than Harif, nodded. His cheeks were dark, Faridah noticed, and his hands looked strong. Dirt blackened his fingernails.

"You bring us blessings," said the *mukhtar*.

"It is I who am blessed. The First, the Last, the One has brought me here," responded the teacher.

The *mukhtar* looked the stranger up and down. "For an Islamic teacher, you look much like one of our farmers," he said, his tone friendly but his words wary.

"I always work at harvest time," responded Kamil. "It seems to me those closest to Allah are also closest to His land."

The *mukhtar's* eyes narrowed as though he suspected deception. "Have you brought any word from my cousin?"

Harif broke in. "Your cousin sends his blessings, and your uncle sent these sheep to you as a present. They trailed us from Bethlehem."

"Blessed be the Beneficent," said the *mukhtar*, smiling now for the first time. The gift seemed to distract him from his suspicions.

In the midst of these introductions, Faridah caught Harif's gaze. She lifted one hand to shoulder level. Harif smiled, and called, "Greetings, Faridah," over everyone's head. She laughed, proud of his boldness.

She doesn't wish to remember that moment, but it floods back. She knows her face betrayed her joy. Harif, too, looked satisfied. His cheeks carried the dust of many days' travel; his eyes burned with confidence won on the sand dunes. Faridah remembers staring at his lips and raising her fingers to her own. She'd felt the villagers glancing from her to Harif and noticing, perhaps for the first time, the deep link between them. Both, after all, had assumed new importance in Ein Fadr and so had become more visible.

Nabeel stepped forward and grasped Harif's hand. "My brother," he said exuberantly, "you have brought us good fortune." Harif nodded at him in a distracted way.

Faridah noticed, then, a woman sitting on a donkey that lingered far behind the sheep. She was young, small, with round face and open smile. She wore a deep red dress in the style favored in those days in the Bethlehem region, with heavily embroidered sleeves and neckline. On her head rested a coin-adorned band draped with simple white cloth. She looked a lady of legends.

The *mukhtar* must have seen the woman at the same moment. "And this is our teacher's wife," he said, "surely weary after her long ride. Nabeel, please see her and the teacher to my quarters. We'll settle them in their own home tomorrow."

"Thank you," said Harif, unable to contain his grin. "But this woman . . . Hannan." He called out her name, and she bowed her head slightly and began to ride forward. "She is to be my wife. Your own uncle's family helped arrange it, may Allah's many blessings fall upon them—and you."

Then Harif—and who can blame him?—was absorbed by the pleasurable task of observing the *mukhtar's* awkward squirming. He noticed nothing else. Not Nabeel's frown caused by the coolness with which he'd been greeted. Not the way Hannan's face colored prettily.

Certainly not Faridah, freezing in place as she absorbed every detail of this Bethlehem woman's face and dress and body. Faridah felt Khalah's hand on her shoulder, but she shook it off. Taking short, quick breaths, she backed away from the village center, unable to unfasten her eyes from the sight of Harif's future bride.

With effort, Faridah pulled herself to the shrine to Alula. There she stayed many hours, burning sheep dung for warmth, pondering the depth of her sins and burying foolish dreams.

He came home with the woman who was going to be my grandmother," Jammana prompts. "You were happy to see him, but not her."

Faridah smiles seriously. "You heard too much in the cave. Here's what you need to know. The wedding was held as soon as your grandmother's family arrived. The *mukhtar* spared no ceremony. He hosted the festivities, during which the women of the village spent a night painting patterns in henna on your grandmother's hands, arms, legs, and feet. Your grandfather led the men in preparing the wedding meal of slaughtered sheep, okra and tomatoes, stuffed eggplants, salads, and even *kibbeh*, a dish that Harif had not eaten since the death of his mother.

"Your great-grandfather Bahir volunteered to break with tradition and give Harif his childhood home in which to live. 'Fresh joy needs to sink into these walls, or they will crumble from sorrow,' he said. He himself moved with Khalah to a neighboring home, so they still shared a courtyard.

"On the day of the wedding, all gathered to sing and dance under the great twisted mulberry. As evening began spreading her fingers in the village, I joined the festivities. I wore a black *thobe* that I'd spent nights embroidering with a pattern of two birds facing each other. Atop my headdress rode a silver chain, and from it dangled the Hand of Fatima. My cheeks were scrubbed, my eyes outlined with kohl. With so formal an entrance, I could not help but silence the villagers. Into the quiet, I spoke. I told Harif and his bride that in my native village it was customary to perform a special dance at a wedding party to ensure happiness for the couple, long life, and . . ." Faridah breaks off a second. "Many children. Then I bowed my head and began to sing about a man and a woman who meet under an almond tree and fall in love. Their fathers both forbid the union. The woman's family promises her to another, but before she can wed, she and the man she loves share the red fruit of a mandrake. They dissolve separately into the night sky and reappear together in the face of a silver moon.

"It was not a song the villagers would favor, speaking as it did of lovers who rebel against the wishes of their elders. But all remained still. Partway through my song, I began to dance, first swaying from side to side, then twirling gently with my arms flung out, finally leaping and twisting. I shook my fingers out as though throwing my song at those around me. The Hand of Fatima bounced against my forehead."

Again Faridah stops talking, and she returns to those last moments of her dance when she saw everything: the villagers' eyes frozen upon her moving form, tension plowing into the square, the uneasy glances that began to run from the dancer to the newly married couple and back again. Hannan smiled innocently. Harif's expression held frightened awareness and, finally, bald desire.

Abruptly, Faridah ended her dance. No one spoke, no one moved. Then Faridah glided toward Harif's bride as though walking through water. Faridah took Hannan's hand and kissed it. "Welcome," she said.

"Thank you," answered Hannan, bringing Faridah's hands to her own lips. "You've helped make my wedding memorable. May the blessings of the Merciful One rain on you."

Faridah nodded once and, without glancing at Harif, left.

That night, the pounding upon her door. That night, the merging of silt and fire, the spell of starlight filtered between dancing arms and legs. The deadly Koranic sin. The veil blown aside.

That single night.

Y̶ou are silent for so long," Jammana says, challenging. "Are you remembering that when my grandmother was ready to give birth to Mama, you decided it must not be?"

Faridah looks up. Four sesame-colored eyes collide in the room's space. Faridah knows she must go forward to the birth. She must go on bravely and honestly.

Into that moment comes a rap on the door. Jammana leaps to her feet, but before Faridah can rise, the door opens.

Ahmed.

Though Faridah has been expecting him, her throat tightens momentarily. Yet, despite the threat he brings with him, both to his wife and to the women who have been hiding her, he looks less imposing than usual, disheveled, awkward in the hut of a village woman. He is accompanied by another man—the merchant who escorted Rafa and Jammana partway to Ein Fadr several days ago.

"There you are, my child," says Ahmed. "Come." He opens his arms to Jammana.

Jammana doesn't move. She doesn't speak. Faridah sees unwillingness in her eyes. Ahmed can see it, too.

"Who's told my girl she need not come when I call?" he asks Faridah curtly. "Jammana, now!"

Jammana wavers. She sways and exhales. Then she obeys the command, moving to her father like a stone rolling down a hill.

Over the top of her head, Ahmed flashes Faridah a triumphant smile.

JAMMANA

A kohl-dark form thrusts open the door and absorbs the room's light. Jammana steps back, trying to still the familiar swell of awe and fear. But as her eyes focus, she sees he's not upright and commanding as usual. He is sagging, as if he might at any moment sink into the earth's skin. The weighty flesh of his face is a lemon shed of freshness, tumbled to the ground and collapsing inward. He's not clad in his crisp medical coat, or wearing his wire-rimmed glasses. He's unshaven. The whites of his eyes are stained the weary red of a late sky.

His forsaken appearance quiets her emotions. An unexpected surge of tenderness runs through her, as though Father were the bewildered boy, she the all-seeing adult. An

upside-down sensation, but pleasant. For the first time in his presence, Jammana is aware of her own untarnished strength.

Even so, even with this surge of affection, she hesitates before his open arms. She has no desire to dash to a parent's embrace. It seems more important that Father understand she is not a child anymore.

In just hours, the terrain of her world has changed. While Grandfather and Mama and Faridah argued in the cave, Jammana teetered as if on a high ledge. The three of them spit their furious phrases somewhere above her head, intending for the words to shoot past before she could catch them. But she stretched high on her toes and grabbed. The serpent inside, awake for the moment, watched as she swayed. He hissed skeptically. Jammana refused to let him confound her. And this time, she captured meaning. She knew that Faridah had emotions no one ever saw. That Mama felt deceived, and Grandfather confused. The serpent reminds her that this clarity will not last, that soon the grown-ups will again be speaking in their foreign tongue. Still—to have achieved this!

She decides to accept Father's embrace, however, when she considers his potential for fury. Then she flows quickly, like the breaking edge of the waves into which he once tossed her. Still, she can't repress private regret. If only he hadn't come now, as Faridah was preparing to explain what Jammana most needs to understand: the moments of writhing shadows, silver in the air. The moments of endless choking with no help offered.

Father holds Jammana in a suffocating grip, his hand pressing her head against his chest. She lifts her chin toward him and inhales his breath, thick and sour. She pushes to free herself as he speaks with ease and authority that belie his bedraggled appearance. "You're not surprised, Faridah?" Father says. "I'm expected, am I?"

If Faridah is uncomfortable in Father's presence, she conceals it. She rises calmly, composed. No sad laughter confuses her lips, no chased look shows in her eyes. She fans the fire embers with the hem of her *thobe*. Her bracelets jingle at her wrist. An oval puff of smoke rises in the room; Father coughs once.

"Under the Blessed Eye of Allah," Faridah says, "you've had a safe trip? We feared a storm was coming. But perhaps you managed to outrun it?" She moves to the wooden table, finds two clean cups. Her fingers dive and swoop as she chooses herbs, adds a dollop of molasses to each cup. Each movement slow, slow as sleep in times of trouble.

"Safe, though uncomfortable. I'm not accustomed to riding such a distance on donkey. I'm not a tax collector who must travel to these trackless villages often." Father speaks in a large voice. "But I'm here on an errand. As you clearly know. So please direct me to my goal."

Faridah addresses the space over her shoulder. "Only three things, Ahmed, are urgent."

Abu Sa'id, grinning, finishes the proverb. "Marrying of a ripe virgin, burying of the dead, and feeding of a guest."

Faridah turns toward Abu Sa'id, but addresses Father. "And whom have you brought for our company? Ah yes, it's the one who accompanied Rafa and Jammana last week. Though he didn't actually introduce himself then."

Jammana watches as Abu Sa'id dips his head, answers in a stately voice: "Forgive me. We each were bent on returning to our homes. I'm Abu Sa'id Barakat. Descended from a long line of Nablus merchants. Also a friend of those in need." His eyes sparkle as though he enjoys participating in this drama. "Praise Allah in His infinite wisdom for granting me the privilege of visiting your village at last." He looks his best, hands smooth and soft as a woman's, cheeks pink, perfumed robe flowing and clean. His health and beauty set off Father's disorderliness even more.

Faridah places cups on a tray and removes a reed bowl from a shelf. She takes down a burlap bag and carefully selects a dozen figs, which she places in the bowl. Father fidgets, but custom—which, for the moment, he adheres to —prevents him from speaking of anything serious while his hostess prepares his plate.

At last, Faridah gestures for the men to sit. Father lowers himself cautiously; Abu Sa'id drops comfortably. Faridah sets the tray before them and sits herself eight steps away, near the door. Jammana stands next to Faridah. The men sip their tea. "Allah bless you with years of grace for your generosity," Abu Sa'id says.

"And may the All-Knowing also bring prosperity to your business," Faridah replies.

"*Inshallah*, all goes well," Abu Sa'id says. Father scowls at him, but he doesn't seem to notice. "Save for the political complications," he continues, "which lead to tear gas and curfews and dampen my customers' spirits. Eventually we shall have war that may even reach the streets of Nablus, I fear. You are fortunate to escape that here."

"The events of the day do occasionally descend upon us," responds Faridah. "We hear explosions in the distance, coming from a new border. But you are right. In Ein Fadr we are more often buried under yesterday's debris."

"I've been told you are the village midwife," Abu Sa'id says. Faridah bows her head, and he goes on. "The scent of a newborn is always a precious gift."

Always? Jammana wonders if Faridah would agree. Faridah doesn't raise her head.

"You are responsible for Rafa herself, yes?" Abu Sa'id continues. "And Ahmed must trust you deeply, as he allowed you to deliver Jammana as well." He smiles between the two of them.

Father clears his throat. Faridah's dancing fingers smooth the lap of her dress. At last she looks up. "And so?" she says to Abu Sa'id, a challenge in the gentle rise of her voice. "Tell me. Whom, then, do you believe to be in need?"

"Ha." Father makes a sound that is more growl than chuckle. "He means me. Because I'm forced to search for my wife as though she were lost livestock." Buried under Father's words, Jammana hears something she doesn't expect. A tendril of fear. A spit's worth of supplication. "Where is she?" he finishes.

Faridah ignores Father, which startles and thrills Jammana. She never imagined he could be ignored. Faridah keeps her gaze on Abu Sa'id until at last the merchant replies. "Ahmed's wife is missing. We have journeyed to find her and pray to the All-Powerful that she is here, safe. Ahmed thought perhaps you—"

"You know why Rafa ran away?" Faridah interrupts.

Abu Sa'id shifts uncomfortably. "Ran away? I don't know that she—"

"You know the circumstances, perhaps?"

At this, Abu Sa'id glances carefully at Father, who leans forward on his crossed knees. "We've had a small misunderstanding," Father says, "Rafa and I. But deserting her home is not the answer. In fact, it is against all propriety and law, as I'm sure every woman in this village knows. They know, too, that hiding Rafa would be a sinful defiance of their own husbands. But you—you would have no such compunction." He takes a deep breath. "Tell me where she is."

"Father." Jammana begins, "if you have grown angry with Mama because she brought me here, you should know it is I who insisted on that. I just wanted a chance to say good-bye, since you've said we're going to America."

"I know all about that. You are not to go anywhere without my permission again. But that is not what worries me now."

Jammana cringes at his dismissive tone. It implies that her words, which she considered so reasonable, are nothing more than a nuisance. After a moment, Faridah speaks. "I cannot help you," she says to Father.

Father smiles thinly as though struggling to pretend Faridah has just agreed with him. "Rafa has been foolish," he says, "but I'm ready to forgive."

"You forgive her?" Faridah laughs as though coughing up something distasteful.

Father rises. "She lost her head," he says, touching his own. "A woman's unclean time, perhaps? You would know better than I." He takes a step toward Faridah. "She even stole money."

"You forgive *her?*" Faridah repeats. The sarcasm in her tone balloons, filling the room. Father's cheeks grow splotched. His eyes darken, turn dangerous. Jammana, frozen in place, suddenly wants to leave. She hasn't been able to stop Father, and she can't bear to see his tongue reduce Faridah as it has Mama. She glances at Divine in his stall, wondering if she could take him outside.

When Father finally speaks, his words are taut but restrained. "Watch what you say in front of the child."

Child. Jammana will not be referred to in such a way. Not now. She knows more than Father. She knows what he doesn't about Mama. That realization exhilarates and emboldens her, and the serpent encourages. "Father?" He turns to her. She swallows hard. "Mama will soon have a wonderful surprise for you."

His eyebrows rise in puzzlement.

"Mama and I, actually," says Jammana. With courage, if not accuracy.

Faridah, standing now, puts a restraining hand on Jammana's arm. But Father seems to be seeing her for the first time. She swells with satisfaction. He appears to estimate her height, then looks her full in the face. "What surprise?"

Here Jammana stumbles a bit. She remembers that Mama wouldn't promise to find a way out of this quarrel, which has mysteriously grown larger than a visit to Grandfather. One statement, however, she can make with certainty. "We want the same thing, all of us," she says.

"What are you talking about?" Father asks, and there's no denying his ridicule now, but Jammana can't stop.

"We're going to"—and then the words rush from her— "to find a way to mend everything."

Father looks back and forth between Jammana and Faridah. "So, things are broken, are they?" His tone lowers. "Well, then. Where is she?"

Jammana detects the menace. Her courage drains into her feet, and they turn heavy. She cannot move her lips. She feels a flash of anger toward the serpent, who tricked her into behaving impetuously. For a moment, no one speaks. Then Abu Sa'id rises to place a hand on Father's arm. "Ah, Ahmed . . ."

Father shakes him off. "Jammana?"

"Leave the child out of this," Faridah interrupts. "Jammana, run to Khalah. Now."

"She's my daughter. I won't have her allied against me. She would never choose against me anyway. She knows better than that. Jammana, where is your mama?"

Jammana is trapped. The power she thought she had drifts away from her, settles elsewhere, a place where people understand the rules and tricks better than she does.

"Jammana?" he repeats.

"I can't say. I promised." Her voice shames her; it quivers.

"To whom did you make such a promise?"

"Don't do this to her, Ahmed." Faridah's voice holds heavy warning.

"Don't ask her to speak frankly to her father?" He glares at Faridah, steps closer to Jammana. "To whom, Jammana?"

Jammana clears her throat, gathers herself. "Mama." She calls out the word defiantly.

Faridah rises, places herself directly in front of Ahmed. "Nothing," Faridah says, "will make Rafa more angry than misuse of the child."

"I would never—"

"You," Faridah interrupts, voice soaring to the ceiling like a fast-growing vine, "will lose any chance with Rafa if you continue this way. If you hope for her return"—she steps closer to Father—"wait. Wait until she comes to you."

He hesitates. In that single moment of uncertainty, Abu Sa'id clears his throat. "May Allah lengthen your blessed life, Ahmed, but we are getting a bit off the path here," he says. "My friend, you've heard your daughter. It is clear that your wife is preparing a surprise for you. You know our wives. They relish their small secrets. This is not a matter for concern. We know she's here, she is safe. Allow the woman her moment of glory, when she will present you with . . ." He waves his hand vaguely. "Something. The surprise, we shall presume. Let us finish this fine tea and taste some figs and return to Nablus, where your work calls, and mine."

Jammana, back on the cliff, stretching to reach lofty phrases, marvels as she understands the gaudy disguises adults place in their conversations. Abu Sa'id talks as though Mama were preparing a holiday treat. And even more amazingly, his perfumed, meandering words seem to calm Father. "I'll be patient a little longer," Father says to Faridah. "Abu Sa'id and I will spend the night in Harif's home. That was our intention anyway." He rises. "But I must return to Nablus quickly, to my duties at the hospital and my patients. I have no time for a woman's nonsense. I don't simply tend a flock of woolly animals. You understand? So tell Rafa to ready her *surprise* quickly and come to me by tomorrow." He pauses. "Make no mistake. If I'm forced to leave Ein Fadr with only Jammana"— he says her name heavily—"by the sight of Allah, Rafa will regret it."

Jammana suddenly knows that what she once believed was wrong. It is not the strong who threaten, but those who are helplessly lost. Father uses desperate words because he has given up on the reasonable ones to bring Mama back.

Jammana also knows, however, that if Mama doesn't come down from the cave, Father *will* take her alone back to Nablus. His anger will propel them all forward. She rubs her arms for warmth.

What will Mama do? Jammana can't guess, but she knows Mama must be protected. Mama is delicate—her nerves as well as her wrists and ankles. She is as slender as Grandfather, though Grandfather's beard provides comforting fullness.

Now, studying Father, Jammana is surprised to see that he also is lean. Nearly as thin as Mama, in fact. It's a shock, because she's always imagined him as large. Gigantic, even. But actually, Faridah is a bit taller.

She glances at Faridah's face. And suddenly the room is ripped by a moan. In confusion, she looks around—Father, Abu Sa'id, and Faridah, their mouths are closed. The moan is rising to a scream, sharp as broken glass, like the sun-colored violet shard in Jammana's vision. Jammana clamps her hands over her ears and looks to Faridah for an answer. Her gaze travels from Faridah's lashes to the hollows beneath her cheekbones to her lips, pursed in concern.

Every feature on Faridah's face is still—except the eyes. As unlikely as it may be, the sound comes from Faridah's sesame eyes, which shine and vibrate.

The scream swells and pierces, finally so loud that Jammana bends at the waist. Beneath the cry, Jammana hears the strident voices of men. Muddled words sometimes break free: ". . . unnatural woman . . ." ". . . unholy alliance . . ." ". . . Star of Bethlehem . . ." ". . . long enough . . ." She straightens to see Faridah's eyes grown sunken, cavelike.

"Stop it!" Jammana implores. All their faces—Faridah's,

Father's, Abu Sa'id's—are discomposed by dismay. Father is
saying something, but Jammana cannot catch the words. She
lurches toward Faridah, reaches up, and covers her eyes,
hides their blaring distress. At last, at last the howling ends.
Jammana keeps her hands in place, and Faridah does not
struggle against her sudden blindness.

"Didn't you hear it? Didn't you?" Jammana demands first
of Father, then of Abu Sa'id. She can tell from their uncom-
prehending gazes that they did not.

"What . . .?" Father sputters. "What's happening to my
child?"

Gently, Faridah takes Jammana's hands and removes
them. Jammana waits, then heaves a breath of relief. All is
silent.

In the keen hush that follows comes a moment of
equally acute perception, as though the scream itself pene-
trated the surfaces of those she loves, peeled them to their
essences. Everyone is made of dust and one other ingredient,
Faridah told Jammana that. Now she sees for herself.

Mama is of the sky, Father stone.

Faridah is from fire, Grandfather the wind.

With those elements, what sort of mixing is possible?

Father has reached Jammana. He touches her cheeks
with the back of his hand, then pushes her hair away to feel
her forehead. Jammana sinks to a squatting position at Faridah's feet. Not long ago, she understood her visions as
glimpses of others' memories. Now they seem to have become something different and to be leading to a destination
she can't yet make out.

Faridah speaks slowly, softly. "She's overwrought. To be
a child summoned into this adult world is no easy task."

"I have not—" Father begins.

"She," Faridah cuts him off, "will stay with me tonight while you are with Harif."

Father opens his mouth as though to challenge, but Faridah's face is closed. Father gives Abu Sa'id an order in his glance, and steps toward the door. Abu Sa'id follows. They leave the door ajar. Jammana, still squatting, watches them. She feels Faridah place a blanket over her shoulders, but she does not move. She is staring after Father, into the heavy air, so she sees the moment it begins. It spills from the blackened sky. An exhausted rain. Drops warm and heavy as spent blood. It drums a hopeless, warning melody.

With effort, Jammana rises. She leans against the door and arches her neck to feel the wetness on her frizzy hair, against her cheek. To let the rain seep into her skin. Then to pray for the ability to forget its message.

HARIF

Lamb sacrificed and cooked over a hot flame, with coriander to give it fire and sweet rosemary to provide slivers of shade. Tabouli with lemon. Beads of rice embraced by softened vine leaves. Fresh bread bursting with puffs of fragrant air. Khalah steps heavily into the courtyard, a tray held sturdy at chest level, each dish bearing the imprint of her enlightened palm.

She turns to Harif, expressionless. "That will keep you?"

Harif knows what she's asking. Quick as a cool night lizard dives for a fly, Khalah must speed to Rafa, warn her of Ahmed's threat. Harif wishes she didn't have to go. He does not want to be alone with the dusty-eyed doctor who wed his daughter, and the well-clad meddling merchant. What Harif wants most to ask—what right did Ahmed have to strike Harif's only child?—is forbidden to him, both by Rafa and by his role as host. To restrain himself and find a different topic will be difficult as grazing sheep on a field of stones. Harif has lost any penchant for idle talk, if he ever had it.

He knows Khalah cannot linger, however. He nods, and she evaporates from the courtyard.

Though he himself eats with his fingers in the traditional manner, Harif offers his guests the spoons Rafa once gave him. The merchant declines, but the doctor takes a utensil. He holds it at a distance, examines it, spits, and wipes it with the edge of his robe. Then the men sit cross-legged on a carpet, all three around the tray next to a fire. In solid silence they reach for food, Harif and the merchant with their right hands. Three minds, Harif thinks, driven to separate ends.

He certainly can't reveal his thoughts, which race among his daughter and his granddaughter and Faridah. He cannot forget Jammana's accusation. He cannot believe it, nor can he dismiss it. It is true that mother and child both nearly died during Rafa's birth. But Faridah put everything she had into saving them, he is sure. She emerged from the birth room pale and flushed by turns, unable to speak. She handed him the baby; then they were lost to each other, he preparing festival food for neighbors, she gathering blood-stained soil and afterbirth to bury. Only the next day did Faridah reveal how Hannan began choking. How Rafa stuck in the womb. How, by miracle—by intervention from Somewhere Unseen—the baby became freed.

Faridah was so haunted by the near loss that she insisted Harif help her when Hannan next became pregnant.

They had to persuade the whole village; nearly all disapproved. But Faridah was determined. And that time—he knows because he was there—they tried every remedy. Hannan was simply too weak, too fragile for a place like Ein Fadr.

Faridah. Maddening woman of hot moon. Of night, ground like java beans. She belongs with him, always has. Yet she opposed their union, even after Hannan died, as he recalls. He blamed her reluctance to be with him on misguided guilt over Hannan's death. But perhaps it had more to do with Rafa's birth than the one that followed. When the sun rises tomorrow, he will find her and insist on an explanation.

I t is a hot fire, fueled with aromatic *arfaj* grasses. Waves of warmth duel with the cool night air. From time to time, a chunk of wood pops or the flames spit burning embers. One lands next to Ahmed's leg. He makes a show of dusting off his knee and scooting farther from the fire, then shoots an accusing glance at Harif.

At last, the merchant Abu Sa'id breaks the silence. "How does your sister do it?" he asks. "I rarely eat such a—" he searches for the word—"harmonious meal."

"Khalah cooks with the angels," Harif says. He won't try to explain further—he's not completely sure himself how her fingers acquired the skill of disarming discontent along with hunger. Despite her efforts, however, he has no appetite tonight. He's eaten no more than a bite. Nor, he sees, has Ahmed.

A village donkey tethered in a neighbor's courtyard sighs heavily. Harif's sheep call to one another in raspy voices as they settle for the night. Abu Sa'id tries again. "It's pleasant in this village," he says, discreetly licking his fingers. "Even the stars seem brighter. Isn't that so, Ahmed?"

Ahmed answers with a glare, and bounds up as though he'd sat on a sharp rock. His spoon falls from his lap. He paces. He is an impenetrable man, Harif thinks. But then, men so seldom understand one another. Harif himself has dragged out his years in Ein Fadr, yet confusion solid as a lifetime of dust resides between him and the others.

"May my father-in-law forgive my poor manners," Ahmed says suddenly, too loudly. "I'm at a loss to understand. We were setting plans for our move when she grew angry over a remote matter and—" He slaps his thigh. "Under Allah, it is wrong. When women try to direct their husbands, the family withers."

Even Ahmed's companion seems surprised by the passion he puts in his words. The merchant's brow wrinkles in puzzlement.

"There are those"—Harif tries to keep his voice mild—"who believe a woman should be free to contradict her own husband."

"Nonsense," Ahmed insists. "Consider Faridah. She contradicts. And yes, she owns her independence. But only that. Not what you'd wish for Rafa, surely."

Harif allows his tone to go icy. "Faridah's spirit is the work of Allah," he says. "My own mother was strong-willed, and Rafa's determination comes from *her* mother."

"Yes, your wife," Abu Sa'id says quickly. He scoops up tabouli with bread. "What was she like?"

Harif knows Abu Sa'id is only politely interested, motivated primarily by a desire to guide the conversation down gentler slopes. Still, he is grateful for the question. He rarely speaks of Hannan—he thought that best for everyone—but since this morning his silence has begun to feel like a betrayal. Another one.

"She reminded me of a single water lily," Harif says. "Delicate. In the desert, of course, they cannot survive."

"I would guess," Ahmed interrupts, "it is women like Faridah who wouldn't last here."

"Yet you see you are wrong." Harif studies him a moment. "Though Faridah's native fires weren't lit here, she secured a place for herself. It is my wife who was worn down by Ein Fadr." He pauses, wondering if outsiders could possibly understand the village's cumulative effect on its own people.

"Whatever the nature of your wife's feelings for Ein Fadr," Ahmed says, "she would never have deserted you."

Harif pulls his prayer beads from his pocket, runs them through his fingers. Ahmed is right, although he won't have the pleasure of hearing Harif admit it. Hannan's determination was of a different sort. One that allowed her to stay, not leave. He recalls their wedding night. The night when what could have been was revealed and snatched away. It will be, he is sure, his final memory before death.

He could not, that night, pull his gaze from Faridah dancing. Her hands—how often had he watched them weave and mold? Now they summoned. The sweet dust she raised with the fall of her heel befuddled him. He climbed her cheekbones to her eyes, lost himself in the twisting of her waist. He imagined beads of perspiration between her breasts. He craved water—at least he thought it was water he needed. He forgot everyone else in the room.

The dance finished. Faridah vanished. Only then did Harif turn to Hanna, recognizing her at last as a stranger he'd desired in order to return to Ein Fadr a champion. Kind and unsuspecting, she didn't deserve such callous disregard. As soon as the guests retired for the night, he walked Hannan to their home. They stepped inside, and she smiled at him with that bold confidence that had attracted him initially. An expression which, though he didn't know it then, he would rarely see on her face again.

He meant to stay with Hannan that night. He thought he would, right up until the moment he left. But suddenly he found himself nodding at her as though they'd reached a decision, and opening the door. Dismissing caution like an old cup of coffee, glancing neither left nor right to see if a neighbor lingered outside, he ran. Bewildered himself, he did not allow his mind to consider consequences.

Faridah opened her door without surprise, without coyness. The hours after that remain engraved on his mind. He'd always thought one act ended a man's boyhood. By the end of the night, he understood virginity was shed in slow and tender layers. The unexpected softness of her eyelashes and her belly. The strength of her thighs. The scent of her neck. The way their bodies, in tune, melded and arched apart. And his grateful surprise that she allowed him this.

He did not return to Hannan until nearly daybreak. He wouldn't have gone at all, had Faridah not forced him. He had no willpower then. Hannan did not weep, though her cheeks were cleansed of color. She stood straight, stiff. "Do you wish me to leave?"

He knelt before her. "I don't know."

His uncertainty was enough for her. His doubts must have been easier to face than the shame of announcing to the village at daylight that her new husband had gone to another. Besides, he would learn later, she loved him. While he watched, she opened a chest of her own belongings, removed a sewing needle, and pricked the palm of her hand. Three times—first timidly, and finally with the force needed to break the skin. She bled, dark drops to tattoo the pure white bedding. She crumpled the sheet, threw it into a corner, and gazed at him, dry-eyed. No accusations, then or ever. Just an abyss that never would be fully bridged.

When Khalah came in the morning to collect the wedding cloth, she had something to display. She held the sheet up in her strong arms. Harif and Hannan both looked drawn and exhausted; the villagers smiled, considering this proof of a successful wedding night. Only Khalah remained expressionless. Only she spoke no words of congratulations. Harif never knew how clearly she sensed the tangled nature of the passion she washed from that sheet.

Seven weeks later, Harif, in passing, mentioned Faridah's name. Hannan, pale, interrupted to say she wanted Harif to accompany her on a trip to the Milk Grotto near Bethlehem. He had never heard of the cave, but Hannan said it was well known among women of Bethlehem—Moslems, Christians, and Jews alike—as the hiding place of Mary and her son, Jesus, right after his birth, as Herod's soldiers killed all the babies of Bethlehem. It was thought to be a sacred cavern of possibilities. More than that, Hannan would not say.

They spoke little on the trip. In the grotto, she broke

off a piece of soft rock and brought it home. She ground it, added oil, swallowed, and passed the cup to Harif. A sip of mixture remained at the bottom. "Faridah must drink it," Hannan told him.

"If she doesn't want it?"

"Make her," Hannan responded, her face hard.

Harif felt he owed it to Hannan to do as she asked. He went to Faridah's room that evening. He opened the door without knocking. She sat on her floor with a basket before her. Again, she showed no surprise at seeing him.

He knew she would refuse the drink if he said it was from Hannan. So he said nothing. He simply held the cup out to her. She studied him silently until, finally, he could not resist. He placed the cup on the ground near her and reached for her neck. She intercepted his hand, moved it to her belly, and stroked it once. For a few minutes, he was aware only of the flesh of his hand pressed between the slight swell of her stomach and her strong fingers. Then she lifted the cup and drank. She drank without question, her eyes on his. She touched his cheek lightly, rose, and walked outside. He stayed, hoping for her return, until he began to fear Hannan would come looking for him.

When he gave the empty vessel back to Hannan, she nodded, satisfied. "Now," she said, "don't speak of her in my presence again."

Harif is brought out of his reverie by Ahmed, who has stopped pacing and is standing over him. "No mother would advise a daughter to involve herself in issues that are a man's concern." Ahmed spews the words. "I'm surprised a father would."

Harif rises. "Rafa came here on her own. I've made no suggestions regarding you." He hesitates. "Except one, years ago, which she ignored."

Ahmed faces him, steps closer. "That was?"

"Ahmed," Abu Sa'id interrupts. He waves a leg of lamb. "We are guests here. May Allah lengthen both your lives. We're still eating. Please." He gestures to the ground.

Harif sits. Ahmed does not. He looks away from the courtyard to the faded hills beyond. He grows hard and oblivious, apart from them. Despite himself, Harif feels a tug of sympathy. Ahmed is a man frozen in mid-step before the power of his bleakest thoughts: fear of losing wife, child.

"It is I who am at fault," Ahmed says suddenly. "I humored her too long. But I paid for it." His voice vibrates. "I've paid. Why do you suppose I lost my sons? Punishment."

Harif shifts his prayer beads from hand to hand quickly, as though they were hot. "Punishment?"

"For failing to control my wife's independent streak."

"Nonsense!" Harif lifts a hand to block Ahmed from his sight.

"Shall we listen to some music?" calls Abu Sa'id, reaching in his robe to pull out his transistor radio.

"My father, may he rest well with Allah, never would have allowed his wife such base freedoms," Ahmed says loudly. "He followed the Koran to the letter. My mother's eyes were always lowered. She never—not once—disagreed with him."

"You believe this caused the babies to die? Then what about Jammana?"

"A girl is permitted me, but not a boy." Ahmed intones

in a voice that seems to Harif to belong to someone else. "A sin against Allah cuts off the descendants."

Harif rises again, incredulous.

"Rafa had the best care for those first two births," Ahmed goes on. "Modern. Hygienic. I watched over it myself. Still, she lost them." He glances slyly at Harif. "I speak of your case also. You lost a son, no?"

Harif can't help wondering, for a moment briefer than a breath, if Ahmed could be right. He cannot deny that he lost a son, or that he swerved from Allah's path. He won't, however, unveil doubts now. He grunts in disapproval. "Hannan was weak by the time of the second stomach. Besides, Rafa is worth as much as any boy. So is Jammana."

"Of course they're not."

Harif steps closer. "This you believe? This is why you thought you had the right?" He straightens. He's still the host, but he doesn't care anymore. He's half a head taller than Ahmed, and he wants it to show. "The right to strike my daughter?"

"You have no place," Ahmed says coolly, "in our affairs."

"I think," Abu Sa'id interjects in a rush, rising and extending his arms to separate the men, "what Ahmed means—"

"Greetings," a voice calls. The three men turn. Nabeel steps forward into the light. "Forgive me, Harif. I did not know you had guests." Nabeel smiles placidly, pretending not to notice the tangible tension. As the years have passed, Harif knows, Nabeel has become skilled at deceiving. The only emotion he unwittingly reveals is smugness. "May the blessings of Allah fall upon your head," Nabeel says.

No one speaks. Somewhere, a donkey brays. Abu Sa'id finally lowers his arms and answers. "Also yours," he says.

"This is Harif's son-in-law, and I'm a friend of the family. We've traveled from Nablus."

Nabeel turns to Harif but does not meet his eyes. "Deepest greetings, and thanks to Allah that I may greet your son-in-law again."

"You must be the *mukhtar*," says Abu Sa'id. "I have a present for you, and one also for Ahmed's father-in law." He reaches into his saddlebag, which lies on the ground.

"What has brought you here?" Harif asks Nabeel curtly.

"I was passing, saw you outside."

It sounds unlikely. Nabeel doesn't pay Harif casual visits anymore.

"Take it with Allah's blessings," says Abu Sa'id, handing both Harif and Nabeel glossy magazines with foreign writing. "This is *Life* magazine, from America. Someone brought them in to trade a few weeks ago. There are wonderful pictures—President Johnson's wife, the astronauts . . ." As no one responds, Abu Sa'id trails off, then coughs and tries again. "Under the eyes of Allah, Harif's sister has prepared a delicious meal. There is plenty." He gestures at the tray.

"Khalah retains unearthly knowledge of food," Nabeel says. "Her meals soothe. At least, usually," he adds dryly. He puts down his magazine and sits on it. The others also lower themselves. As Nabeel rolls rice into a ball with his right hand, Harif wonders how long he will stay. He squeezes the prayer beads in his palm and glances at Ahmed, who is staring into the fire. Ahmed's body carries an inner restlessness; his face is tense. Harif follows his gaze and spots an object in the flames.

It is the doll Faridah made for Jammana, the one she named Asima. It must have fallen there. He reaches for a stick to push it out, but when he turns back, it is gone. Could it have burned so quickly? Or do his eyes play with him, so that he sees troubles where none exists? "In the name of Allah," he mutters, hoping to frighten away unpleasant thoughts.

No one has noticed him fiddling with the fire. Ahmed is standing. Nabeel is speaking. "So, you left Rafa home on this trip? Perhaps that was wise. Travel has become more dangerous in recent weeks."

Ahmed coughs. "May Allah grant you a long life, but I'm suddenly weary," he replies. "Please excuse me." He goes inside.

An awkward silence sits. Abu Sa'id, reaching for more rice, stops himself. He rises with clear reluctance, gazing at the food. "I should sleep, too," he says. "I return to Nablus at first daylight."

Harif walks to the edge of his courtyard. Nabeel follows. After a moment, Harif turns. "Why have you come?"

"As I said. I saw your fire."

Harif sinks the fingers of his right hand into his beard. "Many harvests have passed since you stopped to visit simply because you saw a fire burning. Why now, after the Bedouin has revealed my deception and I'm regarded with such distrust by your clan and the others?"

Nabeel studies Harif. "Perhaps for that very reason. You made a mistake in lying, Harif. You could have told the truth about your visions. That would have been my advice."

Harif does not welcome Nabeel's views now. Nabeel fails to mention that if Harif had been honest those many years ago, he would have been chased from Ein Fadr, forever an outcast. "Is that all you want?" he asks.

Nabeel shakes his head. "I love this village, you know. It's part of me and of my father and grandfather and his father, too—every stone and olive tree. I never wanted to be *mukhtar* the way Adil does. But once I had the job, I used it to protect you, several times. I sought, too, to keep Ein Fadr safe through another generation, and I accomplished that. All our young have stayed—except Rafa. I'm proud of that." He glances toward Harif with a smile that holds a touch of shyness, as though he hopes for a word of praise. When none comes, he goes on. "The villagers feel you betrayed them." His eyes turn bleak. "They won't be appeased. They search for your vulnerabilities. This time it's out of my hands. Absolutely beyond me."

"*It?*"

Nabeel looks down at his feet. "If only you'd taken advantage of my friendship instead of disdaining it."

Harif looks out at the darkened olive fields. "Nabeel," he says, "we were friends half a lifetime ago. Since my first vision, my only friends have been Faridah and my sister."

"And your wife, of course. You haven't forgotten her?" Nabeel's voice arches challengingly. His heart, Harif sees, has grown cold as January water.

"Your message has been delivered," Harif says. "Or, should I say, your father's."

Nabeel's eyes grow sharp; his lips tighten. "You brought us to this. Don't insult me by blaming others."

"Good night, Nabeel," Harif says.

Nabeel steps in front of Harif, refusing to be dismissed. "One more thing," he says. "I know your nature is stronger than my counsel. Nevertheless, I urge you. Rise tomorrow and take your sheep out, Harif, to a green and distant field. Rise with the first light. Stay out."

Harif tips his head, speaks slowly. "Why do you so advise?"

Nabeel's eyes narrow. He shrugs. "By midday, we'll have a bad storm. I'm sure of it."

FARIDAH

The women wake early. A mist clings, and the cold earth emits the concentrated scent of almonds, cumin, mushrooms. The women rise in shadows. They knead and heat, stroke and smooth and stack. Silent as breath. The men, sensing the women, resist at first. Then they shrug to shed sleep. Shrug again, their thoughts dragging reluctantly into today's sharp corners, tomorrow's bold lines. The women, all, are thinking of the fullness of yesterdays.

The sun comes up bitter. At one fist high, it blinds. Faridah, squinting outside her home, kisses the top of Jammana's head. "Look, they're back," says Jammana, pointing to the black tents of the Bedouin, which appeared overnight.

"On their way south again," Faridah says. "That trouble-

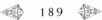

toting Bedouin will probably visit Harif this morning. You will see him one last time, and then he will be forever gone." She pats Jammana's shoulder. "Now, off with you."

Khalah, waiting, nods. *"Yallah,"* she says. "Let's go."

Jammana lingers. "And Father?" she asks. "Will he take me away today?"

Faridah shakes her head. "Your mama will come first, I'm sure. But I cannot wait for her. You saw the ill one last night. I must gather herbs."

Faridah hates to think of Baraka, who seemed sicker than ever when Jammana and Faridah visited. As she coughed, her body lifted from the mat. She shifted heavily, unable to find a comfortable position. Milk the color of first dawn beaded uselessly from her breasts. Her skin felt hot and dry, her pulse rapid. Most frightening of all was the onset of confusion. She seemed to recognize no one save her sister, Manara. Manara gripped Faridah's sleeve, her eyes wide and wet. "I've been thinking, Faridah. What if Adil failed to praise Allah when he entered my sister? If so, she will surely die."

Faridah, infuriated by the superstition, shook her head. "No, Manara. One has nothing to do with the other."

"Then, please! Do something," said Manara, her face full of doubts.

But what? Faridah cannot understand the nature of the symptoms taking turns in Baraka's body. The woman, it seems, is being slowly, capriciously sacrificed. Faridah considered nightshade, with its leafless stem and spray of white flowers. The bulbs blanket certain hills. Could Baraka have eaten a rabbit fattened by the poisonous plant, as a child did in Ein Fadr once? But Adil said Baraka had not eaten in days. He blamed Faridah's poor care. "You are not doing enough," he'd bellowed, his arms moving like branches in a gale. "And whatever you do try is wrong." Faridah had turned away.

Something she can't yet see is poisoning Baraka, an illness she can't name. While she awaits clarity, she can only treat the cough and fever and infection as she always would, except more diligently. Whatever other responsibilities crowd her, this morning she must find the finest herbs. And she knows where they grow greenest, their leaves swollen, their petals proud. Alula's shrine. The villagers say plants that mature in that soil are infused with the life of one taken too soon; Faridah simply credits cliffs that provide extra shade and rain runoff—both so necessary in this driest of seasons.

"And—my questions?" Jammana asks, her chin jutting out.

"Yes, Jammana." Faridah smiles slightly, resigned. "When I'm back, we'll finish it." Faridah glances at Khalah, gesturing her head toward Jammana. "She waged war with sleep all night." She reaches to stroke Jammana's tight curls.

"It was a dream," Jammana says. "A dream I keep having."

"And you?" Khalah asks Faridah.

Faridah shrugs. "I, too, lay on a bed of stones."

Khalah turns to Jammana. "Bring Divine outside for Faridah," she says. Then she tucks her arm into Faridah's, leads her through the door. "What troubles you?" she asks.

Faridah waves her hand to dismiss the question, but can see from Khalah's intense expression that a gesture won't satisfy. It surprises Faridah—Khalah has never asked her anything this personal. Now she is insistent.

"I'm forced to deal with old stumblings," Faridah says at last. Khalah waits, silent and intense. Faridah takes a deep breath. "A plant used to grow within me. Though it blossomed from rich soil, it was poisonous. It directed me falsely one day, and I had to yank it out. When I destroyed it, I sacrificed love along with the hate. That should have been punishment enough, but it wasn't. I'm still paying."

Khalah touches Faridah's cheek with the back of her hand. "You are warm," she says.

Faridah shakes her head impatiently. "My words are clumsy. Still, you understand. I think you always understood."

"All I know is what it has cost you both to live this way," Khalah says. "More is not for me to say."

Faridah reaches to squeeze Khalah's hand. Both of Alula's children, she thinks, are so dear to her. Jammana enters the courtyard, leading Divine. "I'll be back by midday, if I can," Faridah says to Khalah.

"You'll come to me then?" Khalah asks. "I'll make sure you are fed before you go to Baraka's side."

Faridah nods, and mounts.

Normally, she barely need direct Divine. With the slightest pressure of knee, twisting of waist, he seems to intuit her destination. It always has been thus. Today, though, he resists her. He slows on the way to Alula's, halts, and turns his head to look at her with solemn eye.

"What's the matter, Divine?" She climbs off and checks his hooves. She pats his rump, then puts a hand on his cheek. "Hush, now. Don't get spooked," she says softly. She climbs back on. He shuffles reluctantly, then starts forward. He's never stalled so before. She supposes he has sensed her mood. He's an intelligent, energetic beast with honest eyes. She's lucky to have him. There have been days—many—when he's been her only companion.

Her isolation has set her temperament over the years, Faridah knows. Who was she before she was so alone? Who can remember? Each life holds hundreds of little deaths. Even her previous faces have become difficult to recall. The girl just married. The woman divorced. The one with desire so intense it had to be visible. The one with child so briefly no one knew. All those old Faridahs are gone. Now she must try to recollect who she was when Hannan first became pregnant. How she chose the road.

One memory returns easily: the sly look in Hannan's eyes as she approached the well, fingers gently drumming belly. The two women never spoke—even in a drop of a village, Faridah knew how to keep clear of those she didn't wish to see. Hannan, too, excelled at avoidance. So Faridah was startled when Hannan began speaking as though in mid-conversation, her words carrying a rhythm of victory Faridah did not immediately understand. "You'll be there, won't you? After all, I remember our wedding night." She paused, giving Faridah a moment to worry about what she would say next, especially in front of the others gathered at the well. "That night, you wished for us the blessing of many offspring. So you'll help me when Harif's baby comes into the world. Won't you?"

"Oh, Hannan!" The women crowded around, letting their water jars fall to the ground, smoothing her cheeks with damp fingers, stroking her dress at the belly.

"You have stomach!"

"Alula's first grandchild!"

"Praise Allah!"

They moved closer, ever closer, to whisper as one the secrets of pregnancy, secrets only those who have had stomach know—no one else, not male, not child, not barren midwife. Hushed memories of new sensations in the breasts and deep between the legs. The throbbing, propelling urgency, the fresh possibilities. The perpetual concert. Hannan nodded and smiled and swayed, and dropped her head demurely—"I think it's a boy, I'm feverish all the time," she said coyly—but not before she nailed Faridah with her eyes, grinned a final arrow directly into Faridah's defeated heart.

What a smile! In less than a year of living in Ein Fadr, Hannan's sweetness had hardened; Faridah knew it then. Hannan's look made her question her decision to send Harif into Hannan's arms that night.

That heedless night when he appeared and held her as if she were polished stone. The joy of her cheek driven into the floor, of everything turning upside down and the slow burn that melted the hardness of life. *Ya, Harif! Habibi!* Mud and moonlight. Each of them a man and a woman at once. That heedless night when he'd tossed back his head and called, "Forgive my stubborn blindness! Now that I see, I will not leave."

Near Alula's shrine, she bends forward to stroke Divine's cheek twice, and he halts. She looks up at the boulder that hides Rafa's cave. She hadn't intended to go up, but she's drawn to Rafa irresistibly. Just to touch her arm, perhaps.

She dismounts, scratches Divine's head, and climbs the hill. Rafa is gone. Only a mat, a water jug, and a few figs show she was ever here. Faridah is surprised Rafa has chosen to meet Ahmed so early. Does that mean Rafa will take the safe path and reunite with her husband contritely? Faridah must gather her herbs quickly and return to the village in case Rafa needs her.

She hurries back to the shrine and turns in a circle. Her conscious mind can never recall exactly where specific herbs grow. But her legs are like divining rods—they lead her there. It always has been so. And now she is sure she will find crawling rosemary.

As she walks over a hill, she tries to comprehend why she sent Harif back to his bride those countless years ago, with such mistaken certainty. The villagers would have gathered in a steamy circle and stoned them for their adultery. That she knew. Their blood would have spilled, merged, pooled, and then drained into the caked ground. Tears would have been shed for Harif, but none for her. No matter—at that moment she would have accepted death, if she had to, in return for the night she'd just been given. But what of Harif?

And if they had, somehow, escaped death? Even if he'd slipped back to his home with no one noticing, arranged a divorce on some excuse or another—what then? She'd seen him suffer when the elders turned their backs on him—when even his friends couldn't keep distrust from their gazes—after the crop failure, the illness of Musa's son. With Faridah for a wife, he would have been hurled from the village circle once and for all. She was able to withstand the punishment of estrangement, but it would have been like death for him.

She had considered all this as she lay on her dirt floor, Harif next to her, the door open for a breeze to dry the moisture on their skin. They lay watching the blackness of the sky become casual. Villagers soon would be rising. She knew she had to hurry. He turned and smiled, but she glared. "Go! Go!" she growled, her fingers lightly peppering his shoulders. He refused once, then again while she tried to explain in words jumbled, hushed. Finally he rose, still bewildered but obedient. He dressed. "Hurry," she said. He left, and she, spread on the dirt floor, too weary to weep, slept until nightfall.

When she rose, she found she'd saved him. Somehow a bloody wedding sheet had been produced, and none was the wiser. Maybe some suspected but none could know for certain, except Faridah, Harif, and Hannan. And in the weeks and months that followed, those three did not speak of it. Not even . . .

Not even when Faridah discovered she was with stomach. Harif must have known of her pregnancy instinctively, for he brought her a chalky mixture to swallow. She waited for him to speak, but he was for once without words, and in this way she understood he felt ashamed.

Her choice would not have been his. A child was within, and she had no wish to deny that. But she knew this was not her decision alone. If Faridah bore a child, wouldn't everyone guess where it came from? And hadn't she already told him to think of himself first and return to his wife? She drank. Three days later, she lost the baby. Afterward, she fought to quell the memory of her single night with Harif.

She'd remembered it, however, that morning at the well as she watched Hannan preening under the murmurs and strokes of Ein Fadr's women. She'd realized with sudden clarity she might act differently if given another chance. And she certainly would act differently if Harif were—by the will of Allah—unwed. In such a circumstance they would be joined, the disdain of the elders be damned.

But of course, she thought as she watched Hannan in the circle of women, that was out of her hands.

And at that moment, she'd seen it. The shadow of a plan. She didn't make it. It found her.

Jericho Rose. The previous midwife called it Snake Bush. Long ago, she'd warned Faridah against its intense powers. A plant strong enough to make its way without human nurturing, to grow even on dry hills, where the earth is too slow to suck in rivulets of rain rushing past. A plant, in fact, that seems to thrive on thirst, that harbors fury at being shunned by man and stockpiles its poison, waiting for its nectar to be chosen by the unwitting, or the wise. Jericho Rose.

She didn't decide, not ever. It was more a gathering in, as the day came nearer when Faridah would be summoned to sit in close proximity to Harif's wife. A collecting of slender branches from the plant that beckons with long narrow leaves. The plant of oily smells one can never wash off, and lush pink flowers that hide depravity.

Faridah had begun traveling far from the village.

Searching for places of barren but blunt desire—rocky out-croppings, the edges of stone fields. There grew the hardiest bushes in whose branches she felt certain deadly substances were most concentrated. She began to snap off shoots and carry them home. They bled on her hands. She stacked them in a corner and then washed each finger carefully. Not thinking much about intentions.

Finally came the day when she used her knife to slice the boughs into slender segments and drop them into a burlap bag. She crumbled the leaves and added them. She slept that night the slumber of the blessed.

When Khalah came to her at midmorning a few days later—"It's Hannan!" Harif was in the grazing fields—she snatched up her healing herbs and the leavings of Jericho Rose, too. She thought she would brew a tea. Sweeten it with honey to make it palatable. But when she squatted near Hannan's heels, a tea seemed too definite. Too clearly wrong.

Besides, there was Khalah. Hannan's mother was not there for the birth, and Hannan did not want the village women to see her during her time. She allowed only Khalah, who wandered in and out, touching Hannan's forehead, murmuring comforting words. At last, Khalah said, "I must prepare the evening meal," so Faridah knew they would have a slice of time alone, she and Hannan. She didn't think of living or dying, killing or saving. She tossed pieces of branch and leaf into the flame of the lantern. She wasn't sure what it would do until she saw silver sparks and smelled suffocating thickness.

In a map so casually sketched, how could she have planned what happened next? She was waiting, withdrawn, when something beyond her intervened. She never believed in spirits that floated through walls. But she couldn't deny that a force of unrelenting determination, a will outside her own, placed the baby on her lap. That will or force or power or whatever it was wanted Rafa born.

Afterward, Faridah felt the torn fullness she imagined belonged to a new mother, the shock of being suddenly disinhabited. She told herself Rafa was a blade of grass, just like any other. But she never believed it.

Hannan was weaker after the birth, so Faridah helped care for the infant, and her own love sank into the child. If the villagers wondered at this arrangement, so uncharacteristic for Faridah, they kept quiet. The elders, too, watched and waited. Feeling time to be on their side.

The rosemary! Faridah locates it, as she knew she would. A dozen bees hover, guarding jealously. She uses her nails to pierce through the stem, to break off the top two inches. Its needles stain her hand with the smell of gray-green earth. She pushes the spines into a burlap bag.

Nearby, she sees comfrey and begins to dig for the root. After many minutes, she extracts it, then straightens, stretches her back. She shields her eyes from the sun, taking stock of where she's wandered. She's on the scrappy edge of a hillside where trees grow discouraged and even bushes become surly. She's traveled about half a circle, and if she continues, she will end up back at Alula's shrine. She's already collected the herbs she needs for Baraka, but perhaps something else will appear. She rolls her neck to loosen the muscles, starts out again.

When Hannan was pregnant the second time and Faridah again had opportunity and even more reasons to wish for Hannan's end, she insisted on Harif's help, knowing that with him there, she would do her best to save the woman.

The villagers were hostile to this plan—men never attended a birth. It was improper. The *mukhtar* forbade it. Hannan herself opposed it. But the teacher at the mosque, an authority on the Koran, said a man's presence at the birth of his child was not specifically prohibited. The debate continued as the day grew near.

Faridah prepared herself, nervous as a new bride. Daily, she cleansed herself ritually. Every two days, she oiled her hair anew. She wasn't one to pray, but sometimes before she fell asleep in those weeks prior to Hannan's second delivery, she found herself muttering words inchoate, unclear. "Please. I won't. But You . . ." She didn't acknowledge even to herself what she was asking for.

When the hour came and Khalah summoned Faridah, Harif waited outside their door. Faridah, with her eyes alone, bid him to enter, and he did. But it was out of their hands. Almost from the first moment, Hannan began coughing as she had when Faridah threw the Jericho Rose in the fire, although of course by now Faridah no longer carried a burlap bag of the evil plant's shavings. And the baby began to stick.

All as before, yet different. This time, when it emerged—a boy—the cord was wrapped around its neck.

This time, Hannan did not have the strength to lift her head and call out a name for the child. Her eyes fluttered open, but this time they held no victory, and they closed again.

Faridah never before had lost both mother and child. Never since.

Weeks later, Harif told her he had dreamed of Hannan's death during childbirth. "In my vision, she looked older," he said, a pleading in his tone. "I thought it was something I could prevent. If she had gotten through this one, I promised myself I would never lie with her again."

But this was later. That day, the day Hannan died, the village elders gathered in a suspicious circle in Harif's courtyard. While he'd been dry-eyed at his mother's funeral, this time, he shed hot tears and no one could doubt they were genuine. Distraught, he cradled Rafa in his arms. She stayed there a few minutes and then ran to Faridah, and Faridah, too, wept as she rocked the girl.

She didn't weep for Hannan. She wept because she understood. The villagers were temporarily appeased by Harif's demonstration of sorrow, but their eyes were narrowed. If Harif were to stand beside Faridah as spouse, if his child ever were to call her Mama, they would be satisfied no longer. Revenge would shower not only on Faridah, not only on Harif, but on Rafa as well. And the one she couldn't risk sacrificing was Rafa.

There was a single moment, though, six months after Hannan's death. Late afternoon. She sat cross-legged in her courtyard, sorting through dried herbs, stockpiling them. She heard stones move under foot. Harif stood right outside her courtyard.

At first he said nothing. He let her read his face, tattooed with longing and regret. "This sight awes and nourishes me," he said thickly, gesturing at her.

She smoothed her skirt and brushed a tendril of hair from her forehead. She studied the palms of her hands, then lifted her chin to meet his gaze. She rose, letting herbs drop from her lap. "Come," she said, beckoning, not certain how they would move forward from this moment but willing to risk it.

A desperate look came into his eyes. He glanced beyond, to the village center, where Moses' Finger loomed. Then he gazed again at her. At that moment, she could see he'd already weighed the consequences of either decision. He already knew his choice. But she waited. This time, she would make him say it. Finally, he swallowed hard. "I cannot." He choked on the words.

Something within her hardened, though she showed no sign. She stood unmoving as he shuddered and began walking away from Ein Fadr's fringe toward his own home. She stood unmoving until the setting sun began to hurt her eyes, waking her up to the world around.

Now, too, she's jarred to alertness. This time it's a bird's odd cry, shrill and fast. She sees broken glass flash in the sun. It blinds her, but just for a minute. Herbs spill from burlap bags.

JAMMANA

W
here is she?" Father's voice marches into the courtyard, each word knee high, riveting. Jammana knows—has known for hours fanned into centuries—that her world is about to be changed forever. For weeks she's seen her parents heaving a boulder back and forth between them. Now the trade-off is done. One must be the stone carrier, the other the leader. Jammana can guess which Father plans to be.

Grandfather, following Father, darts to Jammana. "My girl." His greeting is a quick caress. His fingers leap over a strand of prayer beads.

At first, Khalah doesn't look up. She appears unperturbed as she rocks a large tin sieve, sifting wheat. When she glances in Father's direction at last, her eyes are mild as a spill of moonlight.

Father stands above her, draws himself up, and glares down as though she were a naughty child. "In there?" he asks with a shudder. He gestures with his chin toward the door to Khalah's room.

Khalah shakes her head once and slowly. Father glances toward Jammana. "She's not . . . ?" He examines the courtyard again. The bright shades of hope painted on his face turn slowly gray, and he stiffens. "I said this morning, or I'd leave without her. Come, Jammana."

Jammana draws back, tugging on a strand of hair. She forces her tightened throat to open so words can pass. "No, Father."

Khalah lets the sieve fall from her hands, and arcs her body with such grace and speed it's easy to overlook how solidly she is built. Before anyone can speak, she takes Jammana's hand and pulls her to the far end of the courtyard into the protected territory of the *taboon*, that cramped chamber with a shallow baking pit at its heart. A woman's sanctuary with smoke hole.

Father strides after them, halts at the oven's entrance. From where Jammana crouches, she sees him only from the waist down. "I said yesterday I would not wait," he calls, as if they were far away.

The lower half of Grandfather's tunic moves into Jammana's line of vision. "You will not take my granddaughter."

"Harif!" Khalah interrupts in a voice that emerges sharply from the *taboon*, cuts through his. "You are not tending your sheep?"

"Not if my family needs me."

"Needs you?" Father's voice sounds stripped of smoothness, heading toward raw. "I'm Jammana's father." Jammana shivers at his proprietary tone.

Khalah thrusts her head out the entrance to the *taboon*, implacable. "Harif, fetch me water. The jar is inside next to the door." Her tone holds a sense of the absolute, as Father's often does.

Jammana inches to the *taboon*'s opening, and sees Grandfather open his mouth as though to protest, then close it. A bemused expression crosses his face. "Beneficent Allah, have mercy on me!" he murmurs. "My women are so determined!"

"Jammana, help your grandfather," Khalah continues.

"No!"

Khalah stares curiously at Jammana, who lowers her voice but aims to mimic Khalah's tone. "I'm better off here," Jammana says.

Khalah smiles slightly. She steps out and dismisses Grandfather with a nod.

"All right," Grandfather mutters. "But Jammana must be here when I return."

"Ahmed?" Khalah asks.

"Hurry, then," Father answers.

Khalah tucks herself back in the *taboon*. As Grandfather goes, Father speaks without looking toward the oven. "Don't force this, Khalah. I've been generous."

"And I would never attempt to advise you," Khalah says. "Still, it's only morning. In the name of Allah, All-Merciful and Compassionate, you haven't even had breakfast yet." She holds her hand above the shallow oven pit to test its heat. "In the moment a leaf spends falling from a tree, I'll have baked warm bread with sweet basil."

Father doesn't reply, which Jammana takes as a good sign. Khalah reaches inside a bowl, picks up a soft dough cake, and allows it to stretch in her hands. "When I was young," she says in Father's direction, "I didn't know how to cook. All thumbs around food." She slaps the dough, spreads it onto the hot pebbles. Father, squatting, studies the horizon. "My mother gave up on me, and I, too, decided to quit trying," she goes on. "I would never cook; I would be the only female in Ein Fadr who refused to prepare food." With a powdery finger, she touches the tear-shaped blemish on her cheek. "Before I could tell her, though, she was gone." She pops the largest air bubbles in the dough and scoots closer to the door of the *taboon*. "After that, Harif went to the fields and I had to cook. But everything I made—my puddings of dates and scalded milk, my pastries filled with *melokhiyyah*—passed down the throat heavily."

Father has taken off his glasses and is rubbing his eyes.

"It changed the day after Harif's wedding," Khalah goes on. "I was in the courtyard washing the wedding sheet."

Father laughs curtly. "All Ein Fadr had already inspected it, I suppose. A barbaric custom."

Khalah shrugs. "Ein Fadr favors the old ways. Anyway, that day I was considering fragments of conversations, the ways people gazed at one another." Jammana feels Khalah glance at her, and senses that Khalah is holding back her words. "It doesn't matter anymore," Khalah says after a moment, "except I was so lost in my thoughts that I scraped my knuckles on the bottom of the wooden tub. My hand began bleeding. I rinsed it in the same water I'd used to wash the sheet." She dusts flour off the back of her right hand. "After that my food took on an unusual quality. Whether I rub my bread with *ghee* or cook it with sweet basil, praise Allah, it seems to encourage compromise."

"And you attribute this to—what?" Father asks, his eyebrows raised in mock interest. "Spirits of the water, perhaps?"

Jammana cringes at Father's tone, but Khalah ignores it. "Something about the act of offering up one's blood," she says.

Father groans. "So, now must we ask our women to cut their hands to improve their cooking?"

Khalah, eyes half closed, seems to search for the words. "Not *my* blood, I mean the wedding blood. Everything that survives seeks a middle way. The one who insists on clinging to his path is finally left behind. That's what seeped into my scraped hand, what now finds its way into my food."

"Are you saying *I* must—"

Khalah holds up her palm. "I'm talking about cooking, Ahmed. And a strange occurrence at a washing tub." She lifts the hot, freckled bread from the oven with a wooden paddle, breaks off a piece, and hands it to Father, then gives another to Jammana.

Both chew in silence. Jammana sees Father's face relax. After a moment, he speaks. "The first time I saw her, I understood immediately how alive she was. I thought Paradise existed under her feet."

His tone surprises Jammana. He is like a fortress whose guards are sleeping. "Eat more, Ahmed," Khalah says.

Father chews. "My father advised against marrying her. I wouldn't give her up." He sighs, drops his head. "How in Allah's safekeeping did we travel so far in such a short time?"

Khalah leans out of the oven chamber, and her voice takes on an urgency. "Rafa must leave here."

"I've been saying that for months," Father answers, his arms spread.

"I mean Ein Fadr, and now," Khalah insists. "She used to be content to keep quiet. But she's changing. She's more like my mother, or Faridah. I can tell by the way she holds her shoulders, how she stands. Soon she won't be able to help herself. She'll name what she sees. Within your household, you can learn to accept that. But women of that kind do not flourish here. So hurry. Take her back to Nablus." She fans her red cheeks with one hand.

Jammana does not know if Khalah is right about Mama, but she *is* certain that Father will grow angry now—he never takes kindly to advice from others, particularly women. He surprises her, though. He is silent. He studies Khalah calmly, takes more bread, eats.

Khalah's cooking is more powerful than Jammana realized. "Will you teach me?" Jammana whispers, gesturing at the oven pit.

"It's not a learned skill, after all," Khalah says slowly. "I can show you how to place the pebbles and mix the wheat, but we each wander toward our own fate." Her shoulders sag; she seems worn by the effort of talking more than usual.

"Ahmed?" The voice is Mama's. Father jumps to his feet. Jammana starts out after them, but Khalah grips her shoulder, holding her back.

Father seems to struggle with his mouth, stroking his mustache as though to force his lips into a frown. But his eyes show clear relief. "You got my message." His voice grows firm, cunningly kind. "I've decided, Rafa. Jammana can stay a few more days. It'll give us time to go home and settle our plans."

Mama doesn't speak.

"Rafa," Father says. "I know it is within my rights under Allah's law to discipline my wife, but . . ." He looks skyward, squinting, and swallows with the grimace of tasting something bitter. Then he gazes at Mama. "I regret my anger." He steps back, then, his face distorted as though his words were unexpected, even to himself.

Jammana stifles a nervous giggle. "I've never before heard him apologize," she whispers to Khalah.

Mama clears her throat. "What happened between you and me is not our deepest problem," she says. "It's what happened between you and the men of Nablus."

"This matter you do not understand," Father answers sharply.

"You're a doctor. It was wrong."

"What was wrong?" Jammana whispers to Khalah.

"Those Christians killed one of our boys," Father says.

Jammana pounces out of the *taboon* before Khalah can stop her. "*What* was wrong?" she asks.

"Jammana!" Mama shoots a reproachful look at Father. "You knew she was there?"

Father takes a deep breath, his eyes still on Mama. "You come from these villagers, Rafa, and they live isolated, in a simpler time. I cannot stand in ignorance as they do." His face hardens. "Allah has not allowed us a son. But He did give one to our neighbors, and that boy was taken. If we failed to retaliate, they would steal all our boys. That's the way of this land."

"What you did was not about a boy," Mama says. "It was

about belonging." Her eyes widen, then, as though she herself has just made a discovery.

Suddenly, it is clear. Father, the finest doctor in Nablus, was among the men who killed. Jammana stared at his hands, trying to imagine them stabbing a Christian. Stabbing a Christian to death.

"We will use your hospital fund money," Mama says. "We will give it to those families."

"Yes," Jammana agrees loudly.

"Absurd. Impossible." Father cuts the air decisively with his right hand, but his tone holds uncertainty.

"You took from those families," Mama says. "Now, under the eyes of the Merciful, you will give."

At that moment, Grandfather, lugging the earthen jar of water, sweeps into the courtyard. He sets the jar down heavily and rushes to Mama. "Are you all right?"

"Of course. But we're talking," Mama says. "Why don't you and Jammana—"

"We'll sit here," Grandfather interrupts, glaring at Father. "Quiet as a kerchief on a woman's head." He summons Jammana with a gesture.

"Not here, Father," begins Mama. Before she can say more, someone else enters the courtyard—a girl with a flyaway look in her eyes.

"Greetings," Grandfather says. "Rafa, you remember Hamid's daughter?"

"Of course." Mama takes the girl's hands. "You are flushed."

The girl looks around, jerking her head from side to side. "I need Khalah," she says.

"I don't know where she is," Mama begins, but Jammana

points to the *taboon* as Khalah emerges. Mama looks at Father. "Has *everyone* been party to our discussion?"

The girl rushes toward Khalah, grips her arms. "She's worse. Talking to people long gone. Reaching for objects I can't see. I left her with the neighbor women. I can't find either Faridah or Adil."

Then Jammana remembers. This is Manara, the sister of the sick woman, Baraka.

"Faridah," Grandfather says in a hollow voice. He puts a hand to his forehead. His face loses color. His eyes seem to age. "Faridah."

"What is it?" Jammana reaches into his beard. "Don't worry. She's only gathering herbs."

Khalah stares at Grandfather. "Faridah is near the shrine," she says after a moment. "We'll fetch her."

Grandfather is stumbling from the courtyard. Jammana tries to make her eyes hard as she looks at Father. "I'm going too," she says in a tone of such unnecessary defiance that Father would have punished her for it once. Now, she knows he will not mention it. She has the sense he'll not dare scold her for some time to come.

HARIF

Harif propels forward, legs aching, throat burning. His eyes strain, searching ahead for the one whose gestures are etched on his soul. A brisk turn of waist is what he seeks, crisp movement of wrists. A certain lift of the chin.

Nothing but boulders and olive trees greet him, and in the distance he sees the Bedouin pitching their black tents. They have returned from Amman. Arudi al-Salman, who once saved Harif from a storm and once unwittingly cast him into one, must be among them. But Harif's thoughts don't linger there. He's slicing the air with such speed that his shoulders no longer keep pace with his feet. His legs, grown reckless, thrust ahead, unwilling to wait for his eyes to survey the ground. He knows he will not stumble. This path lay unmarked and strewn with sharp stones the first time he hurled himself down it to find Alula's body, but now it is smooth as a woman's thigh. The hardened heels of mothers, wives, and daughters have seen to that.

At last he reaches the shrine and the hole where the earth breathes. There is Divine, tied to a tree in that precise way of Faridah's. At the sight of the donkey, Harif is suddenly embarrassed by the leaping in his chest. Allah help him, he's lost in the senseless panic of an old man, almost as ridiculous as the overconfidence of the young. Faridah will stroll up any moment, and no matter how quickly he smoothes his brow, she'll spot the memory of worry in his eyes. She'll laugh, tell him not to be so nervous. He thinks for a moment he hears her voice. But no. It's the caw of a crow.

He sinks to the ground, only now aware of the others who have trailed him. He's jumpy, that's it, but no wonder. He spent an evening created by the devil Iblis himself. He suffered through Ahmed's company and Nabeel's visit, and then he lay down to a night crowded with unholy dreams.

Manara paces in a circle. "Is she here?" the girl asks, left hand pressed against blotchy cheek.

Khalah nods. "Somewhere." Divine's ears rise. He paws at the dirt with a front hoof. "Rafa, Jammana, go that way," Khalah says, pointing. "Manara, over there."

"I'll wait for her here by the donkey," Ahmed says.

Harif tells himself not to search for meaning in his nightmares—after all, every one of his visions has been wrong lately. The haunting dream of glass and anguish came to nothing. And when Khalah appeared as he herded his sheep in that recent evening, he'd had a premonition that something terrible had happened to Jammana, when, in fact, his granddaughter had been fine. It had been his daughter who needed him.

He's lost his gift, no doubt about it. So his heart needn't continue to beat so demandingly simply because just moments ago, he envisioned . . . He stops himself. Over time, he's become adept at making his mind as empty as the evening alleyways of Ein Fadr.

Once they find Faridah, he's going to take his sheep out for a long graze. Spend a night beyond the village, somewhere under the stars. He'll come back restored.

"Fa-ri-dah." Harif hears Jammana stretch the word. It separates into three perfect syllables above their heads.

As he rises, Harif takes in the horizon: endless blue folding under dirt and stone, cupping the earth in warm embrace. There'll be no rain, despite Nabeel's odd prediction. Before them, a cautious lizard inches under a bush, seeking shade.

"Harif," Khalah calls. "You and I are going this way."

He lifts himself and trails Khalah toward the base of the hill pierced by Rafa's cave.

"Faridah." Manara throws the word in front of her. "Faridah," she calls again urgently.

Khalah is shoulder-to-shoulder with him. He looks sideways at her. She returns his gaze, raising her eyebrows and jutting out her chin in a way that seems intended to instruct him to pay attention, to keep scanning for Faridah. Then she breaks off to the left, gesturing for him to continue straight.

Faridah could be anywhere. She often wanders to distant ravines and follows hidden *wadi*s when she hunts for herbs, especially in dry periods such as this. She is of the hills, so closely joined to the soil, that she knows instinctively where to find her healing plants.

H arif."

He turns toward Khalah, but her back is to him, her hand resting on a boulder. *Ya, Khalah! You are so imperial today!* Now she insists that he search exactly where she directs.

"Harif," she repeats, her voice thick. She turns then. Her stark expression is a slap.

What is she telling him? What does she know? Nothing. Everything is well.

"Coming." He gets the word out, then moves forward, letting his feet drag. She's pointing, but he closes his eyes just a second before allowing his gaze to follow the path of her finger.

Russet-colored earth. Not like the blood a woman releases in childbirth. Browner.

Another step and he can see a curved shape, casually crumpled.

He begins, reflexively, to chant. "To Allah belong ninety-nine names. The First, the Last, the One."

He has reached the shape and it has a neck, but not a regular one. Painted with a jagged line the color of sunset. He cannot bear to touch it. Squatting, he puts his fingers below it. Probing for a heartbeat in the hollow between the clavicles.

He knows there is one. He's felt it before.

Now, though, it refuses him.

"The Vigilant. The Hearer."

He searches out her eyes, but they are closed. Her lips are dark purple. He gently lifts her head. He smoothes spilled, tempting hair away from the soaring cheekbones. Sand sticks to one side of her face; he brushes it away.

"The Originator. The Producer. The Beneficent."

He reaches down to straighten her legs, which are bent under oddly. He hides them neatly under her dress.

"The Seeing. The Raiser. The Enduring. The Relenting."

He is breathing fast now, and he puts his hands over his eyes to calm himself. In the blackness of his lids, he sees a young girl, shyly drawing lines in the dirt with her toes.

"The Irresistible," he intones. "The Opener."

He envisions a woman twirling in dance, strands of damp hair revealed at her forehead.

"The Majestic. The Gatherer."

Her arms encircle him, push him away. They extract life, over and over again. Her fingers, shiny with olive oil. Her voice, molasses and lemon together. "You old dung beetle," she called him last week. How that made him laugh!

"The Accounter," he mumbles. "The Truth."

He opens his eyes and finally touches it, that crooked line. Blood stains his finger. He wipes it onto his beard, then uses his upper lip to clean his whiskers.

Something hovers over him. Someone murmurs. "What has this village called upon its shoulders?"

He looks up. Khalah. Dear Khalah, she is always with him when he most needs her. "The Judge," he tells her. "The Kindly. The Well-Informed."

Khalah kneels before Faridah and strokes her cheek. She lifts Faridah's right arm gently and removes Faridah's seven bracelets, slipping them into her own pocket.

"Khalah?" The voice is Manara's.

"Stay there," Khalah orders.

Harif hears a shuffling, an intake of air. The sound of a body dropping to the ground. "In the name of Allah, what have they done?"

Manara's words startle him, wake him up. He turns. She is on her knees. "Who?" he asks, breathless. "Who?"

"Allah, forgive me, for I have failed You." Manara is rocking back and forth, groaning as she mumbles. "Courage fell from me, and in Your eyes I have sinned. I am not deserving. When the moment came, I let it pass."

Harif stands over her. "Which son of a viper?"

Manara looks in his direction but clearly does not see or hear him. She trembles, presses her fingers against her cheeks.

He grabs her shoulders, shakes.

"Harif!" Khalah pulls him. "Look at her! You'll not gain anything this way." She kneels before the girl. "Manara?" Manara looks up, large-eyed, cowed. "You know something? How this happened?"

"How what happened?" A voice coarse, cool. Unexpected. Adil, husband of the ill woman, has approached unnoticed. The one who once sought to be joined with Rafa. How long has he stood there?

Adil is frowning, his shoulders held in close to his neck. "What's happened?" he repeats. He glances around, then sucks in air and walks to where Faridah lies. He stands above her in a way she never would have permitted in life, like he owns her. His gaze is directed downward though he holds his head stiffly upright, as though trying not to look but unable to stop himself.

The intimate, insolent way he studies Faridah angers Harif. "You . . ." Harif takes a broad, threatening step toward Adil. Khalah grabs his arm, stopping him.

Adil does not appear to notice. He stares at the form on the ground. His voice is like a stiff wind. "I needed to find Faridah. Because my wife—"

Manara has risen. Her eyes are unfocused, but she interrupts: "Baraka?"

Adil finally looks toward the others. "She was ranting. Then she seemed to fall into a distant space."

"Oh, Merciful Allah," Manara groans. She unties the cloth belt from her dress, walks to a nearby tree, and ties the belt around a branch. "Stay there, thou evil," she says. "Stay there." And a third time, "Stay there." An old superstition to rid a loved one of illness. Harif knows Faridah would hate for it to be carried out in her sight. Perhaps, he thinks, Faridah will rise and rail at Manara.

"Why would you leave Baraka's side?" Khalah asks, her voice heavy with doubts.

"Faridah, I said," Adil replied impatiently. "I came to fetch her. She told me last night she would gather fresh herbs this morning near Alula's death spot." Adil stares at Harif. "She told many that she was coming here."

Khalah addresses Manara. "I thought you couldn't find him."

"I went outside." Adil hesitates, then stammers: "To, to get some twigs for the brazier. I was gone only a few minutes. Right, Manara?"

Manara drops her head.

Adil kneels over Faridah. Harif feels a longing to strike. "Get away," he says to the younger man.

Khalah's hand restrains him again. "The snake with two heads will slide out from under the rock soon enough," she says. "Do not rush revenge, Harif. Speed comes from the devil."

"He shouldn't look at her," Harif says.

"Harif." Khalah gestures skyward. A vulture circles in the distance. "We've got to get her to the village. She must be washed. And we must make . . ." Khalah breaks off. After a moment, she finishes. "The burial shroud."

Adil ignores them. "What's this?" he asks. He holds up a shard of glass. Violet colored, triangular. The size of a little child's hand. One end smeared in a single coat of nut red.

"Blessed Mohammed," murmurs Khalah.

Harif turns away. "Why weren't we with her?" he says. "Why would I ever leave her alone?"

"She always looks for herbs alone," Khalah says. "Everyone in the village knows that."

Suddenly, Adil becomes abrupt. "Let us go," he says to Harif. "Khalah, you stay here. We'll send help."

Khalah blows into her hands as though to warm herself. She looks at Adil through tight, accusatory eyes, though she says only, "Hurry. The day is warming. We must get her inside."

But Harif doesn't turn away from Faridah, not yet. For a second, he allows himself to believe that Faridah will call out to him. That she will say it all has been a teasing prank she played to repay him for the painful reminiscing in the cave. She'll stand up, ready to forgive, and they'll laugh together at the foolish, arrogant Adil. Then she'll smugly ride Divine back to the village, allowing Harif and the others to walk.

She doesn't, of course. Doesn't rise. Doesn't speak. The

only movement is a winged shadow that falls on her face. It takes effort for Harif to breathe.

"Let's go," says Adil.

Rafa calls out, then, though at first Harif thinks it must be *her* voice in his dreams. "Father?" she says.

With difficulty, he looks away from Faridah, toward his daughter. His grandchild is there, too. He shudders. Jammana must be protected from this. "Keep the child away," he says. Khalah nods, and swoops toward Jammana.

"What's happened? I want to go to Grandfather," Jammana is protesting. But Khalah, arms spread, shoos Jammana back toward the village as though she were a baby chick.

Adil's eyes are wide. "I did not know you were in Ein Fadr, Rafa," he says.

Rafa, striding forward, allows a disdainful glance to skim past Adil. "Father?" she asks again.

Harif stumbles over words. "Life is measured, Rafa, from the start. A precious swallow. No more."

Rafa studies him, puzzled.

"Then the cup is empty," he says. "The moment spent."

"What do you mean? What's happened?"

"But the ones who sin against Allah," Harif goes on, "will face a night black as tar. We must . . ." His body suddenly heavy, he drops to a squatting position. "We must take comfort in that," he says, head down.

Adil steps closer to Rafa. "The old man loves to talk in circles," he says in an intimate voice. "Look over there. Near the hill."

Rafa inches toward the area Adil indicated, then freezes.

"When, exactly, did you arrive in Ein Fadr?" Adil goes on.

Rafa turns. Her eyes, Harif sees, show incomprehension.

Harif rises. "My daughter, you must stay with her." He gestures to the vulture flying closer now, a little to the east.

Rafa groans. She wraps her arms tightly around her body.

"You have heard my wife is ill, surely?" Adil says. "Yet you did not come to visit?"

Rafa steps sideways, farther from Adil, Harif, and the shape on the ground. "How?" she asks, gagging as she speaks.

"I don't . . ." Harif shakes his head, unable to say more.

"It's not fitting that you failed to call on us," Adil says. "Have you heard I am to be the next *mukhtar*?"

Harif stares at Adil. "You have odd obsessions," he mutters.

Adil takes a deep breath, filling his chest with power. "Enough of this. Let's go." He is so dismissive. So young.

Rafa's elbows are pressed into her ribs. Her chin is on her chest. "You'll stay?" Harif asks her. After a moment, she nods without lifting her head.

Harif sets out after Adil. Just once, he pauses to look over his shoulder, to drink in Faridah. He knows, according to custom, he will not touch her again. He will not be allowed near. The women will prepare her, carry her, place her in her grave. This is his last look. After this, everything is never again.

Khalah must have alerted the village. All have been pulled to Moses' Finger as though the tree were a powerful magnet and the villagers tiny grains of iron. Not just the children, who might be expected to notice some excitement. Not only the women, whom the children would call first. The elders are here, the *mukhtar*, the farmers, streaming from the gardens and the hills and the mosque. Men still clutch their tools; women balance earthen jars against their hips. Babies doze, heads slumped on their mothers' shoulders. It's as though they have been summoned for a witnessing.

Let them gather, Harif thinks. Who should be accused is still unclear to him, but let them be ready to step forward and criticize the character of the guilty. He remembers witnessings of the past. A new mother who failed to return to her household duties quickly enough was brought before the villagers and punished, as were two brothers engaged in a disruptive argument over an inheritance. A baby finger was cut from the mother, and the two men had to give a year's worth of crops to the *mukhtar*. Whenever a witnessing is held here, the accused is always denounced and punishment always swift. There can be no mistaking the deep-seated intolerance of Ein Fadr. Now, with a death involved, Harif is sure retribution will be fast.

Harif sees Nabeel striding toward them. Adil grabs Harif's arm and tugs him forward. Harif tries to jerk from his hold, but the younger man is strong.

"Let him go," Nabeel orders, and Adil reluctantly obeys. Nabeel leans close to Harif, speaks so only he can hear. "I searched for you this morning. Why didn't you take your sheep to the fields?"

Harif looks at him wearily. "You know what's happened?" he asks. "How can you worry about my sheep now?"

Adil has reached Moses' Finger. He rests one hand on the old twisted trunk and speaks in a ponderous voice as though he were already the *mukhtar*—although it occurs to

Harif that Nabeel himself has never spoken this way. It sounds more like Nabeel's father.

"A woman came into our presence as a stranger-wife," Adil says. "Then she was no longer a wife, only a stranger. Still, she remained among us. At last she is gone." His words are formal and strangely practiced.

Murmurs set the leaves of Moses' Finger shivering. "What's happened?" a woman calls.

"That's why we are gathered," Adil says. "To find out." The men shuffle forward, making an inner half circle around Harif, Adil, and Nabeel. Many tuck their thumbs into the belts of their robes, waiting.

Harif cuts in. "My daughter. She's near the shrine. She needs help."

"Khalah has taken care of it," a man calls. "She gathered some women."

"So nothing further need distract us," Adil says. He seems to swell. "Harif, tell us. What occurred?"

Harif doesn't answer at first. Adil means nothing to him. He glances toward Nabeel, who nods, urging him to go on. Perhaps this is how Nabeel hopes to train his nephew to lead the village, though Harif disapproves of the timing. Still, he decides to reply. "We found her on the ground," he says. "Khalah and I. She was . . ." He swallows. "She was as you saw her yourself."

"And before that?"

"We were in Khalah's courtyard, and Manara came in. She—"

"No!" Adil cuts him off. "I mean, how did this happen to Faridah?"

Harif can't prevent his voice from rising in disgust. "How should I know?"

Adil looks around at the assembly, wide-eyed and half smiling, as though they share a joke. "You've forgotten? We know the truth, now. Your Bedouin told us. You have the ability to foresee. You have gifts even Mohammed couldn't have dreamed of. You know who did it. In fact, you've known many things that you've kept from us."

"Praise the Merciful. Adil speaks the truth," a man calls loudly. Others begin nodding and murmuring. "If he knows, let him tell."

Unconsciously, Harif steps back. "No," he says. "It's not like that."

"What *is* it like?" a farmer asks in a voice thick with sarcasm.

"It's finally time to be clear," adds another.

Harif always knew he would be punished for the falsehood the Bedouin exposed. He'd felt the shadow of the old *mukhtar,* Nabeel's father, taunting him from village alleyways, biding its time. But he could not have guessed payment would be exacted on Faridah's back. She's been taken, and now, if he can't satisfy his neighbors with an explanation for her death, they will brand him a lying, cursed mystic and expel him from their midst. What revenge that will be!

"Don't tell us you know nothing," Adil warns. "We are not so easily tricked this time."

Harif reaches in his pocket for his prayer beads. He touches them lightly, one by one, but he is not reciting Allah's names. He's trying to imagine Faridah in this crowd. What would she do? What would she urge him to do? He cannot imagine anyone killing her, but he could easily make a list of those who disliked her. What if he gives the name he wants to, and lets them all assume his gift informs his accusation? Will the others believe? Would his lie be so wrong? He tries to decide.

"You are silent?" Adil's tone is calculated, respectful in a way so clearly false that it becomes condescending. "Let me tell you what I know, then." He raises his voice so it can be heard by all. "You were arguing with Faridah two days ago, near the very place where she was killed today. You took her hand. She shook you off."

Harif examines him incredulously. "You were watching?"

Adil ignores the question. "You were angry."

Harif laughs, though weakly. "She's an infuriating woman. Intoxicating woman."

Adil smiles at him in a conspiratorial way, as though they shared that memory of Faridah. This brings Harif up sharp. No one understands Faridah as he did, certainly not Adil. This young man should stop pretending.

But Adil is talking again. "And so," he says, and he scans the crowd to make sure all are listening. "And so you acted."

Instantly, Hari comprehends Adil's meaning. In the name of Allah! Adil doesn't seek simply the name of a murderer. He seeks a confession.

Everything freezes. Harif, breathing deeply, notices the heavy, sour smell of assembled bodies. But he sees only Faridah's face, feels only the pulse of blood at his own temple. "We were as the salt to the sea," he says. "I hurt her, yes, but unintentionally. And not in this manner." His voice is low. He realizes he cannot be heard beyond the first row of faces.

"Unintentional?" Adil reaches into his pocket to re-trieve the glass shard and lift it above his head. "He slit Fari-dah's throat." He yells the last three words to the crowd.

Harif opens his mouth to deny. But he is halted by a fa-miliar voice, one he knows well, raised in an unending groan. A summons of distress he cannot ignore.

JAMMANA AND HARIF

Khalah's voice is hushed but insistent as she tells Jammana to wait, wait in the courtyard, not to go anywhere until they fetch her. Khalah's fingers rub obsessively at her blemish. Her cheeks are damp with perspiration. Something has happened, and Jammana is not to be told. As usual.

"Something bad?" Jammana demands for the fiftieth time.

Khalah answers in a rush. "Not now, *faraashe*." It's the first time Khalah has ever used Mama's nickname for Jammana. Her eyes skim back to the olive groves. "Soon."

"How soon?"

"You must keep your mind on these things," Khalah says quickly. "You are fine. So are your mama and father." She

bends to touch her cheek to Jammana's, and Jammana feels the moist warmth. "Plant those words. Tend to them. They must be enough until later." She nods as though satisfied with herself, and leaves the courtyard without a glance back. Disappears as thoroughly as the yeasty scent of the bread she baked this morning.

They are not enough, Khalah's meager words. Jammana wants to cry out in frustration for the litany of things she does not understand: the faltering tone of Khalah's voice, the nature of Faridah's secrets, the reasons grown-ups deceive. Her sketchiest memories of others' pasts are clearer than what is happening now. And worst of all, they decide that with an embrace, they can order her to wait.

Jammana counts silently to ten, then darts from the courtyard. No sign of Khalah, but she hears voices coming from the village center. She runs.

The villagers are gathered beneath the broad arms of Moses' Finger. The men are in close and tight like the seed of a fruit; women and children sprawl around them as flesh and skin. Jammana searches but cannot find Khalah. Nor Mama. Then she spots Grandfather's friend, the Bedouin who threatened Faridah. He does not notice her. He is rubbing his hands; he looks troubled.

She pushes forward, hoping to find Grandfather among the men. They're pinched together so tightly she has to struggle to reach the front. With effort she shoves her head between two elbows. And there he is, facing everyone, his skin pale as bone, his eyes empty, his mouth slack.

Jammana must reach him and tug his arm, weave her fingers through his beard. Then he will smile and stroke her short hair and be well again. And when she insists, he will tell her what has happened. Her breathing quickens as she inches forward.

A voice cuts the air. A man holds something aloft in one hand and points at Grandfather with the other—the man with brash eyes who she remembers from Grandfather's courtyard when the Bedouin visited.

"He slit Faridah's throat."

Faridah. Slit. Throat. Grandfather blurs, and the words float, their meaning unclear. She thinks of Asima's neck. Of screaming eyes. Of arms spread to block her view.

Who did *what* to Faridah? As the question forms in her mind, she sees Father. He is swooping toward her, falling in her direction. She feels the warm pressure of his hand covering her mouth but—thankfully—leaving her nose free. Only then does she realize she's been moaning. With a great effort, she stills her noise to a hum, low notes like the call of the *muezzin*.

"What are you doing here?" Father hisses into her ear.

That man with the unpleasant eyes was mistaken. It wasn't Faridah. Faridah will be back by afternoon to explain Mama's birth. "She hasn't told me everything yet," Jammana says to Father.

"Take the child," someone calls.

Father grips her arm, and they move as a single, uncoordinated body until they reach the outer wall of a home. Jammana searches the crowd, looking for Faridah.

"Go to Harif's courtyard," Father orders. "Stay there until I summon you."

Jammana stares at Father. "Where is she?" Jammana demands. "What are they doing to Grandfather? I heard something but—it was wrong."

Father rocks on his feet, awkward. "Child," he says at last, "we cannot talk now. I am needed under Moses' Finger."

"It was wrong, about Faridah. Wasn't it?"

Father goes on as if he hasn't heard her. "You are old enough to go by yourself to Harif's courtyard and wait. We will explain everything, your mother and I. Later."

Jammana glances at the crush of villagers around Moses' Finger, the tree rising above them like a threat or a promise. She looks back at Father. She must know what has happened. But she has learned from the grown-ups, and it is time to put those lessons to work. "Fine," she answers. "Yes. Of course. Grandfather's courtyard."

"Good," he says. "That's my daughter." Still, he scrutinizes her as though trying to gauge her sincerity.

She steps away from him, walking backward. "If they need you," she says, her face lowered in compliance, "don't delay."

He hesitates, then nods, and strides off. Raising her head, Jammana watches him merge with the women at one side of the crowd, then slip past them into the knot of men. After a moment she no longer can see him, only the backs of others. She darts to the opposite edge of the gathering and begins to push her way to the front again.

"You've made your points, Adil," Nabeel is saying. "Now, let Harif speak."

"I've offered him a chance—" begins Adil.

"Quiet," Nabeel interrupts.

Harif's dizziness is replaced by a floating, weary calm.

Rafa is not here, and Ahmed has led Jammana away. Faridah is gone, too. So they will not have to bear whatever is to come, whatever it shall be.

The *fellahin* wait for Harif. But when he opens his mouth to speak, he becomes thick-tongued as a thirsty man, the way he was when he lost his way in the desert. *Ya*, how he would welcome the rough hands of the Bedouin now, lifting him, carrying him to a tent to sleep! If only he could return to that moment in Arudi al-Salman's encampment, when he had just been rescued and was dense with relief and possibilities.

He thinks, then, of the many times he has seen these men slaughter his sheep. Before holidays, weddings, when special guests arrive. The flesh is cooked, the blood used to polish the dirt floors of Ein Fadr's homes. Hours in advance, his sheep sense what is coming. They hear the scratching of knives being readied, perhaps, or smell the villagers' pungent anticipation. They stare at him with sharp, accusing eyes, and he is sure they comprehend that he is the one who selects, that the men always ask him—which one? Because he knows which are too old with toughened meat, which still have breeding years ahead. Which are too thin beneath their full coats. And which one is ready. Ready for the knife. Sometimes they struggle once he's pointed his finger. But it is useless to fight. It is to no purpose.

"He says nothing," Adil mutters.

"But someone must speak in his defense," Nabeel says. "Otherwise, this is not a proper witnessing. Where is Rafa's husband?" Harif's gaze is drawn to a movement in the crowd, a rustle. Some men move aside. There stands Ahmed. Harif is sure he is gloating. "Step forward," Nabeel says. "Tell us where you spent the night."

Ahmed clears his throat. "In Harif's home," he says after a moment.

"I saw him there." Nabeel looks toward his villagers as though to make sure they are paying attention. Then he turns back to Ahmed. "And this morning?"

"We went outside together. Khalah was baking bread."

Nabeel nods. "And you stayed together the whole time?" Harif is touched, remotely, by a hopeful tone he detects in Nabeel's voice.

"No." Ahmed's voice is hard. "He went to fetch water."

Harif would like a drink of water now; his throat feels parched. Better yet, coffee. Yes, that's what he would like. To be sitting in a *wadi*, preparing coffee.

"How long was he gone?" Adil asks.

Ahmed examines his wrist. "Maybe half an hour," he says. "Perhaps forty-five minutes."

Adil's brow wrinkles. It is clear that he has only the vaguest idea of the sort of time Ahmed is discussing. Ahmed wears the only watch in the village. "As long as it takes to plow three rows, would you say?" Adil asks.

Ahmed considers the question. "Yes, perhaps."

"So." Adil's voice holds a ring of satisfaction. He holds up the violet piece of glass again.

And Harif hears the scratching of knives, smells anticipation.

Jammana pushes close to the man holding the shard of glass. He doesn't notice her. He is looking over her head. His lips are curved in a silly smile.

"What are you doing to Grandfather?" she asks him. She turns to face the villagers. "Why do you allow this?" she calls. "Where is Faridah?"

Only then does Adil glance down. "Who is this child?" he asks. "Oh yes, Rafa's. Will one of the women lead her away?"

Jammana feels hands on her arms again as she is pulled and passed back to the part of the crowd where women and children stand. And though she shouldn't accept the way Adil treats her, she doesn't resist this time because, staring at Adil's face, she's had a sudden realization. When they finally let go of her, she turns to the woman next to her. "The violet glass," she mumbles in confusion. "But how? How could I dream the future? That's what Grandfather does. *I* remember the past."

"Hush, child," the woman whispers.

"No, I have to . . ." Jammana breaks off. She kneels, holding her stomach. She knows now that she failed Faridah. Failed her completely. Grandfather is still here, however, still in need. She presses her palms to her temples, trying to think.

Someone calls her name. She rises and turns with relief. Mama! Her eyes are glazed, her face streaked with dust, her fingernails chipped and dirty, but it is Mama nonetheless. Jammana flings herself against Mama's chest, but Mama firmly pushes her away. "Someone . . ." Mama begins, then breaks off.

Jammana already knows; but what she knows cannot be right. "Can't they make Faridah better?" she mumbles. "Maybe Father could . . . ?" She knows her question sounds foolish. Still, perhaps there's a chance.

"No," Mama says.

Jammana's stomach clenches again. Nothing could have happened to Faridah. Not her. Not someone that strong. Jammana grips Mama's skirt, leans heavily.

Father has seen death hundreds of times. Many are the evenings when he has returned home from the hospital to disappear into the parlor. Jammana would hear him pacing. After dinner, he would try to lift his spirits by recounting for Jammana how modern medicine had put an end to the grimmest days, when illness could devour dozens under a single moon. "In those times," he told her, "the Nablus valley would often glow with dung fires lit to signal mortality gone out of control. Of course, Allah still takes men when He must, but He is slower at it, allowing us a few more chances."

Father smells metallic and sterile, so that is the scent Jammana has always associated with death, the scent that makes her afraid. But the odor that now lingers around Mama, she realizes—the sour smell of perspiration and urine—must be what truly emanates from the newly departed.

"They didn't know what to make of her," Mama is saying in a stiff voice. "She offended everyone. She had no family to protect her." Mama shakes her head. "Your grandfather," she says. "Where is he?"

Her words jar Jammana, bring her back to the moment at hand. "They're blaming him," she says. "You must stop them."

"Blaming?" Mama looks at Jammana directly for the first time. "Him?"

"For Faridah," Jammana says as Mama hugs herself

tighter. Jammana reaches to shake Mama's shoulders. "They'll listen to you, Mama! Tell them."

Mama sways as though she might fall to the ground. She groans. "A village of retributions," she mumbles. "A cursed village. There's no restraining them."

Mama is too stunned to act, and if Jammana waits for Mama's recovery, it will be too late. She straightens and approaches a pair of women. She stands in front of them. She takes a deep breath. "The men are lying."

The women exchange looks.

Jammana tries again. "You know Grandfather," she says. "He's Harif of the *taboon*. Alula's son." One woman nods slowly, uncertainly. "Grandfather wouldn't hurt Faridah," Jammana says. "It's time. Time to speak up."

Jammana moves on. She weaves through the outer layer of villagers, taking her message to each woman. "It's a lie," she says. "Go stop them." She doesn't wait for replies.

"I found the glass right next to her," Adil is saying. "Blood everywhere."

Harif will try not to listen further to Adil. That, he decides, is what Faridah would advise. He is aware of fatigue pulsing through his forehead. He's argued with these men, one way or another, for long years of his life. *Go ahead, eat from the bowl*, he thinks. *Empty it, all of you. Leave it bare.*

Adil is still talking. The villagers, Harif sees, are intent. They swell out with a raspy noise, then draw in deeper, a breath inhaled.

"We must consider carefully," Adil says. "After all, she's been among the *jinn* for years. Besides, there is no family to pay blood wages. And don't forget, it is lawful to hew a tree which fails to bear fruit."

What utter nonsense he speaks, but it occurs to Harif to wonder at how carefully Adil has thought it all out.

"Still," one man calls, "he must be punished."

"Granted," agrees Adil. "We cannot allow it to stand. *How* to punish is the question."

More muttering—the men arguing among themselves, Harif thinks. Then he realizes the current sound comes from behind the men, like the wind gathering force. The women. Separate, overlapping voices.

"No."

"Stop this nonsense, Nabeel."

"Harif did not do this."

"Be silent," Adil calls. "This is a matter for the men."

The women are pushing forward. Never before has Harif seen them step in front of their men during a gathering at Moses' Finger. But this time, with eyes and hands, each hushes her own husband, her own sons. The men wait, watching Adil. They seem to sense their women's determination. Better to let Adil accomplish their needs and allow peace to reign in their own homes.

"Back to your places," Adil calls.

The women do not move. Children press forward now, emboldened by their mothers. One barefoot toddler sucking his thumb stands in the front, staring curiously.

"Some must clean the body," Adil says. "Others make burial clothes."

A woman passes a whimpering infant to her husband's arms before she pushes closer. Others follow.

Adil glances at Nabeel with a look of entreaty, but Nabeel is silent. Harif scans the crowd and sees his grand-daughter back among them. He closes his eyes, ashamed before her. Ashamed to be so discarded. And knowing it means that she, too, will find no haven here. She'll be a descendant of the impure.

"Let Harif go," one woman says. "Then we'll bury our midwife."

"Let him go?" Adil laughs uneasily. "Yes, his clan has lived in this village for countless generations. But we always uproot evil wherever we find it. That's why Ein Fadr survives."

"He is innocent," a woman calls.

"He lied to us for years," Adil says. "Why is it so difficult to believe that he has killed?"

Jammana's voice is heard above others. "Because Grand-father loved Faridah." She pronounces each word clearly.

"Can't someone remove my granddaughter?" Harif murmurs to Nabeel and Adil.

"Sisters, gather yourselves," Adil demands.

There's a movement at the front of the crowd. Ahmed pushes through and strides toward Adil. "I can help," he says. "I was at the death site, waiting by Faridah's donkey. I heard my wife wailing and went to her. That's when I examined the body. She'd been dead an hour maybe, no more. Give me a moment. Perhaps I can put this issue to rest."

Harif detests his son-in-law's tone, his all-knowing arrogance. Still, he doesn't resist as Ahmed steps forward to take his hands. He is past resisting.

Ahmed stares at Harif, expressionless. Then he turns Harif's palms up. He brings them close to his face and studies them, sniffs them. Nabeel motions the villagers to step back from Moses' Finger. "Give him some room," he says.

Ahmed is mute. He inspects Harif's right palm first, then each finger. Next he concentrates on the left hand, smoothing it with his own. He bends the fingers so he can look beneath Harif's nails. At last he releases Harif. He straightens his neck and shoulders, nods, and turns to face assembled Ein Fadr.

"The women," he says with unmatched confidence, "are right."

Adil grunts, shakes his head. "Though you are Rafa's husband," he says loudly, "you are an outsider to us. We don't believe in guilt or innocence writ on palms. Under the eyes of Allah, I don't wish to insult you. But one of our mothers should be serving you coffee while we, the men of Ein Fadr, attend to this matter."

Several men murmur agreement. Ahmed ignores them. "You think this was used to kill her," he points to the glass, now held in Adil's lowered hand. He shakes his head. "Maim, perhaps. Not kill."

"You were there?" Adil asks arrogantly. Harif realizes that he and Adil are, for an odd moment, in accord in their dislike of Ahmed. It is an amusing thought.

Nabeel yanks Harif closer. "Don't smile," he hisses in Harif's ear.

"I'm a doctor," Ahmed says. "The cut in her neck was not deep enough to have killed her. Her throat was cut afterward."

These foolish men. This ridiculous conversation—as

though any of it mattered. Harif can't wait to tell Faridah about it.

But of course, he won't be able to. That realization takes his breath away.

"Allah Himself knows there would have been more blood if her heart had still been beating." Ahmed hesitates a moment. "She also has a large bump on her head."

A murmur runs through the crowd. Adil looks momentarily confused but struggles to maintain control. "So then Harif—"

Ahmed holds up a hand. "You will argue that Harif struck her on the head and then slashed her throat." He nods. "This is feasible."

"Ridiculous," several women call. Harif hears Rafa's voice among them.

Ahmed goes on. "But even this did not cause her death."

"What, then?" Nabeel asks, impatience creeping into his tone.

"A plant. A desert flower."

Adil sucks in a short breath. Then he looks out to the men, sarcasm painted on his face. Some laugh.

"Star of Bethlehem, I believe," Ahmed adds coolly.

Harif knows the bulb. Hannan always admired its stunning white flowers, but Harif has been wary of it ever since one of his lambs ate of it and died.

Some men are chuckling uneasily, now, others arguing with their women. Children, hearing the overlapping voices of their parents, grow restive. The noise is rising to the level of a harvesting party. But when Ahmed speaks, the villagers fall quiet.

"Her lips," Ahmed says. "That's the proof. Faridah's lips

were stained. It probably took only a few sips and a few minutes. Star of Bethlehem works with enormous strength and speed. Someone knocked her out with a rock, I'd say, then poured the juice from the bulbs into her mouth." He adjusts his wire-rimmed glasses with one hand. "The poison is what killed her. I don't know why her throat was cut afterward."

Adil shifts uncomfortably, then straightens. "Harif must have done it all," he says with a shrug.

"In that case," Ahmed says slowly, "his hands would be tinged from grinding the bulbs. At least slightly. The juice must be fresh in order to kill, and the stain is strong enough to last for days. But Harif's hands are absolutely clean."

"So," says Nabeel with finality. "Harif did nothing wrong."

Adil looks confused. Harif himself is struggling to digest the fact that this detested son-in-law has exonerated him. The men surrounding them have grown still, waiting. Everything seems frozen. Harif hears the sound of his own breath.

"Then," a woman calls at last, "let's examine everyone's hands."

Jammana, who has been standing near Arudi al-Salman, feels the Bedouin whirl suddenly and stride from the crowd. She turns to watch him go, and sees Khalah pushing to the front, her cheeks still flushed. "I don't know what has happened here," Khalah calls once she reaches Moses' Finger, "but we have no time for it. We have two graves to excavate."

"Two?" someone asks.

Khalah nods. "Baraka."

"Baraka too?" an old woman mutters. "What evil is at work here?"

Jammana strains to follow a confusion of sound: lamentations to Allah, ululations of sorrow, the ripping of a dress. The man Adil, Baraka's husband and Grandfather's chief accuser, covers his face with his hands. His shoulders shake. He steps back, moves behind Nabeel.

"I need help." Khalah spreads her arms.

"Check him before he goes," one woman calls to Khalah.

"Who?" Khalah asks.

"Adil. See if his hands—"

"He's gone," someone else says.

"His hands," Grandfather calls, "are unstained. I saw them." Jammana notices that Grandfather's voice quivers slightly.

"We worry now over dirty hands?" Khalah shakes her head. "The day is lengthening. If we don't honor these women, the sin will be writ on each of our ledgers."

The women turn to leave, a few still trilling or crying. "We'll need some of the men to excavate the graves," Khalah is saying. "As Faridah had no family here, we'll bury her near Alula's shrine."

Still the men remain in place.

"Nabeel?" Khalah appeals.

At last the *mukhtar* nods, and the men stir and depart, mumbling.

Jammana heads for Grandfather. Mama is already by his side. "Come," Mama implores.

Grandfather shakes his head. "I'll help prepare the grave. Then I must pray."

He takes a step toward the olive groves. Mama blocks his way. "Let the others. You're exhausted."

"Don't ask that of me, Rafa," Grandfather answers.

Jammana hugs Grandfather. She pulls his head down to hers. "You're free now," she says softly.

He is stiff, unresponsive. She tugs on his beard, hard. But if his chin hurts, he doesn't show it. "The past, Jammana," he says at last, not quite meeting her eyes. "Help me dream it."

HARIF

The quiet. So dense that Harif, sitting on his roof with only Allah between him and the top of the sky, imagines his ears plugged with cotton, as Faridah's are. His mouth hushed by the very weight of the earth. As is hers. After a night of ululations and chanting, it seems right that silence sweep through the wound of morning. The rising of the sun is the sacrilege.

The village is empty now, or nearly so. The *taboons* are cold, baskets left unwoven, and wheat unground. The women departed before sunrise, their voices a low drone, their glances preoccupied and wary. They hold vigil today to ease the loneliness of the dead. They will sit first at one grave, then at the other until nightfall, sharing their stories with the departed, eating bread and figs, singing the mourning songs. They brought their children, in arms or grasping skirts, even the little ones silent, large-eyed. Jammana, holding Rafa's hand, glanced toward Harif as she passed, and shot up her arm in greeting. He'd waved back.

Not long after light reached Ein Fadr, the men hurried to the fields. They walked with short, fast steps and lowered eyes of concealment. Harif, sitting on his roof, watched them go. No gaze met his.

Last night, Harif carried a pile of stones up to the roof. Now, from time to time, he tosses one into the courtyard and observes it bruise the earth with a satisfying thud. The only other sound comes from Harif's sheep. They are grumbling, impatient to graze. Ahmed paces near them. It is partly to escape his officious flow of words that Harif has remained above.

From his perch, Harif sees Nabeel stride into the courtyard. He greets Ahmed, then motions Harif to come down. Harif doesn't move at first. He allows himself a few heartbeats more in relative peace. As he rises at last, he notices his lower back aches. His legs tremble with exhaustion. Haltingly, he descends the outdoor steps, aware of Nabeel studying him and then looking away out of what must be, Harif decides, a sense of guilt.

"Let me take the animals today," Nabeel says, spreading his hands, his voice sonorous. "I will send them out with the boys."

"Which?" Harif asks evenly.

Nabeel raises his eyebrows in puzzlement. "All of them."

"Which," Harif repeats, "of yours did it?"

Nabeel's face tightens in anger. "You blame me when

I've tried only to help?" He raises an arm, gesturing to the sky. "In the name of the Beneficent, you're a difficult man." He sighs heavily before speaking again. "What is writ on His forehead must be. None can prevent it. You know that better than anyone."

"Don't blame Allah!" Harif presses his fingers between his eyes. His forehead is clammy. "Men carried out this death," he says. "And you are the one who knew the future."

A haggard dog darts into the courtyard like a shiver, swings his head right and left, then turns heel. Nabeel rubs the back of his neck and smoothes the cloth of his robe over his stomach. His eyes look as though he's had as little sleep as Harif. "It's the day after the funerals," he says. "Allah Himself would honor us for pausing before trying to assign blame."

Harif steps closer. "Adil didn't do it. At least not alone." His voice sounds raspy to his own ears. "His hands were clean."

Nabeel looks toward Ahmed as though seeking commiseration. "I should have expected this," he mutters, "but I didn't. I thought he could help calm the villagers."

"Calm them?" Ahmed asks.

Nabeel nods. "Some want me to inspect each palm and question each man publicly. A handful think Baraka's death is suspicious, too. Four men came to me this morning to complain their wives won't even lie with them. It's going too far."

Harif removes his prayer beads from his pocket. "Faridah was right," he says. "You see through the eyes of your father."

The space between Nabeel's eyebrows narrows. "If you mean I did not admire her, that's right. She was a branch lopped off a distant tree, blown here to litter our alleys."

Harif, gathering strength, steps toward him, but Nabeel holds up a hand. "Still, if you think I'd sit by and allow her to be killed, you understand nothing. I live by Allah's laws."

"Then tell me."

Nabeel doesn't shift his gaze. "Do you lead a donkey, or does it lead you?" he asks. "There is much about which I am not informed. Much which avoids me."

Harif grabs the shoulder of Nabeel's *jallabiya*. "I don't care to balance facts on a camel's neck. I just want to know." He shoves his face closer to Nabeel's, hoping to frighten the truth out of him. "Clean your eyes. Look at the women. The distrust in their faces. This will hang over Ein Fadr. Eventually it will stink up every home, cripple us all. If you don't punish the killers, Faridah will damage this village more in death than she ever could have in life."

Nabeel squints, seeming to consider. "Let me go," he says at last. Harif releases the cloth of his robe. Nabeel glances at Ahmed. "There are several possibilities."

Harif nods. "I've already thought of the one suggested by Ahmed."

"*I* suggested?" asks Ahmed.

Harif doesn't take his eyes off Nabeel as he answers. "The villagers say a *ghouleh* must be killed three times before she dies. Someone pounded her head, fed her poison, and slit her throat. Three times." He turns slightly aside and spits on the ground.

"But how do we know it was a villager?" Nabeel asks smoothly.

"Who, then?"

"Anybody." Nabeel gestures east to west. "Others have

always passed by the shrine, and now there is movement through all of Judea and Samaria. Jordanian captains in Jeeps. Our own distant neighbors on donkeys. Your Bedouin friend and his brothers who are camped outside the village. Any of them could have done it."

"But why kill an old woman gathering herbs?" asks Ahmed.

"It's a violent time," Nabeel says. "Every group is quarreling with another. Revenge is exacted in unlikely places."

Harif stares at the prayer beads that lie in the palm of his hands. "So wickedness from elsewhere drifted near our village. That's the story you'll offer? That's how you'll bury our sins?"

"Yes, it is what I'll tell the villagers tonight." Nabeel takes a deep breath. "And it's what I believe. If you think there's a chance it happened that way, you should persuade the women. Because agitation will not help us now."

"I won't be your messenger." Harif turns away. "This village consumed Faridah, and now it's consuming you."

Nabeel looks out to the fields, his face unreadable. "All this passion of yours—it's not only about who killed her. I know that." He pauses, moves a hand to his heart. "But hear me, Harif. She was not of us. Never like us. And it's always best to be with one's own. So you should have no regrets about your choices. You made the right decision, the only one."

"You know nothing about right."

Nabeel stiffens. His voice becomes formal. "Let me take the flock for you," he repeats.

Harif walks to the side of his lead sheep. *"Ya-aaaah."* His voice breaks. He forces himself to resume. *"Ya-aaaah-ah-yaaaa looooooh li."* Hearing his signal, the sheep stir.

They move quickly, Harif and his animals—the sheep driven forward by the subtle scent of green, Harif pushed by a desire for what once was.

When they reach a field, the sheep scatter, no longer interested in their master. He stands straight among them, not seeking shade. As he looks skyward, he realizes he doesn't think of Faridah's essence as resting where the rain is born. He believes not only her body but her very soul is with this earth.

He kneels, bows his face to the dirt, and inhales her. Faridah. He lies, belly flattened to the ground, fingers digging grooves in the dry soil, dust coating his lips. He has the sudden sense that he is responsible for what happened, though he cannot understand at first where the thought comes from.

Nabeel is right: Part of his despair stems from his recognition of his own weakness. In the end, when death comes, it will not matter what status he held—whether outcast or *mukhtar*. And as for the haven he'd hoped to preserve for his only child, she soon will be living in America. Allah save him! Faridah forgive him! To keep his family's meager place in this village, he allowed her to slip from his grasp. She already was the outcast. He refused to join her.

Lying in the dirt, he tries to pardon himself. He acted for the right reasons, surely. He sought acceptance not just for himself but for the memory of his clan, the future of his daughter and granddaughter.

But his pleading rings hollow.

Suddenly, within the dirt, he recognizes the scent not only of Faridah, but of Alula and Bahir and even the old *mukhtar* who hated him so. The earth is tied more loosely than man to the rules of time, and its memory is broader. Finally, each story loses its singular importance and combines as one. Each victory crumbles and merges with loss.

Harif notices the wetness of his cheek. It shouldn't be so hard for an old man to control his emotions. Strange about this aging. It has left him only unclad and ignorant.

Crippled by a vast absence, a departure as binding as Alula's, Harif remains at the field until mid-morning. Then he hurries his flock because he wants to be back before any *fellahin* return from the gardens for the noon meal. He doesn't want to meet anyone. He doesn't want anyone to see his shame.

Harif summons the sheep into the courtyard, and they file obediently into the room below his. Only then does he notice Ahmed, sitting in the corner as though he hasn't moved all day.

"Coffee?" asks Ahmed.

Harif shakes his head. Coffee is too dear to be tasted right now. "I owe you thanks."

Ahmed raises his eyebrows in question, although Harif is sure Ahmed knows what he refers to, and even if Ahmed doesn't, this is as much as Harif can manage for now.

"I think," Ahmed says at last, "the *mukhtar* would have interceded if I hadn't."

Harif feels an intense need to lie down. He starts for the door.

"Wait." Ahmed's edgy voice interrupts. He speaks quickly. "We must leave. Soon. I don't want Rafa and Jammana trapped in this."

"In what?"

"What the *mukhtar* spoke of this morning. The villagers are in no mood for generosity. I want my family removed from this—animosity."

"We make our own choices," Harif says wearily. "If my daughter will go with you, I will not interfere."

"But Rafa would be more willing if you were to come with us," Ahmed says. "To Nablus, for a visit of a few days while we finish our preparations to leave the country. Nothing more."

Harif does not have the strength for this. "Later," he says with a wave of his hand as he heads for the door of his home. But before he can reach it, Khalah strides into the courtyard, her face taut.

"Come." She tugs on Harif's arm.

"Khalah," he says, "I am heavy. I didn't sleep all night."

"Ahmed," Khalah says, "Rafa and Jammana will be home soon." She begins to drag Harif as though he were a recalcitrant child.

"I don't want to see anyone," Harif says. "I need rest." She doesn't glance at his face, let alone acknowledge his words. At last he gives up and allows himself to be led. "Will there be no end to this day?" he mutters.

It takes him a moment to realize which way she is taking

him. Along which path. Lined with which memories. He stiffens his legs. "I do not want to go." Khalah yanks harder. She is breathing in rapid pants from the effort of pulling him forward. "I'll find no comfort in this place, if that's what you're hoping," he warns after a moment, but she doesn't answer.

At last he hears a tremble of noise ahead. All the village women, it seems, are here. At Alula's shrine. The boulders women lean against have been shoved over the hole where the earth breathes, suffocating the soil like a hand over a mouth. The shrine's centerpiece, the stump, has been yanked from the ground. It is chipped, as if someone tried to chop it to pieces and then gave up, discovering it to be stone now, instead of wood. Women are pulling it upright again, smoothing it with their hands. Soothing hands. But harsh words, he can tell by the guttural sounds.

Staring at the stump, he relives the day he found Alula here. Once again he is running through the fields, knowing what he will find yet not allowing himself to know. He is lost in the mindless impulse of needing one's mother. "Who," he whispers, "would do this?"

No one answers. Women he has known all his life meet his gaze. Some look curious, others cold. He sees Rafa, inscrutable. Next to her stands Jammana. He sees the hostile faces of the other women, their knotted fists. Some have shed their headdresses. Others have tied up their sleeves, revealing the length of muscled arms. The air smells of rosemary and jasmine and dry clay. The women step closer, grow silent, eyeing Harif. He is deeply aware of being the only man there.

He takes a step forward, stumbles. "How could they do this?" he asks, directing his words at Rafa and Jammana, who stand at the edge of the group. He looks over his shoulder at

Khalah, as though she might be the translator of a strange language.

"It happened when the sun was straight above," Khalah says. "Most of us were at Baraka's grave. Others went back to the village long enough to set their daughters to cooking the evening meal. When we returned to Faridah, we found this. We did not see who was bold enough to sneak behind our backs, quiet as a snake. You must go to Nabeel. Tell him we want whoever did this."

Then many speak at once.

"This has to stop."

"Let Allah see the wrongs made right."

"No," an older woman disagrees, her voice loud.

"Best leave it alone," says another. "Say not a word, and hope this evil will leave our village."

"It is the work of a man."

"The work of a spirit."

The women argue among themselves, their voices braided together, lifting skyward. Overnight, they have been transformed from the sap that binds the village to a force within it.

Khalah turns to him. She doesn't speak loudly, but at the command of her voice, the others fall quiet. "Go to Nabeel," she says again.

Jammana steps forward. "Grandfather," she says, "these women helped you. Now you must help them."

Harif pulls Jammana close, kisses the top of her head. He looks up at the others, struggles to speak. "Nabeel blames someone from outside the village for Faridah's death," he manages. "Someone wandering past the shrine."

"And someone from outside did this, too?" a woman asks. "To our shrine? To your mother?"

"It's what he will say." Harif feels an exhaustion deeper than any he has ever known, a failure more far-reaching. "He won't listen. He will not listen."

Rafa steps away from him, her arms folded around her. The silence ferments. Harif looks at those around him. Tight faces, puckered inward.

Khalah leans toward him. "Go, now," she murmurs into his ear.

"Khalah—"

"I thought you might be able to help," she says with resignation. "You can't. Best leave."

He backs away. He knows Khalah trusts him. Surely Jammana and Rafa, too, though they seem so distant now. But not these others, not really. He has broken the rules for too long. Been neither one sort of person nor another. The fate he hoped to escape by refusing Faridah has become his anyway. Men, women—he is disconnected from them all.

Nabeel speaks that evening at Moses' Finger. Many villagers wear amulets against the evil eye, fragments of the Koran written on paper dangling on their chests. Most of the women stand scattered, apart from their husbands. Jammana surprises Harif—she comes to take his hand. She doesn't smile or meet his gaze. Nevertheless, Harif feels her strength passing into him. He thinks of the two of them as a bridge. Male to female. Past to future.

"Abandon your suspicions. It was not one of us who killed her," Nabeel is saying. "Baraka's death, too, was Allah's will. It's not our place to question the movement of the sun." He does not mention the destruction at Alula's shrine.

After he speaks, Khalah steps to the front. "We must find a way back," she says. "I'll bring bread to each of your homes tonight so that we eat together."

The men nod their heads, pleased. The faces of the women are blank as sand.

In their courtyard, Khalah begins to mix and bake, beads of sweat at her temples, her eyebrows merging above her nose. That night, the women serve her bread. The men eat heartily, confident that their wives and daughters soon will see the need for harmony, that all this has been a brief disruption, an overnight, overwrought windstorm.

Only Harif is suspicious. Khalah does not meet his gaze when she delivers the bread to him. "Eat, Harif," she murmurs. He wraps the bread in cotton cloth, leaves it next to a pile of stones.

He sleeps on the roof that night. Khalah, Rafa, and Jammana bed inside below. Ahmed lies in the courtyard.

Harif wakes suddenly to a sound soft as a spider shifting in her web. He turns over, not wishing to be roused. The wind whistles too shrilly, a warning. He rises to see a shadow shift in the tiny alleys that run between the courtyards of Ein Fadr.

One person. A girl. At first he doesn't recognize her, because she moves like olive oil poured on flesh, and normally Jammana bounds from place to place. But it is surely his granddaughter. He identifies the shape of her childish shoulders, the outline of her short, frizzy hair. She seems to carry a bundle in front of her.

Jammana might be delivering something, but what, at this hour? And wouldn't Rafa run such an errand instead of Jammana? Then Jammana glides out of sight. He stands perfectly still and listens. The hoot of a screech owl, nothing more. He shakes his head. Perhaps he has dreamed the daughter of his daughter passing in the night. Allah knows he is tired to his very core.

He is about to lie back down when he sees a flash of light in the charcoal sky. It grows and lengthens like fury. Wafts of milk rise. Harif is confused. Who has lit a large lantern? Who has sent a mother's milk afloat?

Then he understands. Moses' Finger is burning.

JAMMANA

Jammana scissors through the night, propelled by an impulse she cannot name. She doesn't stumble. She doesn't think. She's aware, only just, of a door's weight, of collapsing into a room, sinking into the scent of donkey hair and damp earth, olives and herbs. Divine is gone, taken into Khalah's care. Otherwise, all is as it has been. She rests head on knees. She waits. It doesn't take long.

A donkey's reluctance. A branch's snap. She is pleased to slip so easily into Faridah's past. The memories drench her. *A scent of rosemary, slowly fading. A sense of being watched, instantly dismissed. An old longing, quickly shed.* It comforts Jammana. Perhaps she can carry these images to Grandfather, too, as a gift. *A bird's call, a flash of glass.* But now a shift, like a spring shower turned menacing. *Unexpected faces, guilt already in their eyes.* Jammana raises her hands to push away the past, and finds she has no control. *A bolt of comprehension.* Stop, she demands. No more! *A stone brought down upon a skull.*

Then a partially formed question—*what sort of Allah . . . ?*—and it's over, and Jammana finds herself holding Faridah's shawl in her arms. She wants to cover herself with it. She wants to vanish into sleep and wake with this horror removed. She lies, eyes shut, and stays for the few minutes it takes to understand that relief will not be found here.

Without a clear goal, she begins to gather Faridah's clothing. A mere armful in all: two shirts, a skirt, sandals, a pair of stockings. She hears Faridah's voice. *If you think to frighten me, you know nothing of my spirit.* She moves to the stockpile of herbs, opens a bag, inhales. *Stay here, fury. Until I need you.* She dumps the herbs into the skirt and folds it into a bundle. At the door, she hesitates, searches the room. *There is only one. Only one person you can be sure of, mine of mine.* "You're wrong, Faridah," Jammana says aloud. She tucks the earthen container of olive oil under her arm, takes the matches Faridah used to light her fires, and points herself down Ein Fadr's alleyways.

Jammana is aware of the importance of Moses' Finger in this village, but that means little to her. She has a fondness of her own for the mulberry, which reminds her of the lemon tree she climbs in her backyard in Nablus. So when she arrives, her first thought is an apology. She touches the trunk, presses her cheek against the dry bark. She is surprised to find that Moses' Finger smells of tomatoes turned acid. Perhaps, then, it already is ill inside, even dying.

She pours the oil on Faridah's clothes, arranges them in a circle around the tree, and adds the herbs. She places Asima on the pile as well before striking first one match, then another. The bark catches quickly, and Jammana starts to thank Allah for the long dry season, then finds she can't. The flames stab upward, rumble a warning.

Her fire is the sole bright streak on the stain of night. The air turns sour and smoky, like the scent of birth in a tiny room. *How pleased Faridah will be.*

"Under Allah's eyes! Jammana, what have you done?" Grandfather's voice slices the night, causing Jammana to jump. By firelight, his face seems a pale moon. He brushes past. "Hurry! We must quench it." He begins stomping on the flames. "Get water, quick." Jammana uses both hands to grip his arm, but he shakes her off. "Hurry! You see how the flames fly? Oh, what this will bring upon our heads."

"Grandfather! Do you still care so much what they think?"

Grandfather slows, unmasked. Then he shakes his head. "It's not only me." He turns back to the flames and resumes stomping.

Jammana must tell him quickly, but carefully. And only partially. "I know who did it," she says. "I know."

He stops to stare at her, eyes black.

"She heard a sound and turned." Jammana hurries her words. "They stood behind her. Two I couldn't see clearly, but the one in front—"

"Yes?" He chokes out the question, his body stiff.

"The husband of the dead woman."

"Adil." Grandfather rummages in his pocket, pulling out his prayer beads. He bows his head as though speaking to the beads themselves. "I will kill him. I will go to him tonight, while he sleeps. I will—"

"No, Grandfather. This is better."

"Burning a tree? From where would you gather such an idea, child?" Grandfather shakes his head. "I want his life."

"But isn't this what Faridah would want?"

Grandfather sinks down, sagging, and Jammana knows she is right not to tell him of the other image. A regal man of romance and revenge. A man of the desert who knew better than Adil where to find poisonous herbs. Who collected a burlap bag of them and handed them over without foreseeing what it would mean to his friend. It is clear to Jammana that to say this name aloud would be too sharp a wound.

The fire gives off waves of heat. A liquid gray hangs over the village. "Look at them," Grandfather mutters, with a gesture that takes in all the village. "Still they sleep. Lost in dreams peopled with the long-departed and comforting as bread from their mothers' ovens." He turns to Jammana. "Khalah's bread," he says. "She knew you planned this?"

"I didn't know myself, not until I felt Faridah's memories." She sits beside him. "I betrayed her, Grandfather. Alula was right."

"What nonsense is this?"

"I saw the glass and the pain."

"I saw images, too, Jammana," he says after a moment. "Also without clarity. Allah must not have intended for us to act."

"Then Allah was wrong."

"No, my granddaughter. Allah is never wrong." He stares into the fire, coughing slightly. Out of the corner of her eye, Jammana sees a movement. A woman stands on a rooftop nearby like a single, distant star. Then another steps from the shadows at the edge of an alleyway, and two more appear in a courtyard side by side. All silent, they hold their distance.

"Grandfather," Jammana whispers, gesturing toward them.

"Hmmm?" he asks absently, lost to her.

She hears a shuffle and turns to see Mama, eyes wide. "In the name of Allah," Mama whispers, "what's happened here?" She studies the blaze a moment, her lips tight. She runs her fingers through her loose hair. "What were you thinking? No, don't tell me now. You must not be found. Come!"

Grandfather stands, shaking his head as though to clear it. "She's right, child. Let's go."

They hurry toward Grandfather's courtyard, Mama in front, her father and daughter trailing. And as they rush forward, Jammana remembers the story of the woman who stole cucumbers.

Khalah is awake. "Moses' Finger?" she asks, and Grandfather nods. The tips of flames are now visible beyond the house. Khalah leans toward Jammana and speaks quietly. "You kept a promise you never even made."

Mama shakes Father awake. "Rafa," he says. "What is it?"

"A fire, Ahmed. You must go. Take Jammana."

"Now?" Father murmurs groggily, unusually heavy with sleep.

"That is best." Mama pulls Father to his feet.

Grandfather leads two donkeys into the courtyard. Jammana hurries to him. "I won't go," she says.

He touches her hair. "Tenacious as a desert shrub, you are. That's good. You will need it. But I am not so strong now. I cannot risk losing you."

Father rubs his forehead. "You want to go *now?*" he asks Mama.

"Just you and Jammana. I'm needed here."

"You're staying? How long?" Father asks stiffly.

"No time for talk. Moses' Finger burns." Mama throws up her arms. "Moses' Finger! Allah save us! Who knows what tomorrow will bring? Jammana must go."

"You mean that Jammana . . ." Father breaks off, staring at his daughter. Mama, murmuring, leads him to a donkey. Khalah is loading food and water on its side. Grandfather helps Jammana mount the other beast.

"All right, Rafa, we'll go," Father says. "But I expect you soon."

"Good-bye," Jammana calls. "Good-bye."

"Hush, *faraashe,*" Mama whispers. "Ride quickly, and by morning you will be home." She pulls Jammana close, kissing her, breathing in her skin.

❖ ❖

As they reach Nablus' edge, the sun rises. It is quickly covered with a cloud, a dubious dawn.

Jammana's home is stripped and unfamiliar. Pictures have been removed from walls. Clothes and books are stacked. Late in the morning, she scales her lemon tree to look over the courtyard wall. The neighborhood, too, has changed. No one lingers. Women scurry from shop to shop, heads down. Men duck furtively inside the door to Abu Sa'id's as if hoping to escape notice. Blood has been smeared on the front of another nearby store, and everyone rushes past, eyes averted.

"Why was it marked?" Jammana asks Umm Mahir.

"Our neighbors say the owner did business with Jews," Umm Mahir says. "This is how they settle."

Together, Father and Jammana wait for Mama. That is the crushing chore of each day. Over breakfast they discuss whether she will send word by messenger or mail, whether someone will phone on her behalf, whether she will simply appear at the door. In the afternoons, without comment, Father brings Jammana surprises: ice cream, magazines, a rolled up Beach Boys poster from Abu Sa'id's shop. At night they sit side by side on the balcony and feel the breeze that comes to heal the desert's burned ground. And they wait.

After two weeks, Father pulls a paper from his pocket at the kitchen table. "A note from Ein Fadr," he says. "Three families have left already. More will soon. The elders are angry. Harif says it's not safe for you, even here."

Listening to Father's voice, Jammana recognizes the gap between intentions and outcomes.

"Retribution is not necessarily wrong," he says. "But we must face the consequences."

"Then what about Mama?"

"Your grandfather doesn't want to leave the village," he says, and looks out the window. "But your Mama will come to us soon."

He would repeat that often.

Father and I settled in a one-room apartment near Boston. In the months after we left, Ein Fadr's villagers scattered, too. Village enmity made it impossible to stay. One by one, then in small groups, families moved to Jerusalem, Nablus, or other villages. Houses that had stood from the time of Abraham were left to jackals and spiders. *Taboons*, olive groves, the caves, the spring, the room where Divine slept and Faridah's tears gave life to feathery dill plants—everything in those wounded, fragrant hills was abandoned, as if it never had been.

Mama and Khalah finally persuaded Grandfather to leave, and the three of them moved into our house in Nablus. Mama called often, speaking briefly to Father but at length to me. "When are you coming?" I would implore.

With Grandfather, I didn't speak of Ein Fadr. He said

my lemon tree was bearing fruit and his sheep were adjusting to new fields. "What would I do without the labor of my flocks?" he asked rhetorically, and I understood how much he missed his home.

With that summer of 1967 came war. A week after the fighting ended, Umm Mahir persuaded Mama to begin working for a humanitarian organization that supported households—Christian and Moslem—whose husbands were dead, imprisoned, or displaced in the fighting.

"It's the work of Allah," Mama told me over the phone.

I did not reply. Her conviction seemed theoretical and distant.

"It's hard to be without you, Jammana," she added after a moment. "I'm hugging you now. Do you feel it?" Then her voice lowered. "I'm arranging for you to come."

"You are?" I nearly shouted.

"Hush. It must be our secret for now. Everything was ready, and then the war—but never mind, now it's settled again. You'll get a call. A friend of a friend."

"How will I know? When will I see you?"

"I'm taking care of it, *faraashe*," Mama said, and her voice sounded confident in a way I hadn't heard before. "Soon we'll be together."

And then, the illness.

In the months after the war, death and disease in Nablus became as commonplace as it had been in the days of dung fires. Medical supplies were scarce, water sources contaminated. In September, Khalah phoned us. Mama had moved in with a Christian family for ten days to care for half a dozen sick children, she said. The children recovered, but when Mama returned, she had a cough. Next she developed a fever. She said she only needed rest. Then, overnight, she became delirious. "We must go immediately," Father said, packing a bag of medicine.

We flew to Amman and hired a taxi to return to Nablus via the King Hussein Bridge. But soldiers stopped us for questioning, made lengthy phone calls, searched our luggage. By the time we were allowed to pass and arrived home, we were too late. Too late even for her burial.

I mourned then in the old way, tearing my hair and pounding my head against the ground. At last Father pulled me to my feet and led me to my old room, where Grandfather lay half conscious, unresponsive. I helped Khalah spoon food into his reluctant mouth and wash his forehead with cool cloths. He would not rise from his mat. He would not speak. I feared he would die and imagined that it was part of a pattern, that Khalah and Father would not be long behind him.

If my days were anxious, my nights were more so, with Mama, veiled and remote, sweeping through my dreams. *"Faraashe,"* she would call as she strode past, "I'm sending for you."

"When, Mama?" I would cry.

Then her voice would become Faridah's. "Not long, mine of mine."

"Wait," I would beg in confusion, and chase after the woman until I was lost in a faceless crowd, my senses suffocated by the murmur of deep voices lowered in secrecy. I woke, chilled.

At last Grandfather rose from his mat and asked, "Has anyone grazed my sheep?" No one had even thought of them. They were in a pen at the edge of Nablus. He ate, rode a donkey to them, and took them into the fields as though the last few days had not happened. As though Mama had not died and he had not lain insensible. In the morning, when he rose again, I asked to accompany him to the fields.

We barely spoke until late afternoon. Grandfather gave me a lunch of bread and dates and sat near me, though he said he wasn't hungry himself. His eyes looked lifeless. I hesitated, then scooted close. "What made you decide to get up?" I asked in a quiet voice.

Grandfather studied me a moment. "I thought I had nothing left to live for," he said. "Rafa and Faridah are gone. You are so far away. Then I realized I have Khalah. My mother's shrine and Faridah's grave. I have my sheep."

"I'll stay with you," I said.

Grandfather shook his head. "I've lost too many here, Jammana. I wasn't able to save any of them." He fingered his prayer beads. "Past and future are no more separate than the tree trunk from its branches. You remember that, don't you? What we were given once, we may always keep." After a moment, he went on. "But time is relentless in this way—missed moments *are* gone forever. We think there'll always be another chance. We are wrong, Jammana. Choose carefully— for both of us."

His words were of little help. I understood only that something precious had been consumed. *Ana antemee ila*, I belong to. *Enta tantamee ila*, You belong to. *Howa yantamee ila*, He belongs to. It was a verb without a direct object.

Back in Boston, Father tried to find work as a doctor. He went out in the mornings carrying his black bag and a stack of certificates and letters of recommendation. But I watched his confidence ebb with the passing weeks. "I can't do it," he said at last. "I can't ask friends to support us anymore."

In this way, he became an Arab physician stocking shelves in an American grocery store, though he insisted that with just a little more time, he would work as a doctor again. "A small practice. That would be fine for a start," he said. "I need only to better my accent."

Some days we barely spoke; Father was exhausted by evening, and I could think of nothing to say to him. I tried to keep the house, prepare the meals, as Mama had. But I hadn't been trained, and many nights we ate yogurt and cereal. Sometimes Father would laugh at our circumstances; more often he grew bitter. "Your mother would be alive if she'd come with us when I told her to," he insisted.

I would rise and leave the room. "She *is* alive," I would mutter to myself. I searched my mind for the details of her face. I pictured her on the divan in Nablus, her fingers combing my hair, her feet tapping out the impatient tune of a woman unable to subscribe to the wishes of parent, husband, or even daughter.

Eventually I absorbed the language and customs of our adopted country, but Father remained isolated. When I went to college, he left for Lebanon. There he remarried. His new wife lacked the mettle of the women I'd known in my childhood, though she gave Father what he'd always needed—obedience.

Grandfather moved back to Ein Fadr, Khalah with him. They grew a small garden. He tended the sheep, and she came into Nablus from time to time to buy or trade. It hurt to imagine them alone in the shell of that village. "Dry bread at home is better than roast meat among strangers," Khalah insisted once when she telephoned me from Abu Sa'id's shop. "Sometimes travelers pass through. Sometimes they stay a day or two."

I should have been among their visitors. I knew that. I kept thinking I would be.

In the summer of 1993, Khalah died grinding wheat in the room where she'd been born. She was seventy-nine years old. The night I learned of her death from Father, I kneaded and baked bread until morning, remembering her in the *taboon*, flour on her cheeks, dough clinging to her fingers.

Father traveled from Lebanon to see Grandfather. "He is not the same," Father said when he phoned me. "No stories, no arguments. He just worries his prayer beads."

"I'll visit him," I vowed, as if Father had asked for a promise.

I'd opened a center in Providence for abused women from foreign countries who were mistreated in ways their own mothers had endured. I hired helpers who spoke a variety of languages, all of us being distant-born ourselves. Arabic, Hindi, and Japanese floated through the halls. In the presence of these alien tongues, I became truly preoccupied, truly American.

I couldn't bear to see what Grandfather had become, what loss had done to him. What my fire had wrought.

The stream of others' memories that paraded through

my mind for so many years had finally dried up. Even my own history, it seemed, had been lost in forgetfulness—until Abu Sa'id's son phoned. Then I learned again that a life lived only in forward motion is not a life at all.

I guessed his news as soon as I heard the Arabic coming across the line, though his words swooped and rambled. It seemed he could express himself only in the crowded, dense style of his father's shop, which he now runs.

"I went to see him, as usual," Sa'id said. "I checked on him every two weeks in keeping with my father's promise to your father. Of course, I thought it unsafe for him to stay alone in that abandoned village, especially as he became weaker. I tried to persuade him many times to leave, but he said he was in Allah's hands." Sa'id's sigh came like a drawn-out hiss. "I found him at the edge of the olive groves by a grave site, some boulders and a ruined ramada. You know the place, perhaps? He'd been dead no more than two days, Jammana. We buried him in the easy hills nearby. He asked me once to make sure his flock was spared slaughter after his death. So it shall be. They'll live out their natural lives." He paused, then. "Jammana? Are you there?"

Funny, I can't recall that son of Abu Sa'id's. He must be about my age. He must have played in the street below our house, one of those children who wanted so little to do with me then. I don't remember any of them. Memory sometimes hides more than it reveals.

Ten days after that phone call, I received a package from him—Faridah's seven silver bracelets and Grandfather's worn prayer beads. I lay them on my bedside table. They should have been dropped together each night on a dirt floor in a home shared by a shepherd and a midwife, I thought. I closed my eyes, recalling that village of poetic tales and tangled passions. Lying there, I smelled dust and smoke and Khalah's bread. I heard a distant call to prayer. When I opened my eyes, Grandfather stood before me. I reached out to let my fingers wander through his beard.

His face seemed thinner, his creases deeper. "Such responsibility you take on yourself," he said.

"I wanted to reduce Ein Fadr. But I didn't mean for you—"

Grandfather pressed a finger to my lips to silence me. He took my hand and squeezed it, and his grip felt as strong as a younger man's. "I failed Faridah," he said, "letting other men determine my course." He moved close. "But my mother said betrayals are accidental, even inevitable. Remember? We deserve forgiveness—all three of us. May we be joined on the other side as we never were on earth."

Before I could reply, he moved a cool hand to my forehead. I lay back, and as I drifted to sleep, he leaned toward my ear. "If I were my mother, that is all I would say," he whispered. "Being me, I have one more admonition. Recall it all, Jammana. Death and birth, dung and jasmine. But recall it gently."